AnnaLise returned her key to a pocket and moved toward the garage. No wonder the lamp was always out. "Batteries don't last forever, Daisy."

However, as AnnaLise reached down to grasp the door handle, the light went off.

"*Y voila.* What did I say?" AnnaLise yanked the handle with the angry strength of the consistently confirmed. The door slid up, but the light from the street lamp above revealed no sign of Daisy's cream-colored Chrysler.

Stepping in, AnnaLise reached for the light, finding and then pushing it.

And on the little dome came.

AnnaLise pulled her hand away as if the thing was scorching hot and took a convulsive step backward, instinctively wanting to be out of this particular cave.

The groan of ancient wood caused her to look up, just in time to see the overhead door come crashing down, The clatter of something metallic on the concrete was the last thing she registered.

Running on Empty

Sandra Balzo

WORLDWIDE®

TORONTO • NEW YORK • LONDON
AMSTERDAM • PARIS • SYDNEY • HAMBURG
STOCKHOLM • ATHENS • TOKYO • MILAN
MADRID • WARSAW • BUDAPEST • AUCKLAND

Recycling programs
for this product may
not exist in your area.

RUNNING ON EMPTY

A Worldwide Mystery/May 2013

First published by Severn House Publishers Ltd.

ISBN-13: 978-0-373-26846-7

Printed in U.S.A.

ONE

Life on Main Street has always been inexplicably hazardous, no matter the season. The skier who choked on her gum halfway down Deer Slope, arriving at the bottom still standing, if not breathing. The fishermen squashed like road-killed possums by a Toyota Land Cruiser against the front of Lucky's Bait Shop. The skinny-dipping White Tail Lodge hostess, dead from hypothermia. And that didn't count the odd tourist or two each year wandering into the mountains, never to wander back out to our High Country version of civilization called Sutherton, North Carolina.

Nonetheless, the day Daisy Griggs reportedly siphoned nearly three pints of blood out of poor Mrs Bradenham during the town's annual volunteer blood drive is generally acknowledged to stand above them all.

It's also what was sending me, Daisy's daughter AnnaLise, back to Main Street...

AG

AnnaLise Griggs stood in a Wisconsin courthouse when she picked up, on the first ring of her cellphone, the call every adult child dreads.

'AnnieLeez? This is Mama,' her mother's oldest friend said on the other end of the line.

Mama was the only person in Sutherton—or anywhere else—who seemed constitutionally incapable of pronouncing AnnaLise the correct way: 'Ah-nah-*lease*'. But, as surrogate-daughter had all her life, AnnaLise let her surrogate-mother's butchering of the given name ride. 'I just have a second, Mama. Is everything all right?'

'Pretty much. Excepting Daisy, she went and drained all the blood out of Mrs Bradenham.'

Well, maybe not the call *every* adult child dreads.

'My mother *what*?' AnnaLise yelled.

Other occupants of the century-old, cavernous lobby turned, en masse, to give the newspaper reporter a dirty look. They themselves might be junkies or prostitutes, purse-snatchers or axe-murderers, but blare into a cell-phone and everybody becomes Miss Manners.

AnnaLise pivoted to face the dirty beige wall, still keeping one eye on a courtroom door in case Urban County District Attorney Benjamin Rosewood emerged through it. The prosecutor had just filed charges against a sixteen-year-old girl whose car skidded on wet pavement and jumped a curb, killing her friend.

Tragic, yes. But vehicular homicide? Not in AnnaLise's mind, but reporters weren't supposed to have opinions. Which is why AnnaLise buried hers in a personal journal, thereby keeping the top of her head from blowing off.

At least, until now.

'Your mother,' Phyllis 'Mama' Balisteri continued, 'she was working the blood drive like always, her being a lobotomist and all. But Daisy made a terrible, terrible mistake this time.'

Despite her occupationally imposed, if personality-driven, need to edit, AnnaLise also let ride 'lobotomist' versus '*phle*-botomist' and cut to the car chase: 'Is Mrs Bradenham OK?'

'Oh, sure.' If anything, Mama sounded a bit disap-pointed. 'But there was blood all over the floor from running out the tube. Daisy up and cut it in the wrong place, you understand?'

AnnaLise didn't understand, but Mama wasn't going to give her a chance to request any clarification. 'Henrietta—the other lobotomist?—she said it looked to her like three, maybe four pints.'

Three to four pints? Didn't the average person have only nine or ten total? AnnaLise tented her forehead against the beige brick, trying to ignore both the explicit graffiti on it and the heightened activity in the courthouse lobby. She did register two videographers lift their cameras and train them on the arraignment session door.

'Where's Daisy now?' AnnaLise asked in a tone that already sounded tired, even to her own ear.

'Don't you worry,' Phyllis said. 'I didn't let the chief's police boys take your mother away.'

Assuming 'the chief' was still Chuck Greystone, AnnaLise's high-school sweetheart, he certainly shouldn't have, at least not without calling.

'She's here at the restaurant with me,' Mama continued. 'But Dr Stanton, he says Daisy might not be quite right.'

'Right?'

Mama lowered her voice. 'You know, like…in the head?'

AnnaLise didn't answer, waiting one, two beats, as DA Ben Rosewood burst from the courtroom and, throwing AnnaLise an apparently offhand glance, exited the lobby via another door, all without breaking stride. Shouting questions, a group of her fellow reporters became more like a pack of wolves, running their quarry to earth.

Feeling even smaller than her five feet of height, AnnaLise stayed where she was, a human lean-to against the building's scarred wall.

'I'm coming home, Mama,' she said softly into the phone. 'Tell Daisy I'm coming home.'

TWO

Friday, Sept. 3, 7:00 p.m. On the road

> *Stopped at the Best Western near Middlesboro, Kentucky, after a long day of driving. About to order pizza for dinner, then early to bed. Tomorrow, I cross into Tennessee and then Sweet Home North Carolina, arriving Sutherton maybe mid-morning. I'm trying to look forward to Mama's cooking and not fixate on what else might be awaiting me.*
>
> *AG*

FOR NEARLY AS LONG as AnnaLise could remember, and even after leaving Sutherton for college, she had called her own mother Daisy, and Phyllis Balisteri, Mama.

Half the reason for that was staring the journalist in the face as she waited on Saturday morning while a black Ford Excursion with Florida license plates backed out of a lined space. Above it, the sign read 'Mama Philomena's' in two-foot-high, neon letters.

The original 'Mama' had been Philomena Balisteri, Phyllis's mom. When Philomena died, her daughter took over the restaurant bordering on Main Street, the boulevard rimming the south shore of Lake Sutherton. 'Boulevard', however, was probably too grand a label for the two-lane road with angle-parking on one side and the revered statue commemorating a loyal local dog on the minimal median strip.

Most of the businesses stood on the same side of Main Street as Mama Philomena's, their front windows facing only the beach and Sal's Taproom across the way. Think of Lake Sutherton—the body of water as opposed to Sutherton, the town—as a figure eight, but with a withered northern loop nearest the mountains. While Main Street lived up to its name, other paved tributaries—like Church, First and Second Streets—fed into it and disappeared.

The driver of the aging but well-preserved Excursion was barely inching backwards from the space, and AnnaLise fought her mounting impatience with the out-of-stater. Growing up in Sutherton, she'd learned that its pace of life was dictated by the ebb and flow—not to mention frequent confusion—of the seasonal population fleeing the oppressive heat and humidity of South Carolina, Georgia and especially Florida.

'Half-backs', they were called, because, as Mama put it, 'They're northerners who go south for the weather, and then come halfway back.'

Half-backs, flatlanders, summer folk—whatever you called the crowds that descended upon the cool, clear lake and ascended into the cooler, surrounding mountains—they were the very reason the town continued to thrive, even during tough times.

Come summer, the population of Sutherton quintupled from a little less than a thousand to 'a little more than bearable' as AnnaLise's high-school friend, Sheree Pepper, would put it.

Winters also brought crowds, but of skiers. There weren't quite the number of tourists as in the summer, but the snow-seekers seemed to take up more room on the streets, wearing their down parkas and armed with skis and poles as they headed toward Sutherton Mountain.

'All tourists, all the time'—another Pepperism.

Not that AnnaLise's friend could reasonably complain. Sheree owned the Sutherton Inn on the far east end of Main Street. Her thirteen rooms were booked solid the entirety of both seasons. This Labor Day weekend beds in Sheree's inn, stools at Sal's Taproom, or booths in Mama Philomena's would be even tougher to get than parking spaces on Main Street.

But AnnaLise hadn't lived in Sutherton—nor the High Country in general—since starting at the University of Wisconsin, and patience was no longer a virtue of hers. She cautiously reversed her gas-conscious Mitsubishi Spyder convertible to give the Excursion more maneuvering room.

The angle-parking on Main Street was always good for a daily fender bender or two as the summer folk tried to back onto it. The less charitable of the natives, nursing beers at sidewalk tables outside Sal's Tap, took bets on which vehicle was going to get nailed next. Mercedes and BMWs brought a special joy to the experience.

As AnnaLise finally wheeled into the space, she cringed at the 'vroom-vroom' caused by a small hole in her muffler that had worsened on the thirteen-hour drive from the upper Midwest. Climbing out of the Spyder, she gave Main Street the once-over, glad—even relieved—to see that it was pretty much the same as she remembered.

With one exception.

Until this past spring, most of the ground-floor storefront on the far corner had been Griggs Market. A small grocery and deli, the family business had become increasingly less profitable over the last few years. Finally, Daisy had thrown in the towel and declared herself retired at the age of fifty. She rented the retail space—but not her home, an over-and-under apartment in the same building—to Tucker Stanton, son of the town's doctor, and after months of renovation, Tucker's 'Torch', an upscale nightclub, was now open.

Turning back to Mama Philomena's—or just plain Mama's, as everybody called it—AnnaLise could see her mother through the restaurant's big plate-glass window.

Daisy was perched on a step stool next to the cash register, feet dangling. The old place didn't have booster seats or high chairs. Kids who couldn't reach the tables sat on the step stool or, when that wasn't available, a pile of ancient phone books.

When AnnaLise was little, she'd climb quietly right to where Daisy was now and watch Mama fill plastic Moo-Cow cream pitchers by twisting off the heads and pouring cream down the plastic cows' throats. Then, if the pitchers were tipped, cream would come streaming out of the animals' mouths.

Which had struck young AnnaLise, who preferred her dish-ware anatomically correct, as just plain wrong. She'd searched the undersides of the creamers for udders and, finding none, resigned herself to the fact that adults apparently were fine with plastic cows spitting into their coffee.

The Moo-Cow pitchers were considered vintage these days, however, and, as they disappeared at the hands of sticky-fingered customers, Mama had locked up the last three—pitchers, not patrons—in a glass display case along with other treasures beneath her cash register.

'Out! Now!' The barked order interrupted AnnaLise's reminiscences as a man with the itchy look of a corporate bigwig embarrassed to find himself just another schmuck on vacation with the wife and kids, pushed out the door ahead of his family.

A second man, about forty with tousled hair, olive complexion and a local newspaper folded under one arm, had been about to enter Mama's, but stepped politely aside to let the squabbling parade pass by.

AnnaLise, intending to follow him in, leaned out to catch the door as it started to swing closed in his face. The stranger smiled his thanks and waved for AnnaLise to precede him, but she shook her head, preferring to take a moment to absorb the sounds and smells that were uniquely Mama's before…well, before she actually *saw* Mama. And Daisy.

Or, to be more precise, before the two women actually saw her.

Shielded from their view, AnnaLise closed her eyes. The très tacky electric chime on the door. The scent of rye toast and black coffee. The clatter of heavy silverware on industrial-strength china.

When AnnaLise opened her eyes, she was somehow in kindergarten again. After school, Daisy and Mama at the cash register, their backs toward her.

'Meh-tass-ta-sized.' Daisy annunciating each syllable as though it were a word all its own. AnnaLise didn't recognize the term, of course, but she heard the fear in her mother's voice.

AnnaLise's father had been sick for what seemed like her entire childhood. In fact, the daughter's first vivid memory was not of home or parents, but a room. A tiny, shiny room filled with black vinyl chairs and magazine-strewn tables, a television in one corner and a coffee urn in the other, the acrid smell of the brew not quite covering the human and antiseptic stew AnnaLise would forever thereafter associate with death.

AnnaLise always sensed her father was just on loan to the small family. That, someday, they would have to give him back.

'It'll be all right,' Mama had said that day at the restaurant, draping an arm around Daisy's shivering shoulders and giving them a squeeze.

'But AnnaLise is so little. And the store. Maybe I should—'

'You hush.' Mama put her left index finger to Daisy's lips. 'But I—'

'No.' If Daisy was as lost as AnnaLise had ever seen her, Mama seemed at her most determined. 'You're not alone, you hear? You and me, we'll make it right. The two of us.'

And they had, somehow. Two women collaborating over nearly a quarter century to keep both Mama Philomena's and Griggs Market afloat. To keep AnnaLise afloat, as well.

And, in return, the five-year-old had done her best to be brave, to be good. And she'd never, ever, told them what she'd overheard, and instinctively understood, that long-ago afternoon.

The man in front of AnnaLise moved toward a booth and Daisy and Mama caught sight of her. AnnaLise took a reflexive step back as the uncertain past became the equally uncertain present. The confused look in her mother's eyes was unnerving enough, but it wasn't as scary as what AnnaLise saw in Phyllis's. *Daisy's in trouble and even Mama doesn't know what to do.*

And, though AnnaLise wasn't sure, either, she knew it was her turn to keep *them* afloat.

THREE

The moment lasted but a second before Daisy's momentary confusion turned to recognition, and Mama's fear to relief.

Presumably at AnnaLise's arrival.

'Hungry?' Mama asked without missing a beat, like AnnaLise had just returned from a hard day in the fourth grade. 'You sit and I'll get you some Bacardi Rum Cake. Or do you want the Baker's German Chocolate one?'

Phyllis Balisteri had never met a brand-name recipe she didn't like. Each had made it onto the restaurant's menu and all were a whole lot better than Mama's mercifully sporadic attempts to make 'home-made sauce' or any of the other Italian dishes she'd tried from scratch.

Since rum cake was as close to a calming cocktail as AnnaLise could decently order at ten in the morning, she gave it a thumbs-up and turned to her mother.

'What a nice surprise.' Daisy threw Phyllis a dirty look as she hugged her daughter.

'Mama didn't mention I was coming?' Or that she'd telephoned AnnaLise in the first place?

'Certainly not. She knows I'd murder her.'

Not likely. Friends since birth, the two women were now just into their fifties. If Daisy had a homicidal bone in her body, Phyllis wouldn't have made it to—much less through—elementary school.

'You OK?' AnnaLise asked gently.

Daisy smiled up at her. 'Of course I am. It's Ema

Bradenham that worries me. I just don't know where my mind was.' A cloud skittered over her face and, as quickly, was gone again.

Daisy Griggs truly *looked* like a daisy. Naturally curly blonde hair and, at the center, a sun-darkened, cheerful face. A daisy face. It was AnnaLise who had first called her mother 'Daisy', apparently profoundly moved by a trip to the High Country Garden Center the spring of her kindergarten year.

People who had known Lorraine Kuchenbacher Griggs all her life gradually just started calling her Daisy, too. And that was fine with AnnaLise's mother, who had never liked her given name much anyway. For AnnaLise, in that watershed year of her father's death, it was more than fine. It meant having some control—power even. Maybe the five-year-old couldn't bring her father back, but she could turn her mother into a flower. And that was enough.

It made the nightmares go away.

Now, AnnaLise and Daisy followed Phyllis and two wedges of rum cake past Mama's private booth to one directly across from where the gentleman from the door was now immersed in his newspaper.

Mama's own table was closest to the cash register and perennially littered with menu-planning paraphernalia: a dry-erase board, red marker, and worn copies of *Best Recipes from the Backs of Boxes, Bottles, Cans and Jars, 1979*, *The Kraft Cookbook, 1977*, and *Favorite Brand Name Recipe Cookbook, 1981*. According to the handwriting on the board, Chicken ala King topped that evening's menu.

AnnaLise dug into her cake, conscious of Mama watching with satisfaction. After all, how bad could things be if baked goods were still enjoyed?

'You want another slice, AnnieLeez? I can put a little butter on top, then grill it up for you.'

AnnaLise shook her head, used to Mama's ministrations. 'Maybe just a glass of milk?'

Mama rolled her eyes and shuffled away. 'Whole milk, then, not that non-fat fluff you girls drink. Always thinking you're going to get heavy. Skinny as a rail, and still…' The muttering faded as Phyllis disappeared into the cooler.

Coast clear, daughter turned to mother. 'So what *did* happen with Ema Bradenham?'

AnnaLise pronounced the first name correctly, as though a second 'm' appeared within it. Most of all, though, she was aiming for 'matter-of-fact' with just a touch of 'concern', but not even the least whiff of 'accusation'.

Daisy, who had been concentrating on her plate, looked up and met her only offspring's eyes squarely. 'I made a terrible mistake,' she said simply. 'When I cut the tube, I must have sliced it above the clamps instead of between them.'

Thinking back to Mama's call and donating blood herself, AnnaLise believed she finally understood what had happened. After you give your pint, the nurse or phlebotomist clamps the tube running from your arm to the bag below in two places. One nearer the arm, to stop the flow, and one nearer the bag, to seal that off. Then he or she cuts the tube between the clamps, leaving the two ends to drip harmlessly empty while the donor relaxes and the technician gathers paperwork and post-donation instructions.

'But wasn't there still blood flowing out?' AnnaLise asked as gently as possible. As she spoke, the dark stranger glanced over, a startled expression on his face. Inadvertently catching AnnaLise's eye, he immediately pretended to once more be engrossed in the local news.

Daisy looked down at her plate again. 'I suppose so.

I mean, there must have been. But Henrietta had left Ema's paperwork on the counter before she went to use the powder room, and so I walked to the back of the trailer to get it.

'The appointment list was sitting on the counter, too, and I remember seeing little Nicole Goldstein's name and musing about the first time *I* ever donated, way back when. The next thing I knew, Henrietta was screaming, blood was flooding the floor, and Ema was unconscious.'

AnnaLise patted her mother's hand. 'It's OK, Daisy. Just an accident.'

But then the teenage girl's car skidding and killing that boy back in Wisconsin had been an 'accident', too, yet that hadn't stopped DA Ben Rosewood from...

'Here's your milk.' Mama dropped a paper-covered straw next to it. 'Now you be sure to drain every drop.'

Daisy shook her head. '"Accident" is a poor excuse, AnnaLise, and you know it. That woman was donating blood for people in need. I had a responsibility to do right by her.'

As though on cue, the door chimed and Ema Bradenham in the flesh—if not quite all the blood—entered. Mrs Bradenham's son, Bobby, who was Sutherton's current mayor, followed. 'Are you sure you don't just want to go home? After all that's happened...'

Although AnnaLise had it on good authority (Bobby's) that Ema Bradenham was six years older than AnnaLise's own mother, Mrs B could still be taken for nearly a decade younger. Of course, standing close to six feet tall—with legs to her chin, plenty of money and a French plastic surgeon on retainer who would enthusiastically lift said chin and anything else that dared to droop—probably helped.

Designer clothes and the vintage K Mikimoto pink

pearl necklace she perpetually wore—and AnnaLise habitually coveted—didn't hurt, either.

Mrs Bradenham interrupted her son. '"After all that's happened"? Bobby, if I have told you once, I have told you a thousand times, when something unfortunate occurs, put it behind you and move on. The blood drive was Thursday and here it is Saturday. Enjoy the holiday weekend. Goodness,' she said, without missing a beat, 'is it warm in here?' She flapped her pearls like they could conjure up a cooling sea breeze.

'You're just going through the change, Eee-mah.' Mama, now at the cash register, butchered Mrs B's name, as she did most others. 'Want a fan?' Phyllis gestured to the display case, repository of the Moo-Cow creamers as well as a handful of orange and yellow paper fans, now brown-edged with age.

The accordion-pleated fans and twenty-three miniature hand-painted tea cups were, mercifully, all that remained of Mama's ill-fated decision to have a couple of glasses of wine before bidding at her very first restaurant equipment auction.

Mrs Bradenham shuddered, though whether at the mention of menopause or the suggested ratty fans wasn't apparent. Then Mrs B—a nearly universal nickname for her among the locals—caught sight of AnnaLise. Turning abruptly, she almost swept the stack of cookbooks off Mama's table with her Hermes handbag. Gorgeous, but if the thing were any bigger, AnnaLise could climb in and latch it closed over her head.

Assuming it wasn't already occupied by a complementing foofy dog.

As AnnaLise looked around for some place other than the handbag to hide, Mrs Bradenham made a beeline for her.

It wasn't that AnnaLise despised Bobby's mother, it

was just that the woman made her feel…well, small. As in miniature. Which AnnaLise knew she was. She just didn't like to be treated like someone's pet.

'Oh, AnnaLise, look how a*dor*able. What a sweet little outfit.' Then to Daisy: 'And you, my dear. I do not want to hear a word of apology about the…incident on Thursday. I am just fine. In fact, I am told a bit of bloodletting is actually good for the complexion.'

'She's right.' Phyllis left the cash register. 'Demi Moore uses leeches, I saw it on the Internet. Imports them from France.'

'Why France?' Daisy asked. 'Don't we have leeches here?'

'We do, for sure,' Mama said. 'Plus, I bet our leeches are every bit as good as those French ones. And probably not as rude.'

AnnaLise, who hadn't even unwrapped her straw, now surveyed the glass of whole milk with dismay. It looked like a vat of cream in comparison to the non-fat she was used to drinking. And the talk of leeches wasn't helping with her queasiness.

'Contrary to popular belief,' Mrs B said, 'I have found the French very accommodating on my many visits.'

Phyllis snorted. Daisy just rolled her eyes and re-addressed her cake. The rudeness—or honesty, depending on your point of view—was pretty much *de rigueur* for Mama. Not Daisy, though. She tried to avoid hurting people's feelings. And to patch up those her best friend had already wounded.

Especially given the recent blood-drive mistake, AnnaLise would have expected her mother to be a little more gracious to Bobby's. The two women, though not close in AnnaLise's experience, had known each other for years.

Now Mrs B gave Daisy a puzzled stare and turned back to AnnaLise. 'As I was saying, Dr Stanton tells me the spill looked far worse than it was. I lost well under two pints.'

Two pints. Better than the three to four Mama had mentioned, but it still didn't seem like only a small matter to AnnaLise.

She opened her mouth to say so, but anticipating another apology, Mrs Bradenham just waved her down. 'Not a word now, Little One. Not even a syllable. We shall not speak of it again.'

Mrs B shrugged her handbag onto her shoulder, unintentionally dislodging a lock of carefully coiffed, ash-blonde hair to show a two-inch scar high on her forehead.

Before AnnaLise could pretend not to notice, Mrs Bradenham quickly covered it. 'Ahh, I see an open booth in the back. Bobby?'

But as Mrs B made her way back to a table, Bobby took his mother's place by AnnaLise. 'Hey, Annie—good to see you.'

Bobby and AnnaLise had met on her first day of kindergarten at Sutherton Elementary. A year older, Bobby and his mother lived in a big expensive house on the west side of the lake. The Griggs family lived in the same building as their grocery store on Main Street. It wasn't surprising the children's paths hadn't crossed until that fateful day in early September, when Bobby stepped in to prevent a third-grader from snatching AnnaLise's snack. Bobby had emerged from the confrontation with a bloody lip; the third-grader with Mama's 'Marshmallow Crispy Treat'; and AnnaLise, with the conviction she could have handled the bully better herself. Nonetheless, the friendship of 'Annie' and 'Bobby' had been cemented.

AnnaLise slipped out of her side of the booth to give him an enthusiastic hug. Then she beckoned the now-mayor away from the table where Mama stood consulting with Daisy over the relative merits of elevating creamed spinach over green bean casserole on the night's menu.

'Shame on you, Bobby,' said AnnaLise, punching him in the arm. 'Where's my protector of old? You just hung back safely and let me deal with all three of them.' Bobby was tall and well-built, with thick, chestnut-colored hair and a 24/7 smile. In other words, the perfect politician.

'Sweetheart, it was a war of words and I never did have any idea what your mother and Phyllis were talking about. And as for Ma?' He gazed skyward.

AnnaLise laughed. Mrs Bradenham hated being called 'Ma' by her sole heir. Which was why he did it, of course.

'Besides,' Bobby continued. 'I didn't see you do much more than try your darndest to get a word in edgewise. In vain, I might add.'

'Speaking of which—the one spelled v-e-i-n—I wanted to tell you how sorry I am about what happened. The blood-letting, I mean.'

'I saw that I had a missed call from you.' Bobby shook his head. 'Only like Ma said, water under the bridge. No harm, no foul. What's past is past.'

'No chorus of "Que Sera, Sera"?' AnnaLise and Bobby shared a love of old movies. 'But there was harm. I understand your mother lost consciousness. It would have taken a whole lot of French leeches to do that.'

'Running on empty or not, think what Ma saved on shipping and handling. Those things don't just slink over here on their own, you know.'

AnnaLise opened her mouth to apologize again, but Bobby waved her down in a gesture reminiscent of Mrs B. 'Let's face it, Annie. Our mothers are getting older. Maybe mine oughtn't to be giving blood anymore and yours—' he touched AnnaLise on the tip of her nose— 'oughtn't to be taking it?'

'They're not exactly ancient, Bobby. My mom's barely fifty. And Ema?' AnnaLise glanced down the aisle to the back booth, where Mrs Bradenham had her smartphone out and appeared to be texting. 'Well, I know she's older, but she looks amazing.'

'It's *The Picture of Dorian Gray.* Film originally released in 1945.'

'Not to mention, a book by Oscar Wilde. His only novel, in fact.' As a reporter, AnnaLise felt it her responsibility to give another writer his due.

'You know how Dorian kept that portrait of himself locked away? Well, I'm the portrait for Ma.'

AnnaLise just stared at him.

A shrug. 'She gets older, but the only evidence of it is yours truly.'

With the popularity of cosmetic surgery and Botox, Bobby probably wasn't alone in that. 'Carbon-dating our baby-boomer parents might be the only way to prove their ages these days.'

'Either that, or cut Ma in half and count her rings.'

'Whose rings?' Phyllis flopped down on the booth bench next to Daisy, sending the smaller, lighter woman into the air like she was on a red vinyl teeter-totter. Before either AnnaLise or Bobby could explain, if that was even possible or prudent, the door chimed again.

Bobby beckoned the newcomer over, while saying, 'AnnaLise, here's somebody I want you to meet.'

An Asian-looking man in his thirties approached them. Despite his relatively young age, he walked aided by a cane.

'This is Ichiro Katou. Ichiro, say hello to my oldest friend, AnnaLise Griggs. And you already know Mama and AnnaLise's mother, Daisy.'

Both women finger-wiggled hello to Katou before returning to their own conversation.

AnnaLise extended her hand. 'Good to meet you, Ichiro. Just visiting?'

Katou shifted the brass-topped cane from his right hand to his left to take hers with a courtly bow.

'Originally, yes. I arrive in Sutherton two months ago as tourist among so many others.' Katou's English had what to AnnaLise's ear was a Japanese veneer. 'But now I find I will stay for some time.'

'How nice.'

'Bobby and I plan a sushi restaurant on the White Tail.'

Sushi in Sutherton. Would wonders never cease? AnnaLise's face must have showed her surprise.

'I know what you're thinking,' said Bobby, holding up his hands. 'It's like the leeches.'

'Leeches?' Katou said, a shocked expression on his finely featured face. 'Those are not, how you say, good eating, no?'

'No. That is, you're right,' Bobby said. 'We were talking about imported leeches earlier, versus the home-grown variety.'

'For medical purposes,' AnnaLise contributed, though it wasn't quite true. No need to subject a newcomer to their admittedly warped slug humor.

Katou nodded once. 'Sutherton people already say, "Raw fish? We have lake just chock-full of them."'

He seemed to be developing both the Carolina High Country accent and sensibility—or lack of the latter.

Bobby laughed. 'Ichiro and I have talked about the possible…challenges, as you can see. But I think you'll be surprised, Annie, by how much Sutherton is changing. Besides, our typical customers may not be local. The tourists, bless them, should be enough to sustain us.'

Spoken like a true…well, mayor.

A clearing of the throat from the rear of the restaurant and Bobby glanced toward its source before lowering his voice. 'Ma disapproves.'

'Why?'

'She hasn't said. But you know my mother. She simply ignores anything she doesn't like. Figures that, without her fueling the issue, it'll go away.'

'I will not go away,' Katou said with a wry smile. 'She cannot repulse me forever.'

'I wouldn't bet on it,' Bobby said grimly, glancing again toward Mrs B's booth.

AnnaLise was confused, and not by Katou's use of 'repulse'. 'Earlier, you mentioned White Tail. Is someone reopening the lodge?'

Owned by Dickens Hart, White Tail Lodge had been built in the Seventies and patterned after the Playboy Club concept. Rather than Bunnies, though, it featured White Tail Fawns—comely females dressed as deer, complete with doe-eyed make-up and, you guessed it, fluffy white tails.

A different era, the end of each high season was marked by the so-called White Tail Games. Fawns—in full, if skimpy, regalia—competed in contests of 'skill' ranging from relay races and target shooting to water-balloon tosses and limbo contests. Surprisingly, Jell-O wrestling hadn't made the list of events.

'Annie, the lodge was torn down a couple of years ago,' Bobby said. 'If you came home more often than every century, you'd know that.'

An exaggeration, but what could AnnaLise say? It was true that while Daisy and Mama had visited her, the last time she'd been in Sutherton was for her mother's forty-fifth birthday. The ill-advised surprise party had culminated in Phyllis declaring, 'Don't you dare go thinking about a fiftieth, AnnieLeez, or Daisy'll have me drawn, quartered and boiled in oil.'

Then, apparently inspired, Phyllis had added 'one quarter of a fried chicken' to the restaurant's entrees.

'I do have to visit more often,' AnnaLise acknowledged. 'But you were saying?'

'I was *saying*,' Bobby resumed, 'that the island is being developed as a residential and retail area called—surprise, surprise—Hart's Landing. High-priced condos intermingled with restaurants, boutiques and entertainment venues.'

'Dickens Hart is developing it himself?'

'Along with a business partner named David Sabatino. He's here with his family from New York.'

Maybe Mr High-Power, saddled with the family for breakfast. Or maybe not. 'So your new restaurant…?'

'Katou's,' Ichiro supplied. 'Bobby believes this is right name for grand sushi place, but I think it sounds too very full of me.'

'It's perfect,' AnnaLise assured him.

In fact, the journalist wouldn't change a thing—not Katou's delightfully thoughtful way of speaking, nor the jet-black hair over eyes that hinted at hazel.

Those eyes lingered on hers until AnnaLise, embarrassed, glanced toward Bobby. But the mayor himself was looking past both of them. AnnaLise and Katou pivoted to see Ema Bradenham waving from her back booth.

'Your mother desires your attention,' Katou said to Bobby. 'Would you like me to…'

'Act as a sacrificial lamb?' Bobby finished. 'Please. And with my thanks. Tell Ma I'll be right there.'

With another grin, Katou bowed to AnnaLise and took himself off.

'What a charmer,' AnnaLise commented.

'Says you and the entire female population of Sutherton. Except for my own dear mother, of course.'

Mrs B, spine ramrod-straight against the back of her seat, seemed intent on establishing as much distance as physically possible between her and Katou, who'd propped his cane next to the booth and slid in across from her.

'You'd best go,' AnnaLise said. 'She looks about ready to explode all over that nice man.'

A mischievous smile. 'You wouldn't want to miss it, would you?'

'Go,' AnnaLise said sternly, hooking a finger toward the booth. 'Before there's bloodshed. Uhh, more…bloodshed,' she amended. 'I'll be in town through the holiday weekend. We'll get together later.'

Bobby was not one to be put off. 'Let's say Sal's then, tonight at seven. We can have a drink and catch up before Sinatra takes the stage.'

'Tonight is Frat Pack Night?' AnnaLise couldn't believe her luck. If Daisy was going to bleed somebody out, might as well be just before Frat Pack weekend. 'I'll be there!'

'Ah, yes,' Bobby said, with a theatrical sigh. 'If only I inspired that kind of passion.'

AnnaLise kissed him on the cheek. 'You do. Now go see your mother.'

As Bobby followed orders, AnnaLise returned to join her tablemates, excited beyond her better judgment. No matter how schmaltzy an evening of Franks—as in Sinatra music and dollar hot dogs—might sound, the event never disappointed.

Mama and Daisy were whispering and giggling like a couple of fourteen-year-olds as AnnaLise slid onto the bench across from them.

Phyllis smiled knowingly at her. 'Never too late, is it, AnnieLeez?'

'Now, Mama, don't—'

'"Now Mama" nothing,' she said. 'Why you and Bobby never went out is beyond me. Such a nice boy, and I hear he's just a little…dickens, to boot.'

'Phyllis!' Daisy snapped. 'You hush!'

AnnaLise was confused. 'A "little dickens"?'

'As in Dickens Hart's seed,' Mama said. 'How else could Eee-mah Bradenham live in that big house? Her baby-papa bought it for her, is how.'

AnnaLise thought, 'Baby-papa?' Had hip hop come to the mountains, or did the mountains come to hip hop? Either way, Mama must have been clipped in the crosswalk.

'Baby-*daddy*—' AnnaLise started to correct, but she was interrupted by Daisy.

'Phyllis, you do not—and could not—know that.' Daisy managed to simultaneously chin-gesture toward the Bradenhams' booth while hurling warning daggers in AnnaLise's direction.

Mama said, 'They can't hear me, and your daughter is plenty old for knowing the truth.'

'The "truth", you say? You're spouting nothing but idle gossip.'

'Eee-mah worked at the White Tail Lodge.'

'So did I. So did you. Dickens Hart was the town's biggest employer. Almost everybody worked at the lodge one time or the other.'

'But *hers* was the "right" time. You remember her winning the White Tail Games that year? The boys from school—Rance Smoaks, when he wasn't even fifteen, and that pimple-faced kid whose folks owned the inn back then. Why, Daisy, even your Tim sniffed around that girl like she was a bitch in heat.'

'Phyllis, you watch your mouth now.'

'What? I'm just talking about a dog. A female one.'

AnnaLise raised her hand, about to explain that, technically, a 'dog' was the male canine, while 'bitch' was the female.

But Phyllis shook her index finger. 'Not a word, AnnieLeez. You hear me?'

Surrogate-daughter dropped her hand and shut her mouth.

'I swear, Daisy,' Mama continued, 'if we had them thought balloons over our heads like in a cartoon, your daughter'd be correcting them, too.'

Time to guide the squeaky wheel back on track. Unlike her mother, AnnaLise had nothing against idle gossip. In fact, it was the reporter's bread and butter. 'So you were saying Ema was…popular?'

Mama snorted.

'Enough,' Daisy commanded.

AnnaLise's mother didn't 'command' often, but when she did, her daughter obeyed.

Phyllis, on the other hand: 'And just why are you defending her, Daisy? It's not like you owe that woman anything…well, 'cepting a pint of blood or three.'

Smiling at her own joke, Mama turned to AnnaLise. 'Your mother's just being overly sensitive like she gets. She was Eee-mah's best friend way back when, at least until Dickens Hart picked her to be a Tail.'

'You were a Tail, Daisy?' AnnaLise teased. Despite the lodge's best public-relations efforts, the Fawns had quickly been dubbed Tails by the locals. Even as a kid, AnnaLise could've seen that coming.

'You know perfectly well that I worked in the kitchen,' Daisy snapped. Then to Mama: 'And *you* know that when

Ema was promoted, our paths just didn't cross much anymore.'

'Probably on account of she was busy *un*crossing other things. Like her legs.'

Oh, boy. AnnaLise again caught the eye of the man she'd helped with the door what seemed like a year earlier. The sections of the newspaper he'd brought to his booth were annotated in red Flair and scattered across its tabletop. AnnaLise smiled sheepishly with a what-can-you-do shrug.

Daisy was trying to shush Mama, for all the good it did.

'Our Eee-mah goes away,' Mama continued, 'and comes back with a baby and her story about a rich husband who died from this automobile accident they'd all three been in.'

'You saw the scars for yourself back then, Phyllis.' Daisy seemed to want no further part of the discussion, throwing worried glances toward the subject of their conversation, still sitting with her son and Ichiro Katou.

'What? That itty bitty one up by her hairline? Sure didn't look "new" to me. And how about the child? Bobby came through this "devastating" crash just fine, supposedly because he was strapped into some kind of baby bucket.'

From the corner of her eye, AnnaLise caught movement at the Bradenham booth. Mrs B was leaving. Or maybe she'd overheard the conversation about her and was just getting up to sock Mama in the jaw.

Before AnnaLise could throw herself into the breach, the restaurant door burst open and an unfamiliar voice bellowed over the chime, 'A body's just been pulled out of the lake!'

FOUR

'HUH,' DAISY GRIGGS SAID. 'A little early in the season, now, isn't it?'

Mouth open, AnnaLise turned to her *other* mother.

'Daisy's dead-on right, I'm afraid,' Phyllis said, rising. 'Classes don't start up at the university till Tuesday.'

The University of the Mountain. Where kids drank too much, went to the water's edge to relieve themselves and tumbled into the lake. With luck, their friends dragged them out. The buddy system of drinking was much encouraged in Sutherton.

Mama was peering out the front window toward the beach across the street. 'Usually be a week or two after that before somebody actually sees a floater going past.'

'A...floater?' said the herald. A man of about thirty, with the tell-tale sunburn of a tourist, he was obviously perplexed by the lack of excitement his announcement had engendered. 'My God, a corpse just washed up on the beach. Shouldn't we do something?'

'Like what?' Mama turned. 'Police chief's car is already kicking up gravel over there.'

'And from what you yourself said, they don't need an ambulance,' Daisy contributed. She was paging through Mama's copy of *The Kraft Cookbook*. 'At least, not right away.'

Mrs B, who had made it as far as their table, looked shocked at the collective insensitivity. AnnaLise seconded the emotion. Her grandmother used to say that, getting older, 'you can finally say what you think. Other people don't like it, that's too damn bad'. But Grandma Kuchenbacher had been eighty. If Daisy was starting now, how would she be in another thirty years?

Mrs B might originally have intended to confront Mama and Daisy about their gossiping over Bobby's paternity, but if so, she wisely changed her mind. Skirting the tourist, she kept right on going.

He followed her out, seeming relieved there was at least one person in the restaurant with a social conscience. AnnaLise could see him trailing, trying to point the way to the action. When Mrs B ignored him and went in the opposite direction, he glanced back toward the restaurant.

Mama waved. 'Y'all enjoy your vacation, now.'

AnnaLise didn't need to see an eye-roll. Shaking his head, the visitor recrossed the street to the beach.

'Ambulance chaser,' Mama muttered.

Not giving Daisy an opportunity to point out, again, that there was no immediate need for an ambulance, AnnaLise stood. 'I'm going to see Chuck over there. Be right back.'

Making her escape, she found Sutherton's chief of police leaning down, talking to the driver of a second patrol car through the window.

Straightening, he saw AnnaLise. 'Hey, Lise—good to see you. Sorry I didn't return your call.'

'No problem,' AnnaLise said. 'I just assumed you were getting an arrest warrant for my mother.'

He gave her a quick kiss on the lips. 'Well, the possibility did bring you back to us.'

Chuck Greystone's face combined the strong planes of his Cherokee grandfather with the auburn hair and green eyes of his Irish mother. It was a devastating combination.

One that still could make AnnaLise's heart melt, despite the fact that she'd literally and figuratively moved on.

She gestured toward the knot of people close to the water. 'College student?'

'Nope, looks like Rance Smoaks. Though he's been chewed on some, so he's got some chunks missing.'

Lovely, if not unusual in the High Country.

Chuck's voice was neutral, despite the fact that he and Rance shared a long history. A long and bitter one, partly because Rance Smoaks was a son-of-a-bitch and partly because Chuck had replaced the man as Sutherton's chief of police.

Rance's father, Roy, had preceded his son in the office. And Roy's father before him. The Smoaks family hadn't taken kindly to Chuck's breaking their line of ascent to the throne.

'I have to tell Kathleen,' Chuck continued.

Kathleen was Rance's wife. She had been a classmate of Bobby Bradenham, which made her a year older than AnnaLise and fifteen years younger than Rance. Plenty young enough not to have seen past the police uniform to the mean drunk that lay beneath.

'She'll be devastated,' AnnaLise said. And the new widow would be. Kathleen Smoaks was a good woman who had the misfortune of falling in love with a bad man. A shame—especially since AnnaLise knew Bobby had asked Kathleen to marry him just out of high school. If only she'd accepted, life could have been so different for both of them.

Not that AnnaLise was exactly a poster child for wise choices.

She gestured toward the blue tarpaulin that was being used to shield the body from onlookers. 'He was plastered as usual, I assume?'

'Probably. We'll know more when the lab work comes back.' Chuck put his hat on, squared it over his forehead. 'You'd think people, at least our locals, would learn to stay away from the lake when they're drinking. Especially someone as experienced as Rance.'

'Chief.' A voice rang out from the waterline. 'We got us an entrance wound.'

'Damn it all.' Chuck swung away and then turned back to AnnaLise. 'I need to talk to you.' A glance toward the tarpaulin. 'When we both have some time.'

A chill ran up AnnaLise's spine. Something to do with Daisy? Maybe the idea of an arrest warrant was no far-fetched fantasy.

'I'll be here through Labor Day,' she said. 'Is this…'

But Chuck was already moving away. 'Good. If I don't see you tonight at Sal's, I'll call you tomorrow.'

'OK, but…' AnnaLise realized she might as well be talking to the wind. All attention was focused on the body.

AnnaLise turned toward Mama's, waiting for a white Mercedes-Benz to dawdle past, the driver rubbernecking the commotion on the beach.

An 'entrance wound' meant that Rance Smoaks had been shot. During hunting season, accidental shootings weren't all that unusual. But deer season didn't commence until the day after Labor Day, meaning three days from now. And even then, only bow-and-arrow, not rifle, was permitted.

A tap of the Mercedes' horn.

'AnnaLise,' Mrs B's voice called from the driver's window. 'Pay attention, please. I have been waving you on for eons.'

An exaggeration, yes, but an explanation seemed in order to appease the woman. 'I'm sorry. I was thinking about this—' she waved back at the beach vaguely, knowing she shouldn't name the victim until after the family had been notified— 'incident.'

'Another drowning,' Mrs B said, shaking her head. 'And, likely, another newspaper editorial tomorrow, calling for fencing off portions of the lake. Whatever happened to personal responsibility, I want to know.'

'In this case, it doesn't appear to be the victim's fault. He was shot.'

'Certainly not on purpose?' The way Ema Bradenham said it made it clear that such a thing wouldn't be tolerated in her tidy world.

Which, of course, made AnnaLise want to muddy it up more. She moved closer to the car, confidingly. 'I don't see how it could possibly be an accident. After all, deer season doesn't start until Tuesday, and as for gun—'

'Please,' Mrs B interrupted with a shiver. 'I know they are held sacred up here, but firearms lost their fascination for me a very long time ago. When Bobby took up deer hunting last year, I was just filled with trepidation. The whole idea is just so...déclassé.'

'My mother doesn't like hunting either,' AnnaLise said, seeking common, yet not too 'common', ground. 'My father's deer rifles are locked in a cabinet, and I don't think they've been touched since the day he died.'

'Exactly where they belong. The thought of hunting one of those beautiful creatures to hang its poor head on a wall...' She shook her own head, as if words failed her.

Apparently it had never occurred to Mrs B that some people actually ate the venison to get some protein into the family's diet, a distinction that made a difference to AnnaLise.

Another horn sounded and Mrs B moved on with a dismissive flapping of her hand at the wrist.

When AnnaLise re-entered Mama's, it was as if she

hadn't left, except that the good-looking stranger in the booth was gone.

'All I'm telling you,' Mama was saying to Daisy as AnnaLise took the bench across from them, 'is that AnnieLeez shouldn't be ruling Bobby Bradenham out as a husband.'

'AnnieLeez' almost got back up. Instead, she took a couple of deep, cleansing yoga breaths. After all, she'd be there only two more days. A person could stand anything for forty-eight hours, right?

'OK,' she said sternly, using her index finger to snake her cake plate back. 'Let's put an end to this here and now. Bobby and I are friends. There's no chemistry beyond that, never was, never will be.'

She could see Bobby, still in conversation with Ichiro Katou. The two seemed to be filling out documents.

'But there was with Chuck Greystone,' Mama said with a sideways glance at Daisy.

They giggled.

Two days *after* today. Which meant more like sixty, sixty-five hours, not forty-eight.

AnnaLise looked up at the clock on the wall. Its minute hand seemed to be crawling backwards.

'Chuck and I are good friends, too.' AnnaLise felt like she was talking to middle-schoolers. 'In fact, I just saw him. Standing over the body.'

AnnaLise expected the bald remark to turn the conversation, but apparently her love life—or their perception that she had none—was infinitely more fascinating to them.

Mama was nodding. 'The Three Musketeers, that's what we called them. You remember, Daisy?'

If it was intended as a memory test, AnnaLise's mother was about to earn a passing grade. 'AnnaLise, Chuck and

Sheree Pepper. Sheree had such a crush on that boy. It reminded me of you, me and Tim. A triangle.'

Timothy Griggs had been AnnaLise's father. From what Daisy had told her, Daisy, Phyllis and Tim had been the 'Three Musketeers' of their generation.

'Phyllis, you always had a crush on Tim, and you know it,' Daisy continued as the front door chimed.

Mama's turn to blush, but she was saved from answering when a wiry woman with cropped, nearly white-blonde hair swooped down on them.

'Move over, girlfriend.' Joy Tamarack plopped herself on the bench. AnnaLise didn't bounce up like Daisy had when Mama sat down, probably because Joy, a physical trainer, weighed about a hundred pounds. And all muscle. She practically crushed AnnaLise's ribs with her hug.

'I'm so glad to see you,' AnnaLise said when she'd regained her breath. 'But isn't this a little late in the year for the Frat Pack?'

Joy and a dozen of her old college sorority sisters took over Sheree's Sutherton Inn annually for a weekend of, as Joy once put it, 'drinking, smoking and engaging in aural—that's a-u-r-a-l—sex. Meaning we just listen to each other lie about it.'

'We pushed back the date, Annie-girl. Everyone's biological clocks went off, shall we say, belatedly yet simultaneously last year, so some of us needed to schedule around spouses and—' she wrinkled her nose— 'babies.'

Joy's expression made it clear that her own personal biological clock could go hang itself.

'No new relationship?' AnnaLise asked. God knows she was asked often enough. It was only fair to reciprocate by torturing others.

'Hell, no. Once was enough. More than enough.'

Joy, mid-twenties at the time, had been wife number

3 of the legendary Dickens Hart. Less than a year later, she'd caught Hart helping himself to, in Joy's words, 'a little Tail.' As in one of the lodge's Fawns.

Joy might have been young, but even then she was a shrewd businesswoman and had come out of the divorce in fine form. Since Hart had plenty of practice with pre-nups by that time, AnnaLise had always wondered if the 'little Tail' was under-aged, providing Joy with additional leverage during the property settlement phase.

'Sal moved Frat Pack Night to this weekend just for you, I presume?'

'Honey, we *are* the Frat Pack.' Joy stuck a cigarette in her mouth. 'You'll be there, right?' she mumbled around the cancer-stick while digging for a lighter.

'Of course. I'm meeting Bobby for drinks at seven.'

'Great.' Joy unearthed a psychedelic pink-and-green lighter and turned to AnnaLise's mother as she thumbed the wheel on it. 'Daisy-girl, I hear you—'

Splat.

'No smoking.' Mama set down AnnaLise's now empty milk glass and got up to tend the cash register.

Joy surveyed the creamed lighter. 'Well, this is one collector's edition Bic that's never going to flick again.'

'Probably for the best,' AnnaLise said. 'The Seventies are dead, and you will be, too, if you don't stop smoking.'

'Says the woman eating rum cake at ten a.m.'

'With a healthy glass of milk,' AnnaLise pointed out. 'At least, until rather recently.'

Joy sniffed, then wrinkled her nose again. 'Oh, my gawd. Is this whole milk? Warm whole milk?'

'Warm, because I didn't drink it,' AnnaLise said defensively. 'Besides, I'm running again. I can splurge occasionally.'

Though it sure as hell wouldn't be on a glass of milk. A

slice of the German chocolate cake that Mama had mentioned came to mind.

'I'm in training, too.' Joy pulled a thin paper napkin out of the dispenser on the table and set her lighter on it. A dribble of milk leaked from where the flame should be.

'But still smoking?'

'Even a journey of a thousand miles must begin with a single step.'

'And a paroxysm of coughing.' She gave Joy a shove so she could slip out of the booth. 'I'll see you tonight, but now I want to drop in on our tenant. You coming, Daisy?'

'Of course. You'll love what Tucker's done to the store,' Mother Griggs said as she followed.

Mama just waved them past the cash register. Not that she needed to. Daisy had long ago given up trying to pay for her food at Mama's and, for AnnaLise, it would be like handing her mother a fiver for making coffee in the morning. The thought never even occurred to her. Which was why learning how to dine in *other* people's restaurants when she went away to school had been such an adventure. Happily, one that ended without jail time.

Joy trailed mother and daughter, making AnnaLise wonder why her friend had entered in the first place. God forbid the woman should ever *eat* something.

'I haven't been to Torch for a show,' Joy said, 'but I've heard good things about it.'

'I'm really glad.' AnnaLise stepped out of Mama's and held the door for Daisy and Joy. 'The Stantons put a lot of money into retrofitting the old market into a nightclub.'

'Starting any new business is expensive,' Joy said. 'And banks are pretty stodgy now about giving loans.'

Joy's tone made it sound like she was speaking from personal experience. The last AnnaLise had heard, Joy—

the smoker—was managing a fitness club somewhere in Indiana.

'So how's *your* business going?'

'Going?' Joy spread her hands wide. 'More like, going, going, gone.'

'I'm sorry.'

'Don't be.' Joy gave her a wink. 'I've got a can't-miss venture in the works.'

'Are you going to tell us about it?' Daisy had been lagging behind, letting the friends talk, but apparently she wanted in on any news.

'Not yet.' An enigmatic smile from Joy. 'But your little hometown here *is* involved.'

AnnaLise's cellphone gave a two-tone ping, indicating a new text message. She glanced at it and hit delete, but not before noting the time. 'It's not quite eleven-thirty. Will Tucker be at work already?'

'Of course,' Daisy said, leading the way down the block. 'Torch is open all day.'

'They're serving lunch, too?' To AnnaLise's knowledge, the Stantons had obtained a liquor license and created a small kitchen in one corner in order to offer light hors d'oeuvres during club hours. She didn't realize they'd put in a full, professional-grade food-service operation.

'I have a hunch Tucker believes in giving the people what they want.' Joy stopped next to a little red convertible with a tan top and nodded down the block. 'Go take a look, and I'll catch you later.'

'Sounds good. I think I'll run the lake path tomorrow or Monday. Want to come?'

'Sure, but make it tomorrow,' Joy said, climbing into her convertible. 'Monday's the parade, as a born-and-bred Sutherton girl ought to recall.'

Of course, the Labor Day parade. With the excitement

of Frat Pack Night, AnnaLise had forgotten the *other* holiday.

As Joy backed out of her parking space, AnnaLise and Daisy continued down Main Street to Torch.

The entrance of the former Griggs Market was set at an angle facing the intersection of Main and Second Street. Around the corner on Second was the residential entrance to the townhouse-style apartment where Daisy lived. And, at one time, her husband, Tim, and AnnaLise, too.

The commercial plate-glass doors of the market had been replaced with rich wooden ones that gleamed in the morning light. They were flanked by newly installed sidelights, each featuring an elongated flame on a matte-black background and the word 'Torch'.

Despite Daisy's assurances, the place looked closed. AnnaLise leaned down to peer through the translucent white center of the sidelight flames. Detecting movement inside, she raised her hand to rap on one of the doors when it abruptly swung open.

'Sorry, man,' a boy of about seventeen said. 'I mean, ma'am.'

AnnaLise, who had backed off just in time to save face, literally, was young enough to prefer the nearly cross-gender term 'man' over 'ma'am'. 'Not your fault. I didn't know the place was open.'

As AnnaLise spoke, she realized the boy held what looked like a miniature to-go cup, just the right size to accommodate a double shot of espresso. And it smelled great.

Before she could ask him where he'd gotten his drink, the kid was halfway across the street and heading for the beach. No matter, the scent of espresso from inside Torch still hung in the air.

Daisy entered and threw out her arms. 'Isn't it wonderful?'

Following her, AnnaLise took in the revolutionary change.

The shelves and counters of the market were gone and the walls of the square room were painted slate gray. In addition to round tables on the floor, a raised bar-level had been installed in front of three walls, giving those seated there a place to set their drinks while enjoying a clear sight-line to the half-circle stage on the fourth wall.

Tucker Stanton was cross-legged on said stage, a scraggly attempt at growing a mustache and goatee against his toffee-colored skin making the eighteen-year-old look even younger. He was alternately slapping splayed fingers on a bongo drum and reciting something that sounded like a cross between haiku and 'There Was a Young Man From Nantucket'.

Mercifully, Tucker caught sight of them before he got to the punch line. 'AnnaLise! Welcome!'

Hopping up, he weaved his way through the tables to give AnnaLise a hug. Tucker Ulysses Stanton might be too young to drink the alcohol he served, but AnnaLise thought he had a great chance of succeeding at pretty much anything he put his mind—and his father's money— to. He was just that kind of kid.

But a bongo? And blue haiku?

'How do you like the place?' Tucker asked.

'It's great,' AnnaLise answered honestly. 'But I thought you were opening a nightclub.'

'It is a club—' Tucker started.

'But not just at night,' Daisy added, looking pleased with herself and Tucker. 'I asked him why he'd spend all that money to be open only four hours a day.'

'And your mother was right,' Tucker said. 'I'd already

decided to put in an espresso bar for the after-work crowd, so opening a few hours in the morning for the caffeine cravers seemed natural.'

'A coffee shop.' AnnaLise was taking in the mostly full tables. 'How does—'

'Oh, don't worry,' Tucker said hurriedly, looking a little hurt. 'I checked with Mama to make sure she was down with it. Besides, Torch isn't a coffee shop, it's a coffee-*house*. The "cool, man" kind, like with Dobie Gillis.'

And Maynard G. Krebs, which explained the sparse facial hair on the guy who looked more like a young Will Smith than Bob Denver. 'There's no way you could have seen *The Many Loves of Dobie Gillis*. That was more Daisy's generation.'

'Excuse me,' Daisy protested. 'Only if I watched TV practically *in utero*. That was late 1950s, I think.'

''59 to '62,' Tucker said. 'It was based on a collection of short stories.'

'By Max Shulman,' AnnaLise said, getting in another shot for the written word. 'But how did you ever see it, Tucker?'

'DVD,' Tucker said. 'If you want, I can lend them to you.'

'I'd *love* that,' Daisy jumped in. She'd wandered over to the stage and was tapping on Tucker's bongo with a fingernail.

'Great. I'll bring volume one tonight.' Tucker turned his boyish charm on AnnaLise. 'Torch is premiering a tribute to Rodgers and Hammerstein, featuring our very own chanteuse. Can you make it? I'll even waive the cover charge.'

It was a thoughtful, showman-style invitation and any other time AnnaLise would have jumped at the chance.

But tonight was Frat Pack Night. You just didn't miss that, show tunes or not.

'I'd love to, but I have a date with some old friends.' She turned to Daisy. 'Maybe my mother…'

'Oh, she'll be here,' Tucker said.

'I certainly will.' Daisy let the drum go silent. 'I haven't missed an opening yet.'

AnnaLise was grateful to hear that she'd found a place to socialize so close to home. As in downstairs. Especially since daughter was abandoning mother on the first of three nights home. In order to be back at work on Wednesday, as AnnaLise had promised, she'd need to be on the road very early on Tuesday.

'Cool,' Tucker said. 'Hey, can I get either of you an espresso?'

Daisy declined on the basis of having drunk nearly a pot of coffee at Mama's, but AnnaLise quickly accepted. 'I'd love a large decaf, non-fat, no-foam latte. With a sugar substitute.'

'Coming right up,' Tucker said, turning to a woman who had just appeared behind the granite-topped counter. 'Sue, one large "what's-the-point", please.'

Daisy laughed and gave Tucker a hug. 'Isn't he just adorable, AnnaLise?'

'He is that,' AnnaLise said, and meant it.

As they left the store with her latte, AnnaLise felt completely relaxed for the first time since Mama's call about the blood drive.

Daisy seemed as sharp as ever. And if that weren't enough, Tucker was an absolute gem—almost like AnnaLise had a younger brother living at home to keep an eye on things—and her mother obviously enjoyed having him there. All was right with the world again.

As AnnaLise rounded the corner onto Second Street,

her cellphone rang. She started to hand Daisy her latte, but the older woman was lagging a bit so AnnaLise set the drink on a window ledge and went handbag-diving.

When she finally came up with the phone it was blinking 'one missed call'. AnnaLise's options were 'view' or 'ignore'. She chose the former and a display came up 'Ben's cell'. She snapped the phone closed and shoved it back into her purse.

'Sorry, Daisy. I should have just ignored it.' Picking up her latte, AnnaLise looked around.

No Mother Griggs in sight.

AnnaLise retraced her steps around the corner and onto Main Street. Daisy was back in front of the coffeehouse/nightclub, one eye pressed to a sidelight like it was the viewing end of a telescope.

'What's up?' AnnaLise called. 'Is Tucker waxing dirty again?'

Daisy turned, a horrified expression on her face. 'AnnaLise, quick,' she whispered. 'Tell your father to call the police. Some crazy bearded man with a drum has broken into our market.'

FIVE

'So what did you do?' Sheree Pepper asked AnnaLise.

'I didn't know what to do, but the moment only lasted for…well, a moment. Then she was Daisy again.'

'Weird.'

'You're telling me,' AnnaLise said.

'Like she was possessed or something.' The two old friends were sitting in the parlor of Sheree's bed-and-breakfast, the Sutherton Inn.

Sheree had redecorated when she bought the place, each room now virtually museum-quality. The parlor featured bright yellow walls, whitewashed woodwork, a floral couch and one cherry-red chair.

Sheree—the third corner of what Mama had called AnnaLise's social triangle—unwound her tanned legs and stood to retrieve an opened bottle of Cabernet from the sideboard. 'More wine?'

'It is past noon, so what the hell. Thanks.' AnnaLise held out her glass, wondering for the umpteenth time why Chuck Greystone had preferred tiny, brunette AnnaLise to statuesque, red-headed, sexpot Sheree. 'I know there's some rational explanation for Daisy's behavior, but it was downright spooky.'

'Rational is as rational does,' Sheree said. 'Just what are you thinking? Alzheimer's?'

'God, no.' AnnaLise shivered involuntarily at the thought. Her friend always *had* possessed a knack for voicing scenarios that AnnaLise would be trying hard not to envision. 'More like a vitamin deficiency. Something easy. Daisy's too young for Alzheimer's.'

Sheree remounted her chair with the grace of a ballerina. 'Early onset, maybe? I've heard about people getting it while they were still in their forties.'

Getting it, AnnaLise thought. Like catching a cold.

Another shiver told AnnaLise that she couldn't get her head, or even body, around the idea that something serious could be wrong with Daisy. AnnaLise looked at the antique schoolhouse clock on the wall. 'It's nearly three and I haven't heard back from Dr Stanton.'

'Give the guy a break, huh? It's the Saturday of a long weekend, and you called him all of an hour ago, right when you came through my front door. We haven't even finished this bottle of wine I popped to calm you down. Besides, Daisy's OK now, right?'

'Fine, so far as I can tell. Or I wouldn't have left her.'

Even as she said it, AnnaLise wondered whether Daisy was indeed 'fine', or prodigal daughter had just convinced herself of that so she could escape to the normalcy of the inn. Bobby Bradenham's mother wasn't the only one capable of ignoring things in hopes they would just go away.

But the fact was, Daisy had shown no embarrassment at her haunted—if brief—detour down memory lane. After an awkward hesitation, AnnaLise—partly from nerves, partly in disbelief that her mother could be serious—had simply laughed off Daisy's panic. 'Are you kidding? Tucker playing a bongo in our old market? Daddy would have loved it!'

Daisy squinted at her, as though it had been AnnaLise who'd departed from the main line, then broke into a laugh herself. They'd gone into the apartment, Daisy to start lunch and AnnaLise to unpack.

So…*could* Daisy have been kidding? Maybe she was

sitting at Philomena's right now, telling Mama about AnnaLise's brain-fart, the way AnnaLise was discussing Daisy's with Sheree.

'This place looks great,' AnnaLise said, trying to be casually social with her old friend.

'So you've told me. Twice.' Sheree was many things, but sensitive wasn't one of them. She leaned toward AnnaLise. 'Now you listen to me, honey. You'll talk with Dr Stanton when he calls you back. Until then, there's nothing—'

Neither of them had heard the door open, but suddenly in the room appeared a man, the same one AnnaLise had seen at the restaurant.

'Jim,' Sheree said, hand to her heart. 'You scared me near senseless.'

A look of apology on the handsome face. 'I'm sorry. I thought all the other guests were off on a frolic.'

He extended his hand to AnnaLise. 'I'm James Duende. Didn't I see you at Mama's this morning?'

Despite the Latin surname, there was no accent in his speech beyond a trace of north-east corridor.

'You did. I'm AnnaLise Griggs.'

'AnnaLise and I went to school together,' Sheree said. 'A pleasure to meet you.'

'Are you visiting for the weekend?' AnnaLise asked.

'And beyond,' Duende said, cracking a grin. 'I have a job that will keep me here for the duration of the winter, God help me.'

'Hey, skiers pay big money for the pleasure of Sutherton's ivory-colored slopes,' Sheree said, before AnnaLise could ask Duende what he did.

'Jim lives above the dining room,' the innkeeper continued with a meaningful gleam.

'Ahh, number thirteen.' AnnaLise turned her own blind eye to the 'gleam' part. 'You're a brave man.'

Room thirteen had become another Sutherton legend after a spurned lover barricaded himself in it and drank poison before throwing himself out the window. His ghost would probably still haunt the place if the 'poison' hadn't been cheap room-shampoo and his fall barely nine feet, cushioned by newly tilled soil below.

But Sutherton didn't let go of its legends easily. More's the pity, since Daisy's siphoning of Mrs Bradenham was destined to become one. Probably *number* one.

'I have to admit, I'm a sucker for a good story,' Duende said. 'Besides, I can stomp around all I want without bothering anyone below, except during breakfast.'

'Nonetheless,' Sheree said coyly, '*some* noises carry.'

Damn, thought AnnaLise. Another one bites Sheree's dust. No matter, though. AnnaLise wasn't in search of a man and certainly not one who was living indefinitely in a rooming house of sorts in small-town North Carolina, and shtupping the innkeeper to boot.

Still, an extra man, no matter whose, would make Frat Pack Night even more fun. 'Are you coming to Sal's tonight?'

'What's tonight?'

Sheree looked put out. Apparently she'd had other plans for the evening. And 'Jim'.

Well, that's too bad, AnnaLise thought. It wouldn't kill Sheree to share. 'I'm sure you've met the Frat Pack.' The sisterhood took over the inn whenever they visited. It would be hard to miss them.

But apparently he had. 'Pardon?'

'Joy Tamarack and her gang,' Sheree explained, a tad sourly.

AnnaLise noticed. 'Why the long face, Seabiscuit?'

Duende laughed, but Sheree's scowl grew more pronounced. 'What are you, five?'

'Sorry. Coming home can regress a person.'

'You don't live around here any longer?' Duende asked.

'No, I went to college in Wisconsin and took a job there after graduation.'

'So you're back to see family. I couldn't help but notice the resemblance this morning.'

Since Daisy was blonde and blue-eyed and Anna-Lise dark-haired and brown-eyed, Duende was probably assuming Mama was AnnaLise's…well, mama. It was a common mistake.

'It's a little hard to explain, but my mother is Daisy Griggs, the blonde woman I was sitting with this morning. Mama is her best friend.'

'Gotcha.' If he did, he was a quick study. Duende changed the subject. 'So, what do you do in Wisconsin?'

'I'm a reporter for the city's daily, the *Urban Times*.'

'General assignment?'

The guy obviously knew something about the biz. 'No, I cover the police beat. Are you a journalist, too?'

But James Duende was backing toward the door. 'Nope. I've just known a couple. Well, I'd better get going. Nice to meet you, AnnaLise. See you later, Sheree.'

And he was gone.

AnnaLise looked at Sheree. 'He was in a hurry all of a sudden.'

'Not always.' Now an arch look. 'Mostly he takes his time.'

The last thing AnnaLise wanted to hear about was Sheree's love life. Or, more precisely, her sex life.

Like James Duende, change the subject. 'Why were you looking so disapproving of Joy and her band of sisters? Did they break something again?'

So far as AnnaLise knew, the Pack had broken one lamp, two chairs and an antique chamber pot. At least as of the last statement.

'No. They just gave me notice. They won't be back next year.'

No Frat Pack? It was unthinkable. Not that it should matter to AnnaLise. You don't live here any longer, she reminded herself. Still…

'I just saw Joy and she didn't say anything about this being their last year here.' A suspicion crept in. 'Are they going to Asheville instead?'

Lying southwest off the Blue Ridge Parkway, Asheville touted its 'arts community, diverse outdoor adventures, a vibrant and inviting downtown, numerous historic and architectural attractions, and unique shopping options'.

Let's just say that if Sutherton and Asheville were siblings, the latter would be the one mom liked better.

'Never.' Sheree was aghast. 'This is Joy and her gang we're talking about.'

True. Imagine the damage the women could do to the art galleries of Asheville. And what it would cost them to make restitution.

'Joy's planning to stay in Hart's Landing,' Sheree continued. 'Free of charge.'

AnnaLise found that hard to believe. 'Does her ex know yet?'

'I doubt it. But Joy usually gets what she wants from Dickens. Makes you wonder what she has on him.'

Echoing what AnnaLise had thought earlier. That didn't stop her, though, from saying, 'Maybe he still loves Joy.'

Sheree threw her a look dripping with pity. 'You really *are* still five, aren't you?'

'Because I'm not jaded and cynical?' Or am, but try not to show it?

'Exactly. Dickens Hart loves Dickens Hart. He created one empire and now he's building another, zoning it mixed-use and naming it for himself. Along the way, Hart's destroyed plenty of people and will destroy more. And I'm betting Joy knows just which of his closets are holding the skeletons.' Sheree sniffed. 'Frat Pack weekend was eighteen "room nights" I could always depend on. I just hope this isn't the start of a slippery slope.'

'You've never had a problem with Hotel Lux or the mountain rental properties, have you?' Fact was, the 300-room hotel and assorted mountain chalets and cottages were essential to Sutherton's tourist business. Sheree's thirteen rooms couldn't accommodate every one of the area's visitors.

'That's different. The Lux is mountain, as are the other private rentals. Discriminating guests, if they wanted to lodge on the lake itself, had to come here.'

'Except those who stayed at the White Tail Lodge, back in the day.'

'I said "discriminating".' Sheree growled. 'Now there are condos—one- and two-bedrooms, with kitchens—right in Hart's Landing. "Where the mountains meet the lake and the finest in shopping, dining and entertainment are right outside your door."'

Sheree said the last as if she was parroting a booming-voiced television announcer. Or Dickens Hart. Anna-Lise had to see this place for herself. It sounded...well, it sounded wonderful.

She felt like a traitor for even having the thought. If the new development was all it was trumpeted to be, Hart's Landing could well sound the death knell for not only Sheree's Inn, but all of Main Street.

Including Torch and Mama Philomena's. 'What kind of rest—'

But Sheree was preoccupied with the housing. 'Dr Stanton's already bought three of the condos. He's living in one, Tucker in another, and I understand he's renting the third to that Ichiro guy.'

'Bobby Bradenham's business partner?' As if there could be more than one 'Ichiro' in a town the size of Sutherton.

'Yeah.' Sheree slowed down. A good man could do that to a woman. 'You've met him?'

'Bobby introduced us this morning. Nice guy.'

'Handsome guy. Those eyes are to kill for.' A thought seemed to strike Sheree. 'Hey, speaking of which, did you hear that bastard Rance Smoaks finally got what he deserved?'

'Speaking of killing, you mean?'

'Well, yeah.' Sheree slowed down another notch. A *dead* man can do that to you, too. 'Though it sounds kind of harsh when you put it that way.'

AnnaLise didn't point out that *she* hadn't put it any way. 'It should. There's a difference between wanting someone dead and doing it.'

'Yeah. Courage.'

At a loss for what to say to that sociopathic revelation, AnnaLise settled for, 'What's he been doing since he lost his position as police chief?'

'Drinking,' Sheree said. 'Honestly, I don't know how Kathleen and he have managed to keep their place on the lake this long. It must be mortgaged up the ying-yang.'

'Certainly is a lot of house.'

Sheree shrugged. 'Familiar small-town tradition. Rance was a Smoaks and so the "good ole boys" down at the bank let him borrow more than he could afford.'

'I never understood the Smoaks' mystique,' AnnaLise

said. 'Rance's nephew River was in our class, remember? Girls were always ga-ga over him.'

'For one thing, he was the only eighth-grader old enough to have a driver's license.'

'And need a razor.'

'Even without being held back three times, he'd have been shaving. The male Smoaks practically come out of the womb with dark beards.'

'And the females, big boobs,' AnnaLise agreed.

'Maybe that's the allure,' Sheree said. 'The whole family is hyper-sexual. They exude pheromones.'

Luring the unwitting. 'Poor Kathleen.'

'Actually, lucky Kathleen. Believe it or not, Rance's father might have been a Smoaks, but his mother was Nanney Estill.'

'Estill? Like the road?' Estill Trail was a major route on the other side of the interstate.

'Like the trail. And the mall. Even the golf course,' Sheree said. 'The Estills, my girl, have real money.'

Smarts, too—at least enough to divorce Rance's father. Though, admittedly, Nanney Estill had married Roy in the first place.

'Are you saying some of the Estill estate came to Rance?' That might explain why Kathleen and Rance seemed to feel they could live beyond their means. 'I didn't realize Rance and his mother were close.'

'You kidding? Nanney wanted nothing to do with her husband Roy after the divorce. Or Rance.'

'Her own son?'

'We *are* talking about Rance Smoaks, remember?'

True. 'But—'

'Anyway,' Sheree continued, 'Nanney married against her family's wishes and apparently it didn't take long for her to see the error of her ways.'

'Meaning her family disowned her.'

'I couldn't say.'

Which meant Sheree could, but wouldn't. A rare show of restraint. AnnaLise tried to pick up the threads of the story.

'So Nanney divorced Roy and functionally abandoned little Rance,'—who'd once set the middle school on fire—'yet left him money when she died?'

'Not on purpose, silly.' Sheree was preoccupied with a rough fingernail. 'Apparently, there was this insurance policy she'd forgotten.'

'With her son being her nearest relation and therefore her beneficiary, unless she stipulated otherwise.'

'Bingo,' Sheree said. 'And now it all goes to his widow. I understand it's a bundle.'

'Lucky' Kathleen, indeed. A little too lucky? 'Are you sure she lacks… "courage", as you put it?'

'Oh, yeah. Kathleen didn't kill him.' Sheree gave up on the nail. 'Apparently he was out shooting with a friend.'

'Smoaks had a friend?'

'Of sorts. Joe Palooka.'

'You're kidding.' But AnnaLise knew that while Joe Palooka was a joke, he was a sad one. Born with the distinguished name of Stewart Chapel, going overboard on alcohol and food had turned the man into a caricature— an overinflated, misshapen punching bag that had gone way too many rounds. But a man who, like the old balloon that was his nick-namesake, kept popping back up for more punishment. Especially from fair-weather friends like Rance Smoaks. Fair-weather, meaning anytime there was no one else available.

'Where were they shooting?'

'At Rance's lake house. Trying to hit liquor bottles at twenty feet.'

'Let me guess, Rance was drinking straight from one such.'

'No, but close. The way I heard it, he'd set up a row of empties on the dock so they could shoot toward the lake and not hurt anyone.'

'Safety first. I'm impressed.'

'Yeah, except one bottle wasn't quite empty. Rance leaned over the line of them to remedy the situation and...'

'Joe didn't see him?' Lovely. Drunken target-shooting.

A shrug. 'It was dark.'

Night-time drunken target-shooting? Doubly lovely. 'And Rance just toppled into the lake?'

'Seems so. Joe's not absolutely clear on the sequence of events.'

Poor, pathetic Joe Palooka. With friends like Rance...

But speaking of friends, AnnaLise checked her wrist-watch. 'Gotta go. I'll catch you tonight at Sal's.'

'You still wear a watch? I use my cellphone to tell time.'

AnnaLise was standing. 'I use a watch to tell time and a cell to make calls. So sue me.'

Sheree was tsk-tsking as she followed her to the door. 'And I suppose you still have a camera, too.'

'With actual film inside, believe it or not.' AnnaLise turned. 'Call me old-fashioned, but what's wrong with that? Look at Mama's: the clunky cash register, the cushioned booths, the comfort food. That's why we love it.'

'Maybe that's why *you* love it. I love the view.'

'The view?'

'Sure. The lake, the beach and the bodies.' Sheree Pepper held open the door and shrugged. 'You know what they say: "eventually, every body comes home to Mama's."'

SIX

SHEREE AND HER 'PEPPERISMS'. Though prone to the sweeping overstatement and occasional outright lie, she'd been accurate this time.

Things *did* come home to roost on Main Street. Or, more specifically, on the public beach across from Mama's, where the constant Lake Sutherton currents deposited everything from wayward flip-flops to sodden advertising flyers blown off the mailboat.

Bodies, at least the human variety, were still infrequent. In fact, AnnaLise had long maintained that Sutherton's widespread reputation for bizarre accidents and untimely deaths was greatly exaggerated.

However, she did concede her having trouble convincing people of that in the future, given Daisy's recent phlebotomy flub and Rance Smoaks's even more recent actual demise.

PASSING THE CINCHED WAIST of Lake Sutherton's figure-eight, AnnaLise slowed her Mitsubishi Spyder convertible so as not to miss the turn-off for White Tail Island. Especially since Daisy, in the passenger's seat, was hanging her head out past the windshield, eyes closed, but otherwise enjoying the breeze like a cooped-up collie.

Good thing the top wasn't down or Mother Griggs would be standing up like a beauty queen in the homecoming parade. Not that AnnaLise would mind. She'd been both delighted and relieved when Daisy agreed to make the short trip with her.

Approaching by water, the fifty-acre island dominated Lake Sutherton's smaller northern loop, but from the road, it never seemed that obvious. AnnaLise needn't have worried about overshooting her mark, though. Always low-key and increasingly overgrown since the lodge had closed, entry to the island was now boldly announced by massive brick pillars, anchoring an overhead wrought-iron banner reading 'Hart's Landing'.

As AnnaLise made the turn, a large 'Phase One' sign appeared, 'Fully Occupied!' slashed across it. The next placard read, 'Phase Two—Coming Soon!' And the third, 'Pre-construction Prices—Better Act Now!'

'Burma-Shave,' Daisy piped up, eyes now wide open. 'You know, this little car makes an awful racket for its size.'

'There's a hole in the muffler, which I'll have fixed when I get back to Wisconsin. But what did you say about Burma?'

'Burma-Shave. The cream became famous because of an advertising campaign that I think started all the way back in the 1920s and ran into the Sixties. The company used a series of roadside signs that sort of interconnected. I don't remember everything clearly, but your Grandma Kuchenbacher would recite them whenever we went on a driving vacation.'

'Signs? Like billboards, you mean?' AnnaLise glanced over at her mother, who was smiling nostalgically.

'No, smaller. Only a couple of words on each sign and then the last one would always read "Burma-Shave". Grandma's favorite chant was "Does your husband / Misbehave? / Grunt and grumble / Rant and rave? / Shoot the brute some / Burma-Shave."'

'I love it!' AnnaLise was giggling. 'Tell me more.'

'I wish I could,' Daisy said. 'I should have written them all down back then. Now, I've forgotten most of what your grandma told me and when I'm gone…' She shrugged and left it there.

'Maybe you should keep journals, like I do,' said AnnaLise. Then, more sternly, 'That way, when you're gone *in another thirty or forty years*, I'll be able to pass the family lore on to my kids.'

'Best find a husband first.'

'Well, that's not very forward-thinking of you,' AnnaLise said, glancing over. 'I don't need a husband to—'

'Speaking of forward-thinking,' Daisy interrupted, 'watch where you're going. Here's the bridge.'

The car bumped onto the wooden span, which to AnnaLise's surprise hadn't been updated like the entrance. Luckily the distance from shore to island wasn't more than twenty feet. If you looked back as you reached the other side, you could just catch a glimpse of the Bradenham house through the trees.

'And soon,' said Daisy.

'Soon what?'

'The husband and children. Have to regale them with our family stories before you forget what you remember of what I remember. Though God knows that's not much anymore.'

AnnaLise threw her mother a startled look. Was Daisy aware of her memory blips? 'Everyone forgets things.'

It was a backhanded way to approach the subject, and AnnaLise was rewarded by an equally vague answer. 'Perhaps.'

Then her mother seemed to think for a moment. 'You mentioned journaling. I've been mulling over this blogging thing on the Internet. Seems that way I'd have a record of what I did, of what happened to me. And you would, too.'

Was Daisy considering a blog as a tool to train her memory? Or to remind herself when it failed?

Or...both?

'Sure, but remember blogging is for public consumption. Journaling, you can keep private.' Before AnnaLise could follow up further, they wheeled into Hart's Landing. It was a little like that scene in *The Wizard of Oz*, when Dorothy steps out of the cyclone-blown house.

'We're not in Sutherton anymore, Toto,' AnnaLise said out loud.

'More like New England.' Daisy was trying to peer three-sixty out of the convertible's windows as they turned into a parking space. 'Federalist, maybe?'

'Maybe.' AnnaLise turned off the engine and climbed out to look around. 'Red brick, white trim, blue-gray shutters. It's pretty, but not exactly High Country North Carolina.'

Daisy joined her. 'Though I'm not sure what even *that* is anymore. Sutherton's getting to be like any other town. People come from all over and they bring their influences.'

'Change,' said AnnaLise, disapproval audible even to her own ear. 'Bah humbug,' she threw in for good measure.

'AnnaLise Marie Griggs. You sound more like eighty-two than twenty-eight.'

'Just because I want things to stay the way I remember them?'

'They can't. And even if they did, your memories would change.' Daisy was staring south across the lake, toward Main Street. 'Take it from me.'

'The hell I will!'

The words hadn't come from AnnaLise, but from around the corner. The voice sounded like Joy Tamarack's and it was joined by others, also raised. Thinking her friend might be in trouble, AnnaLise signaled Daisy to stay where she was.

Hart's Landing consisted of three long four-story buildings forming a squared horseshoe, the opening facing the mountains. As AnnaLise traced the sidewalk from the parking lot, the center of the landing came into view—a town square of sorts, complete with gazebo bandstand. Though mostly still empty, the first floors appeared designated for retail, with residential apartments above.

Three people were standing on the sidewalk, arguing. A lot of noise for such a small group. As AnnaLise got closer, she recognized Dickens Hart. He stood only about five foot nine and had to be in his late sixties, but he still had the looks and bearing that had attracted Joy and countless others. Dark hair, now salt-and-pepper. Deep brown eyes.

Sort of a pocket Sean Connery.

Joy was standing toe-to-toe with him, obviously angry, though AnnaLise couldn't yet make out individual words. The third person, staying to the side and seeming to listen intently, was the father of the family AnnaLise had seen leaving Mama's restaurant that morning. Presumably David Sabatino—the developer Bobby had mentioned.

AnnaLise was about to retreat to save everyone embarrassment, when an apartment window quietly slid closed above the trio. It might as well have sounded like a thunderclap for the reaction it elicited. The three people sprang apart as Daisy rounded the corner, too, joining AnnaLise.

Dickens Hart was the first to catch sight of mother and daughter.

Since it *now* would be more rude to turn tail and run, they walked up to the group.

'AnnaLise,' said Hart. 'It's been a long time. Can I hope you're moving back to town? Maybe looking for a nice place to live?' He swept his hand toward the buildings. 'It's a prime time to buy in.'

'Unless you're me, of course.' This from Joy. Somehow, without AnnaLise noticing, Sabatino had disappeared.

Like James Duende, entering the Sutherton Inn as a silent shadow.

'I said *buy* in,' Hart snapped. Then he apologetically addressed Daisy. 'I'm sorry. Family squabble. You know how it is.'

'*Ex*-family,' Joy snarled.

'Family stays family. Forever.'

A life sentence. The way Hart said it made AnnaLise very glad she wasn't related to him. And, despite Daisy and Mama's gossiping, she dearly hoped Bobby Bradenham wasn't either.

AnnaLise had been very young when she first heard the term 'womanizer'. Her father had been talking about Dickens Hart, and though AnnaLise hadn't known what the word meant, she knew it wasn't a good thing to be. Growing up, AnnaLise had always kept her distance.

'The subject of family reminds me,' Hart continued, turning to AnnaLise. 'I was going to email you on your newspaper's website.'

'You were?' Granted, AnnaLise was a reporter, but on an urban daily newspaper nearly eight hundred miles away. What possible good could she do Hart? 'Why?'

'I'd like to publish my memoirs. I've been piecing together notes and journal entries. I'm looking for someone to help me with the project.'

'In what way?'

He looked puzzled. 'To collaborate. You know, in the writing of it.'

'You want me to collaborate on your autobiography? I'm a journalist not a...a book author.' God help her, she'd almost said 'novelist'. But in truth, what better way to blur the line between fact and fiction than for a journalist to help an egomaniac twist his memoirs?

'I've read your work,' Hart persisted, looking her straight in the eye. 'And while I've interviewed a couple of highly-recommended ghostwriters, I really need someone who knows both the High Country and Sutherton's place in it. To make things simpler.'

And probably cheaper for him. Which meant that the best way to say 'no' would be to quote a fee so high Hart would have to be an idiot to agree. Like a bluff bet in poker.

'Well, thank you for thinking of me,' AnnaLise said, glancing over at Daisy. 'I'm afraid, though, that I'm very busy right now and I couldn't possibly take on something of this magnitude for less than a hundred thousand, upfront, whether we're the only ones who ever read it or not.'

Hart's mouth opened.

Better up the ante. 'And I'd want fifty percent of any advances and royalties from the publisher if the book is accepted, of course.'

'Umm...'

'Before agent commissions and my out-of-pocket expenses.'

'Uh...'

Raise him again. 'Plus, I'll work only on my own timetable. From Wisconsin.'

'But—'

Now call *his* bluff. 'And I'm not ghosting this, Dickens. I demand full collaborator's credit on the jacket cover.'

'Done,' said Hart.

Shit, girl. You've negotiated yourself one hell of a deal. Or…the deal from hell.

SEVEN

'WHATEVER WERE YOU THINKING?' mother asked daughter as they stood with Joy, watching Dickens Hart walk away.

'I never imagined he'd go for it.' AnnaLise was torn between horror and elation. The obvious horror was having to work with one of the most despised men in any valley. But a gig that, at minimum, would pay twice her annual salary? Which she could do while still making her annual salary?

Wow.

And, as a bonus, if Hart truly had an interesting story, AnnaLise knew she really was a gifted enough writer to…

'Why, you self-important asshole.'

'That's a little harsh, isn't it?' AnnaLise said to Joy. 'I just responded to what—'

'I was talking to Dickens. Or at least his back.' Joy gestured toward Hart, who was nearly out of sight. 'The big shot can pay that kind of money to massage his ego—which, by the way, is the biggest part of him. But I ask for space to open a spa and a measly one-bedroom condo to live in above it and what does he say?'

AnnaLise and Daisy just looked at her.

'I'll tell you what he said. No. Flat out. Under the circumstances, he should be on his knees thanking me for trying to inject some life into this place.'

'You expected him to just give the properties to you?' AnnaLise asked. Whatever Joy thought of the memoir fee, at least AnnaLise was willing to work for it.

'Well, yeah.' Joy glared at her. 'What's wrong with that?'

AnnaLise raised her hands palms out. 'Nothing. Nothing at all.'

'You bet your ass there isn't. That man stole my youth!' She stomped away.

'Weren't they married only…about a year?' Daisy finally managed.

'Apparently, Joy's was a very short youth.' AnnaLise cocked her head and looked at her mother. 'So did I just make an awful mistake with Dickens?'

'Probably. But it's an awful, well-paying mistake.' Daisy grinned. 'And who knows? Maybe you can turn it into a best-seller.'

'I doubt that, but I'll know better after I go through his notes and journals. Maybe beginning tomorrow.'

Now Joy came stomping back. 'And another—'

'Hello!'

Startled, AnnaLise, Daisy, and even Joy looked around for the source of the new voice.

'You see up.'

AnnaLise did. Ichiro Katou was waving from the second-story window she'd seen close. Apparently, it was even quieter going up.

'Hello, Ichiro. Have you met my friend, Joy Tamarack?'

The limits of his window-frame confined him to a half-bow. 'A pleasure. I did not mean to overdrop your earlier conversation.'

'It's either "overhear" or "eavesdrop",' AnnaLise said, trying to be helpful.

'Thank you,' accompanied by another little bow. 'It is good to know the correct way for me to say these things.'

'Sure, sure,' Joy said before AnnaLise could respond, 'but you don't need to apologize for listening.'

'Thank you,' Katou said again and hesitated. 'You mind I ask a question?'

'Shoot.'

The Japanese man looked nonplussed for a moment and then seemed to understand the idiom. 'Oh, yes, I see. "Shoot", as in go forward.'

Joy nodded encouragingly. She, like Sheree and AnnaLise herself, seemed charmed by him.

'You say to Mr Hart that the water rises.' He spread his hands wide. 'Is it safe here? Must I leave the island?'

AnnaLise looked at Daisy. 'Is the lake level up?'

'No,' her mother said, wrinkling her brow. 'In fact, it was an unusually dry August. We've been worried about fires, not floods.'

'No, no, no,' Joy said, turning red. 'Ichiro, you misunderstood. I didn't say "flooded". I said "underwater".'

'Underwater?' AnnaLise echoed. 'As in, owing more than a property is worth? But Ichiro doesn't own the condo.'

She tipped her face up to where he was now hanging out the window. 'You rent from Dr Stanton, right?'

'You are correct,' Katou said. 'You are saying I do not worry?'

'Not about drowning,' Joy muttered. She seemed to regret having opened her mouth at all. She appealed to her friends on the ground. 'You two have to keep quiet about this.'

'What's the big secret?' AnnaLise asked. 'A lot of people bought when housing prices were high and now that values have dropped, they're stuck. It's not something to be ashamed of.'

'Besides,' Daisy said. 'Tucker and his father, certainly, don't seem to have anything to worry about.'

AnnaLise thought she saw something cross Joy's expression. 'But it wouldn't be just the Stantons, would it? All of Hart's Landing could be in jeopardy.' Along with— easy come, easy go—AnnaLise's 'memoir' contract.

'Pfft.' Joy must have read her mind. 'Dickens Hart will always land on his feet. Just press him on your book deal and get the money upfront.'

'I'll do that,' AnnaLise said, though it might be like insisting the devil sign on the dotted line for your soul. 'But back to you: your spa idea could be a real boon to the development. I assume that's the project you have "in the works"?'

'Yup,' Joy said.

'Well, don't worry,' Daisy said. 'You'll think of something.'

'Oh, believe me.' Joy squared her shoulders. 'I haven't given up.'

'Good for you,' Daisy said, slapping Joy on the back as the prospective spa-owner turned to leave. Again.

'Hello,' Katou said again from on high.

'I think you mean goodbye,' AnnaLise said. 'Joy's leaving.'

'No.' He pointed. 'I speak to him.'

Sure enough, a new arrival. Bobby Bradenham was passing Joy on the sidewalk from the parking lot.

'I thought I heard your car go by our house,' Bobby said to AnnaLise when he reached them. 'You better get that muffler fixed. Especially with out-of-state plates.'

Sutherton's police department was notorious for ticketing. It, along with tourism, had provided an important stream of income for the town over the years.

'The municipal coffers down?' AnnaLise asked.

'You'd be surprised how much law enforcement, when properly motivated, can bring in.' He looked around the group. 'What's everybody doing here? We only need Mama for a quorum.'

'And *your* mama,' AnnaLise said. 'Assuming we want to re-create the restaurant scenario from this morning.'

'I dropped Ma off at Hotel Lux to get a mani-pedi.'

'Your mom is primping for Frat Pack Night?' AnnaLise knew better, but she loved Bobby's imitations of his mother.

'Please.' Theatrically, he threw out his hand, palm-up. 'I despise crowds, as you well know. If I want to enjoy the lake, I will do so from the comfort and privacy of my own lovely deck, not some noisy hole-in-the-wall.'

'Does your mother ever use a contraction?' AnnaLise asked, curious.

Bobby's hand had migrated to the imaginary strand of pearls. 'Why ever would one use a single word where two will do? And apostrophes—' a denigrating flap of the hand— 'so common, no?'

'Your mother,' Katou said, looking puzzled. 'AnnaLise asks if she hires someone?'

'Hires someone?' Bobby repeated, looking at Anna-Lise.

'Oh,' she said, understanding. 'Contraction, root word contract. Leading to contractor, perhaps. Very good reasoning, Ichiro. However, a contraction is—'

But Bobby cut her off, presumably having heard enough of AnnaLise's lectures in the past. 'I was just saying that my mother will be staying home tonight.'

'Your mother does not enjoy…the company?' Katou asked.

'Only her own,' Daisy said under her breath as she moved into the shade thrown by the building.

'That's not entirely true,' Bobby said with a grin. 'She tolerates me at times.'

'And me, as well,' Katou said. 'Tomorrow for the lunch. I look forward to seeing your home and learning of your family.'

'Ma will be *delighted* to show you the place,' Bobby said, 'but don't expect any family sagas. Ma's so evasive, I've always wondered whether I'm adopted.'

'You, me and every kid who doesn't look like their surviving parent,' AnnaLise said, glad Mama wasn't around to put her two cents' worth in about Bobby's paternity.

'I think that's why I was always fascinated by the subject of heredity in school. I even tried to blood-type myself once. I thought Ma was going to hit the ceiling when she caught me with a knife and two lenses I'd taken out of her reading glasses to make a slide.'

'Now you scrape.' Katou disappeared from the window and returned with something that looked like an oversized cotton swab.

AnnaLise's eyes widened and Bobby laughed. 'Ichiro and I are taking part in a worldwide genome project. It uses DNA, which is the reason for the giant Q-tip.'

He gestured toward the door of Katou's building. 'Want to see?'

AnnaLise glanced over at Daisy, who was hovering none too patiently. 'I think not. We both have plans for tonight, and I need to iron something to wear.'

'To Sal's?' Bobby asked. 'You might want to add a couple wrinkles and maybe a mustard stain. Help you fit in.'

A buzzer sounded and with a wave, Bobby entered the building. AnnaLise stepped back to say goodbye to Katou, but he was gone, too, presumably having been the one to buzz Bobby into the building.

That left just AnnaLise and Daisy on the quiet sidewalk. 'This place really is a ghost town.'

But Daisy didn't seem to be interested in Hart's Landing. 'Should they be messing around with DNA?'

'They're not exactly creating a monster, Dr Frankenstein,' AnnaLise said as she led the way back to the car. 'I did some research for an article about *National Geographic*'s genographic project. They're trying to collect hundreds of thousands of DNA samples from people around the world in order to trace human migration. I think it would be fascinating to find out where the ancestors in your lineage were a thousand years ago and how they got…well, here.'

'And paternity?' Daisy asked.

AnnaLise shrugged. 'I don't know which program Ichiro is involved with, but from what I've read, lineage tests are much more general than paternity tests. They might show that your parents came from European descent, for example, but not provide specifics. Once you had the DNA, though, I'm guessing you could test for whatever you wanted.'

'Wouldn't you need samples from both father and child?' Daisy stood waiting while AnnaLise climbed into the car and leaned over to unlock the door.

'As I understand it.' AnnaLise put the key in the ignition as Daisy slipped into the passenger seat. 'But remember I was doing an article on the genographic project, not paternity testing.' She looked sideways at her mother and grinned. 'A little information, in the wrong hands, can be a dangerous thing.'

'Amen to that.'

EIGHT

SEVEN THIRTY AND Frat Pack Night was already in full swing.

'I'm so sorry,' AnnaLise said, sliding into a seat opposite Bobby. 'My watch—'

'Was still on central time,' Bobby said, signaling Sal's bartender to draw AnnaLise the local brew—a Pisgah Porter. 'Don't worry, I figured you'd be late.'

Fine reputation to have, re-cultivated after less than twelve hours back in your own hometown.

A sliver of sunlight slanted across Bobby's face and continued its travels around the room. AnnaLise glanced over her shoulder to see Sheree Pepper, Sutherton's favorite innkeeper, slip through the door. Since sunset wouldn't be for another twenty minutes, it was still bright on the beach outside. Inside, more like another world.

The room was dark, the only illumination coming from the red plastic mesh-covered candle holder centered on each table and a klieg spot directed at the stage. There, Sal Goldstein, brown hair slicked back and showing a lot more scalp than AnnaLise's last visit, crooned 'Mack the Knife' into the microphone.

AnnaLise had once made the mistake of suggesting the tune was made famous by Bobby Darin and gotten an earful.

'You telling me Frank Sinatra never sang that song? Huh? You telling me that?'

Nope. Not me. Forget I ever said anything.

On a stool next to the bar owner sat an opened laptop computer so he could control his own playlist. A digital version of the old one-man band, sans cymbals strapped between knees or tambourines tied to limbs.

Sheree took the third of four chairs at the round table. 'So, where's your friend?'

Bobby and AnnaLise exchanged looks as she stood to pick up her beer from the bartender. 'You field this one,' she told him. Then: 'Sheree?'

'Cabernet. Something with a cork, if that's remotely possible.'

AnnaLise didn't bother to point out the folly of ordering wine in a place like Sal's. Sheree already knew better.

Behind her, AnnaLise heard Bobby ask Sheree, 'By friend, do you mean Ichiro?'

AnnaLise told the barman Sheree's unwisely optimistic request and turned, back to bar, to watch Bobby and Sheree.

'Of course I'm talking about Ichiro.' Sheree was looking around like she'd find the man hiding under a table. 'Where is he?'

Bobby shrugged. 'He'll be here about ten. Why?'

Sheree, of the push-up bra and pushed-down neckline, said, 'No reason.'

AnnaLise snickered as she returned with her mug and slid a tiny bottle of wine like they serve on planes to Sheree. 'What's wrong, one guy's not enough? Which reminds me, where *is* your "tenant"?'

Sheree grinned. 'One, much like once, is never enough, AnnaLise. You should have learned that by now.'

AnnaLise reflexively glanced at her purse, where a cellphone with two missed calls and three texts from Ben was buried. 'Sometimes, one can be too many.'

Especially when that 'one' wouldn't take 'it's over' for an answer.

The eye movement wasn't lost on Sheree. 'Honey, do we need to talk?'

'Later. Maybe.' AnnaLise lifted her mug. 'But tonight, dear friends, a toast. To Frat Pack Night.'

'To Frat Pack Night,' Bobby echoed, raising his glass.

'Hold up.' Sheree removed the clear plastic glass which had been upended over the neck of the bottle and checked the label. 'Cab/Merlot blend. Indeterminate vintage.'

She clinked the bottle itself against first AnnaLise's and then Bobby's brews. 'To impertinent little wines.'

'And impertinent little friends,' Bobby said with a grin.

'I'll drink to that.' Sheree took a swig from the bottle and then poured the rest into her plastic cup. 'So why's Ichiro going to be so late?'

They both looked at her.

'What? I just hate for him to miss the show.'

'He'll catch an hour,' Bobby said. 'That's probably more than enough for anybody's initiation to Frat Pack Night.'

'An hour? Are you saying Sal stops at eleven now?' AnnaLise said, taking an appreciative sip of her rich North Carolina brew. 'Since when?'

'The place has closed at eleven for a couple of years now,' Bobby said over the lyrics '...*line forms, on the right dear...*'

'Sal tries to get home for Leno,' Sheree said, tugging at her top.

'Unlike Daisy,' AnnaLise said. 'She's going to Torch tonight and told me not to wait up. You'd think my mother's getting younger and I'm getting older.'

'Pretty soon the two of you will cross.' Sheree waved at someone in the crowd. 'There's Chuck.'

'Oh, good,' AnnaLise said, turning to beckon him to their table. 'He said he needed to talk with me about something.'

The police chief put up his index finger in a 'just a second' signal while he finished a conversation. AnnaLise turned back to her companions.

They didn't say anything. Just looked at her.

'What?' she asked.

'Nothing,' Sheree said. 'But…how long has it been since you and Chuck spoke?'

'Quite a while, I'm afraid. I saw him this morning on the beach and we exchanged voicemails after Daisy's—' she looked at Bobby— 'and Mrs B's accident, but we haven't really *talked* in ages.'

'In addition to refusing to change your watch to the time zone you're in,' Bobby said, 'you're lousy at keeping in touch.'

'I know.' AnnaLise felt herself flush. Truth was, she'd been so immersed in her Wisconsin life that she'd let her relationship with childhood friends slide. Daisy and Mama provided the Sutherton version of CNN Headline News, but when it came to protracted conversations… 'I'd see a message and think, I'll call back when I have the time to truly reconnect, but…'

'There's never that kind of time,' Sheree said. 'And then, eventually, we just forget.'

'Putting us all in the same boat.' Bobby leaned across the table toward them. 'So did you hear it was Rance Smoaks they found on the beach this morning?'

'Good riddance,' Sheree said.

'Ahh, we must be talking about Rance.' Chuck had finished up and sunk into the chair between Bobby and AnnaLise and across the round table from Sheree. 'I hate to

say it, but the only person who's broken up on that issue
is Kathleen.'

'And she's the one who should be most grateful,' Sheree
said.

AnnaLise, mindful of Chuck as police chief, added,
'Not that she is.'

'Grateful to the shooter, you mean?' Chuck asked.

'No, no…I just—'

'Stop torturing her,' Sheree said. 'We all know Rance
was a tool. And a dull one at that.'

'True.' The door opened and Chuck glanced up, his
eyes following the newcomer.

AnnaLise twisted to see James Duende. With the nodded permission of the couple at the next table, AnnaLise
snagged one of their chairs.

Oblivious, Sheree set down her wine. 'Whoever's that
for?' gesturing at the chair.

'Your "one".'

'Jim?' Rubbernecking now. 'Where is he?'

'Right over where'd he go?' AnnaLise looked around,
but Duende had disappeared.

'The guy who just came in?' Chuck said. 'Dark wavy
hair, olive complexion, military physique?'

'Good eye,' AnnaLise said, turning back. 'I wish I was
as naturally observant as you are. I have to make myself
study people and places, and then take notes.'

'It's a gift,' said Chuck. 'In my line of work—'

'Work, schmurk,' Sheree interrupted. 'You think he's
hot.'

'But straight,' Chuck said.

'Straight?' AnnaLise stopped and looked at her long-
ago boyfriend. 'Chuck?'

He scrunched up his eyes and then stared back. 'Yes,
Lise?'

'You're…gay?'

'Got it right the first time, Annie,' Bobby said.

If you didn't count the nearly two decades AnnaLise and Chuck had been friends. And more.

'Sorry,' Chuck said, covering her hand with this.

'You don't have to be sorry.' AnnaLise blinked. 'I'm glad you, umm…'

'Found himself?' Sheree supplied. 'I was glad, too, when he came out. Explained all those years he ignored me.'

'You, my lady, scared the shit out of me,' Chuck said.

But I didn't, AnnaLise thought. Figures. I'm one of those women guys make 'buddies' of. Watch the game with. Confide in about their wives and girlfriends.

She cleared her throat. 'Came out? So everyone knows?'

The 'but me', was unspoken, but not unheard by Chuck. 'I called you five, six times.'

'I know. I've been a bad friend.' She turned her hand over to squeeze his. 'So, what's been the reaction?'

'Good.'

'Except for Rance Smoaks, the homophobe,' Sheree said. 'Like I said, good riddance.'

Bobby explained. 'Rance tried to get Chuck ousted last year, to retake the office. It got pretty nasty.'

Chuck shrugged. 'He thought the town would prefer even an active alcoholic to a gay guy. He was wrong.'

Dead wrong, as it turned out. 'I can't believe neither Daisy nor Mama told me,' AnnaLise said.

'I asked them not to.' Chuck withdrew his hand and tented his fingertips. 'That I wanted to call you.'

'And they listened?' Harder to believe than the news that her old boyfriend preferred men.

'Sure.'

'And then promptly forgot, probably,' Bobby said nodding. 'Just like we were saying before you got here, Chuck. Life moves on, even in Sutherton.'

Before AnnaLise could agree or disagree, the front door was yanked open.

Sunset shafts of orange, rose and purple sliced through from outside, triggering a chorus of '*Start spreading the news...*'

The Frat Pack had arrived.

NINE

Sunday, Sept. 5, 2:00 a.m.

*Combining the Pisgah Porters at Sal's with Mid-
night Espresso Martinis at Torch was not, in retro-
spect, a good idea.*

AG

A RUN, IF ANNALISE survived it, might salvage the rest of
the day from her hangover.

'You're shitting me, right?' Joy said when AnnaLise
called her cell. 'It's barely eight a.m.'

'You said you wanted to run this morning,' AnnaLise
protested. 'Besides, Sal's closed at eleven last night.'

'That doesn't mean we stopped drinking.' The tone of
Joy's voice added, 'you idiot.'

'Granted,' AnnaLise said. 'But think how much better
you'll feel after you exercise.'

Nothing but the chilly silence of a cell connection that's
been broken.

'What? No click? No dial tone?' AnnaLise said into
the phone before flicking it off. 'Oh, for the days a girl
knew when she'd been hung up on.'

'What, dear?' Daisy stuck her head around the corner, all smiles.

How did she do it? When AnnaLise had finally tracked
her down at Torch, the woman had been pounding down
vodka gimlets.

'I was just calling Joy,' AnnaLise said, holding up the phone. 'She's decided not to run.'

'And, if elected, not to serve?' Daisy chuckled. 'I'm sorry, dear. Want to come to the restaurant with me? Mama has Savory Scrambled Eggs today.'

The thought of eggs, savory or not, was stomach-churning. Nonetheless, AnnaLise couldn't help asking, 'Is that the one with chipped beef in it?'

'Don't be silly,' Daisy said, lips pursed. 'That's Company Scrambled Eggs. The Savory have Philadelphia Cream Cheese.'

'Oooh, I like those.' AnnaLise actually thought about it for a second. Then: 'No, I really do need to run.'

'Well, your choice, but you can run anywhere,' Daisy said, gathering her handbag and moving toward the door. 'You can only get Mama's Savory Eggs here. Today. With me.'

Mother Griggs was being insidious, but AnnaLise stayed strong. 'Don't try to guilt me into it, Daisy. I'll exercise, *then* stop in at Mama's.'

'Suit yourself,' her mother said, stepping out onto the sidewalk, 'but don't you mean "shame you into it"?'

'Nope,' said AnnaLise to the closing door. 'I'm pretty sure I mean "guilt".'

She had gotten as far as the front sidewalk when a thought struck her: the bicycle.

As AnnaLise wheeled out on her old powder-blue, five-speed Huffy, sporting her matching blue bike helmet, she congratulated herself on finding just the right exercise for the morning. Not only would she eliminate all that jarring impact of sole to concrete, AnnaLise would also spare her stomach the nauseating jostling and, with luck, feel well enough and get back soon enough to have break-fast with Daisy.

Not guilt? My ass.

The trail was asphalt and nicely level along the south and west sides of Lake Sutherton, so AnnaLise decided to bike clockwise until even with the White Tail Island bridge on the north shore and then retrace her route counterclockwise. With the exception of Dickens Hart's mini-mansion, summer rental cottages lined the eastern waterfront, and the trail maintenance there was at best hit-and-miss. Mostly miss.

For the sake of this morning's hangover, AnnaLise planned to steer clear of both the uneven eastern trail and Hart himself, lest he press her to fill her cute little bike basket with his journals and notes.

Yes, better to see Hart this afternoon, she thought, riding past Sal's Tap and onto the trail entrance marked by the statue to the Faithful Dog.

'You poor pooch,' she said to the granite retriever. 'Your master went away and all you got was this lousy statue.'

Paralleling Main Street west of town, she ticked off the impressive properties that lined Lake Sutherton. Unlike the nameless canine depicted in stone, the homes had impressive titles: Miller House and Preston Place, Watkins Nest and Cranswick Cottage.

North of the residential stretch was the Sutherton Post Office. It was situated next to the north launch for the convenience of the mailboat that serviced the homes and cottages along the lake. In the winter months, when the lake was frozen, the courier discharged his appointed rounds the less colorful way. By four-wheel-drive truck.

But in the summer, much to the delight of tourists who paid fifteen dollars each for the pleasure of riding along, local college students would deliver the mail, hopping off the mailboat on one side of the property and catching up with it on the other, just in time to jump back on.

Each delivery was accompanied by the sound of passengers cheering on the kids and, on occasion, the splash of one of them landing in the drink, usually in a not life-threatening, but immensely entertaining way.

Truth be told, the shtick was mostly about entertainment, which explained why tourists were boarding the boat, even sans mail. Today the vessel carried thick Sunday newspapers instead. Hell, in order to keep the visitors—and their fifteen bucks—coming back, the mailboat would deliver pizzas if necessary.

As AnnaLise rode by, the excursion was readying to head out with Sal's granddaughter, Nicole Goldstein, as the designated mail-runner. AnnaLise waved and nearly lost control of her bike, hitting a tree root that had pushed its manifest destiny heavenward through the asphalt.

AnnaLise couldn't see who was at the wheel, but she assumed it was Bob Esmond. Cap'n Bob had helmed the boat for as long as AnnaLise could remember.

As she'd experienced when first returning to Main Street, there was a definite comfort in things remaining the same. But also, AnnaLise had to concede, in things changing. Like Sutherton embracing an openly gay chief of police. AnnaLise was proud of her hometown and proud of Chuck. It couldn't have been easy to grow up gay and closeted in such a small, closely knit community. It must have been even tougher to open the door and come out.

All in all, AnnaLise's world was shaping up. Daisy seemed sharp this morning and her daughter was feeling better by the minute. There was a lot to be said for crisp mountain air over warm tomato juice and Tabasco sauce as the preferred hangover cure, though AnnaLise did wish she'd thought to take a couple of aspirins.

Just past the north launch and Lucky's Bait Shop, serving it, Main Street veered away from the lake. The walk/jog/bicycle path AnnaLise was riding on, though, continued to parallel the shoreline. She rode under a bridge of hand-hewn timber and found herself in front of the second-most impressive house on Lake Sutherton, Bradenham.

Yes, just 'Bradenham'.

Hart wasn't the only narcissist on the lake.

AnnaLise paused, putting one foot down to stay balanced on her bike. Should she stop at the house and see if Bobby was around? Tempting, but she really wasn't dressed for visiting and if Mrs B happened to be lurking…

'AnnaLise!'

OK, so Mrs B *was* lurking.

AnnaLise shaded her eyes and turned, trying to locate the woman. Her mistake was looking at the house instead of toward the lake.

Bobby's mother waved from a lounge chair on a wide, wooden deck cantilevered over the water. It was connected to the house by the bridge AnnaLise had just passed beneath.

'Wow,' she said, looking up. 'This is gorgeous. New?'

'It is, and I must say I am very proud,' Mrs B said. 'Leave your bicycle and come have a lemonade with me, so I can show off my outdoor living space properly.'

How do you pass up an offer like that? And an 'outdoor living space', no less. AnnaLise leaned her bike against one of the bridge supports and looked both ways. 'How do I get up to you?'

'Take that flagstoned walk to the house,' Bobby's mother said. 'The stairs to the first deck will be on your right, and then you'll have to cross the bridge.'

'When I come to it,' AnnaLise muttered, as she climbed

the steep flight of steps. She'd been a flat-lander long enough that the elevation of Sutherton, around four thousand feet above sea level, could literally take her breath away.

Ashamed to be laboring, she grasped the stair rail for assistance. The wood under her hand looked like mahogany, but the spindles below were iron, as in black and wrought. Some might say *over*wrought, for the setting. Sure was nice, though. And sturdy.

The deck AnnaLise reached from the staircase had replaced the simpler one she remembered being off the living room's French doors. Pausing to catch her breath, she looked around. Where Bobby's fishing rods and other outdoor gear—always banished from the house in AnnaLise's memory—had nestled, a wall of cabinets now stood neatly labeled with a brass plate centered on each door: 'Fishing', 'Hunting', 'Hiking' and—who *doesn't* have one of these?— 'Miscellany'.

Except at my Wisconsin apartment, AnnaLise thought, it's called 'junk', lower case. And it's a single drawer, not a mahogany cabinet.

But this was, after all, Bradenham. The new deck had a trellis overhead to support the leafy vines that shaded the big sunken hot tub and all-weather kitchen. The whole arrangement just cried out for a party. But why would someone who never entertained and, according to Bobby, disliked crowds, need or want such a space?

Other than to impress those boating by it. Or, in this case, bicycling.

AnnaLise patted the giant stainless-steel grill on its shiny hood. 'If I owned you, you'd already have a lovely sheen of barbecue grease, and margarita dribbled down your front control panel.'

The bridge that connected the 'house deck' to the 'lake

deck' was about five feet wide, with high wrought-iron railings on each side, presumably for safety. The bridge then opened onto a round platform, planks set at a diagonal to the bridge. The railings were lower here and airier, so they almost disappeared into the foreground when you looked out onto the lake.

'Breathtaking,' AnnaLise said. Mrs B was resplendent on a chaise that up close looked like something Cleopatra would have owned if she'd had it custom-made in North Carolina and God had financed the lay-away plan.

No pearls and Hermes bag today. Bobby's mother was wearing a pair of walking shorts and a crisp, tailored white blouse. As she stood up, she slipped her feet into woven sandals with kitten heels.

'It is a glorious view, is it not?' She waved AnnaLise toward a table where a tray with glasses and a pitcher of iced lemonade stood. 'Please, help yourself.'

Does the woman sit here every day, AnnaLise wondered, a full pitcher of lemonade and glasses on the table, in the event she has a visitor not immediately deemed banishment material? Perhaps a 'gentleman caller', as in *The Glass Menagerie*?

Seemingly reading her mind, the older woman said, 'I am expecting Bobby and his friend, Ichiro, any moment now. They will be so happy to see you.'

Nice. Not only had AnnaLise forgotten the planned luncheon Bobby and Ichiro spoke about just yesterday, but she'd been unkind to Mrs B, if only in her thoughts. 'I'm so sorry. I didn't mean to interrupt your Sunday.'

'Oh, not at all, dear,' Mrs B said, gesturing her toward a chair. 'They want to talk to me about their restaurant venture.' She lifted her eyebrows or, given her cosmetic work, tried to. 'I have my doubts about sushi in Sutherton, but then what do I know? I have only lived here for most of my adult life.'

'So you are not from Sutherton originally?' Anna-Lise asked, unintentionally mimicking the other woman's speech pattern.

'Heavens, no—wherever would you get that idea?' Mrs B actually 'harrumphed', something AnnaLise had previously seen only in print. 'My father was in the foreign service, so, though I was born in the South of Florida, I traveled extensively throughout Europe and Asia.'

South of Florida? Like the South of France? And AnnaLise was pretty certain 'foreign service' would translate more into 'army brat', but who was she to say? Her international travel extended as far as Toronto, Canada, just over the US border to the north and Tijuana, Mexico, ditto to the south.

'What brought you to the High Country?' AnnaLise asked, raising her voice to be heard over a passing, reverberating waverunner.

'Sorry, my dear,' Mrs B said, turning to glare at the offending speed demon. 'I told Bobby he needs to ban those annoying machines.'

Ema Bradenham wasn't alone in her feelings. In fact, Sheree Pepper might best have expressed local opinion on personal watercraft that buzzed around Lake Sutherton like giant mosquitoes: 'Can't kill 'em, can't stick 'em up their asses.'

AnnaLise wasn't much of a fan either, but Mrs B's tone did smack a bit of 'if I were king'. Or, more precisely: 'if my son was mayor—which he is'.

'You were saying, dear?' Mrs B was looking at her expectantly.

'Oh, I'm sorry. I was asking you why you moved to Sutherton.'

'Work, originally,' Mrs B said, an unexpectedly nostalgic cast to her face. 'In fact, your dear mother was my very first friend here.'

'Really?' The intonation rang wrong, as if Daisy had told her daughter otherwise, so AnnaLise muddled on. 'I didn't know you were so new to town when the two of you met.'

'Oh, yes.' Mrs B looked lost in thought for a moment. Then: 'How *is* your mother, Little One? I hate to ask her directly, lest she think I…'

'…was concerned about the blood-drive incident?' AnnaLise set down her glass. 'You have every right to be. Daisy made an awful mistake.'

The other woman waved the subject off like she had in Mama's restaurant the day before. 'Not at all, dear. But, Lorraine and I spoke yesterday and, frankly, she seems…different.'

Lorraine. AnnaLise hadn't heard her mother's given name spoken out loud for years, maybe decades. 'Different? She *has* had a couple of…I guess I'd call them spells, when she became disoriented. I phoned Dr Stanton to see what he thinks.'

Which reminded AnnaLise that she still hadn't gotten a return call from her mother's physician, and that suddenly seemed inexcusable under the circumstances, even over a holiday weekend. 'I'm hoping that he'll tell me it's as simple as a vitamin deficiency of some kind.'

'Or mineral,' Mrs B said. 'Even something as apparently unrelated as a urinary tract infection can cause behavioral changes and delirium as we grow older.'

'But Daisy's not old,' AnnaLise protested. Or delirious either. At least not most of the time.

'I know, Little One. I know. But chemical imbalances can affect us at any age.'

The more they talked about it, the more agitated AnnaLise was becoming. In fairness, not because of Mrs B
per se, but because her questions indicated other people
were noticing Daisy's 'spells'.

Which meant they were real, not something vaguely
imagined by AnnaLise or Mama.

AnnaLise had to talk to Dr Stanton and soon, because
she'd need to leave on Tuesday at sunrise for the drive
back.

While making the thirteen-hour trek to Sutherton in
two days and leaving that last stretch of rural and mountain roads for the morning of the second one made sense,
the return trip could be done in a single, albeit very long,
day. Once on the interstate, AnnaLise would have straight
sailing and be back in Wisconsin by ten p.m.

So today it was, and no physician excuses regarding
availability.

'I understand Dr Stanton's bought a place in Hart's
Landing. Do you happen to know where?'

'I do not, but Bobby might. Would you like me to call
him? I should find out what is keeping them, anyway.'

'Would you? I didn't bring my cell.'

Mrs B obliged. After the push of a no-doubt speed-
dial button, she said, 'Hello, Bobby?' A listening pause.
'Really?' Again. 'Well, certainly. I expect you for lunch,
with or without Mr Ichiro Katou.' Another pause. 'Just
leave him a message to meet you here. If he…yes, of
course. But listen, Bobby, I called for another reason.
AnnaLise is here…on her bicycle…well, I thought so,
too…wait and I shall.'

She put her hand over the phone's mouthpiece. 'Would
you join us for lunch, AnnaLise? Bobby is on his way
now.'

But AnnaLise had already risen to her feet. 'That's

very kind of you, but I think I really need to track down Dr Stanton as soon as possible.'

'Absolutely, my dear. Very wise of you.' Back to the phone. 'Bobby, AnnaLise is looking for Dr Stanton. Do you know which of the condominiums...uh-huh, uh-huh... I shall tell her...no, she cannot stay—' a smile— 'I will tell her that, too. Goodbye, dear, and see you soon.'

She set down the phone. 'Goodness, what a production. Bobby says that you know where Mr Katou lives, correct?'

'Correct.'

'Dr Stanton's unit is on the fourth floor, right-hand corner as you face that same building.'

'Got it,' AnnaLise said. 'Thank you so much for the lemonade. And the conversation.'

'My pleasure, Little One.'

AnnaLise was climbing onto her bike when she heard from on-high, 'Oh, and AnnaLise?'

'Yes?'

'When you reach Hart's Landing, would you knock on Mr Katou's door for me and tell him he is to meet Bobby here? To borrow your applicable phrase, "as soon as possible"?'

Not one to risk Mrs B's wrath, the first thing AnnaLise did in Hart's Landing was to try and figure out just how one knocked on Ichiro Katou's door.

She could toss pebbles at the window he'd filled, though the last time AnnaLise had done something similar, it had ended badly.

So, putting the gravel option on a back-burner, AnnaLise's problem was getting there from here, 'here' being the sidewalk on which she'd stood with Daisy just yesterday.

Storefront, storefront, storefront...ah, of course. The

'lobby' door she'd seen Bobby use on Saturday. Trying the doorknob, AnnaLise wasn't surprised to find it wouldn't turn, since Katou had buzzed Bobby in. OK, simple enough. She checked the list of apartments and pushed the button next to the handwritten name 'Katou'.

Nothing. She stepped back to look at Katou's windows. They looked like they had yesterday, except the man himself wasn't conveniently framed in one. 'Ichiro!' she called up.

Still no response. Katou was probably en route and, like AnnaLise, had simply left his cell behind.

Duty attempted, if not done, AnnaLise shifted her gaze to the corner unit Bobby had identified as Dr Jackson Stanton's.

No visible lights, though she wouldn't have expected them in the daytime.

'Hello?' she called up. 'Anyone there?'

No answer from that corner, either.

She pushed the button next to the 'Stanton' label.

In the distance, AnnaLise could hear sirens—likely the Sutherton Volunteer Fire Department readying their trucks for the Labor Day parade. But here on the island, nary a sound. Nor a flicker of any other life forms.

If AnnaLise had her phone, she could have called Tucker at Torch to get his father's number. But, of course, she'd left the cell at home. A lesson to be learned for both AnnaLise Griggs and Ichiro Katou, it seemed.

She climbed back on her bike.

MAYBE THE ELDER Stanton would be at Torch, AnnaLise thought as she pedaled away from Hart's Landing. Dr Jackson Stanton was an owner, after all, and word had it that father and son had grown very close since the physician's wife—and Tucker's mother—had died.

Theresa 'Terry' Stanton had been the one who insisted when Tucker was still a baby that her husband take the month of August off from his Miami practice each year to enjoy the mountains of western North Carolina. The cool, crisp weather, the many lakes and streams and, perhaps, most of all, the serenity of just doing nothing.

'That man would cut people open twenty-four/seven if I let him,' Theresa had once famously said.

That's why, Daisy had told AnnaLise by phone, the male Stantons' arrival in Sutherton six weeks after Theresa's death last year was widely assumed to be father and son's final visit. Instead, that August turned out to be the first month of their permanent residency and Tucker's enrolling at The University of the Mountain.

And, unfortunately, his expulsion before the semester's end. One would think it must have stung his father, just named Chief of Medicine for the affiliated University Hospital. But all Jackson said was, 'Terry always maintained Tucker was just like me,' a bemused smile trailing the doctor's remark.

Then he rented Daisy Griggs's storefront for his son to start a new business.

It seemed to be working out splendidly so far for both Tucker *and* Daisy, AnnaLise had to admit as she passed back under the Bradenham Bridge. Who knows, maybe Daisy could even go back to work. Serve coffee and cocktails, if not brew and mix same, respectively. Then beat on bongos during band breaks.

The thought made AnnaLise smile. Maybe the reason Dr Stanton hadn't returned her call yesterday was that he just wasn't that concerned about Daisy. After all, the man undoubtedly had other patients who were in much more dire straits.

Up and over the tree root, around the bend.

AnnaLise skidded to a stop.

In front of her in the combined north boat launch/post office parking lot was a tangle of emergency vehicles, bubble lights revolving.

Another drowning? Two in two days would be a lot even for Main Street. AnnaLise just hoped this one wasn't aided by a bullet. That sort of thing could put a real dent in any town's tourism.

Chief Chuck Greystone was talking to a tall, slender African-American man.

Dr Stanton. Seek and ye shall find, only it appeared that AnnaLise would need to take a number if she wanted a chance to speak with him. Even then, pressing for an appointment might be bad form under the circumstances. Whatever they were.

The crunch of tires on gravel drew AnnaLise's attention as a panel van pulled in. She recognized the county's long-time medical examiner at the wheel.

Chuck moved toward the newcomer's vehicle as Dr Stanton turned and caught sight of AnnaLise.

She toed down the kickstand on her bike, making sure it was set on asphalt instead of the soft earth, and went to meet him. Still in his early forties, the widower had aged noticeably in the five years since AnnaLise last saw him, his graying hair now more salt than pepper.

AnnaLise had sent a note when his wife died, so she decided against offering her condolences again.

'It's good to see you, Doc,' AnnaLise said instead. 'And I got a tour of Torch yesterday. You and Tucker have done a wonderful job with it.'

'Hey, it's all Tucker,' the doctor said. 'I've been tied up with a special project at the hospital, so I hope you'll accept my apologies for not getting back to you yesterday. I had my hand on the phone to call you this morning and then…well, this.' He pointed toward the pier where AnnaLise could now see the mailboat docked.

'Oh, goodness,' she said, Daisy forgotten for the moment. 'Was there an accident with the boat? I saw Nicole Goldstein on it earlier. Is she all right?'

'Nicole's fine,' Dr Stanton said, pointing to where the college student seemed to be holding court amongst a gaggle of tourists wearing shorts and bearing digital cameras. 'It's Bob Esmond who's badly shook up.'

AnnaLise followed his hand to see Cap'n Bob sitting on the rear bumper of the EMTs' truck. He was holding a clear mask over his mouth and nose—oxygen, presumably—but was upright.

'Heart attack?' AnnaLise guessed. Esmond had to be pushing eighty.

'No, just shock. It's hard to believe, given Main Street's reputation for…misadventure, but he's never snagged a body before.'

So AnnaLise had been correct in her prediction when she pulled up. Not that it was all that hard in Sutherton. Just imagine the worst and nobody would bet against you.

'Quite the Labor Day this year,' AnnaLise said.

'Since most lake accidents are alcohol-related, it's not unusual to see a peak over a long weekend.'

'So this one involves drinking, too?' AnnaLise was thinking about Rance Smoaks.

'That, I don't know. I was called just because Bob's been a patient of mine. Cause of death, thankfully, is the medical examiner's bailiwick.' He shook his head. 'It's always harder, though, when it's someone you know.'

A chill crept up AnnaLise's spine. 'The floater is a local?'

Dr Stanton looked taken aback at the term 'floater'.

'Sorry,' the reporter said, flushing. 'I cover the police

beat for my newspaper back in Wisconsin. The...term is part of their vernacular.' And Mama's, as well—not that AnnaLise would mention that.

'Understood,' Dr Stanton said. 'We use terms in medicine that would sound pretty callous to lay people, as well.'

He nodded toward emergency personnel hefting a humansized tarpaulin up to the deck surface. 'But to answer your question, the victim is relatively new to town.'

'How new?'

'Just a few weeks. You wouldn't know him.'

AnnaLise was getting a bad feeling about this.

Stanton said, 'The only reason I do—'

'Is that he's renting an apartment from you,' AnnaLise finished for the doctor as they watched Ichiro Katou's body sling being gently laid onto a gurney.

TEN

'I'm so sorry,' said AnnaLise.

Knowing that Bobby would be at his mother's house by now, she'd biked back to Bradenham where she found both of them.

As she broke the news, the rays of a noon sun shimmered on the choppy surface of Lake Sutherton, almost as though the small waves were 'dancing' in strobe lights.

'This seems very odd.' Mrs B was sitting on the oversized chaise longue where AnnaLise had found her the first time that day. Bobby, at AnnaLise's request, had taken a seat next to his mother. 'Mr Katou—despite his use of that cane—seemed otherwise a healthy young man. How did he drown?'

Mrs B had taken the news in her stride, in keeping with both her general attitude toward life and her specific attitude toward Katou. Lips closed in a straight line, projecting neither sympathy nor satisfaction.

Bobby, on the other hand, seemed devastated. 'How could it have happened? And when? Geez, somebody has to notify his family. He told me his grandfather died of cancer earlier this year, but that's all I know.'

'Easy, my dear.' His mother patted his hand. 'I know Mr Katou and you were friends, but you cannot be expected to—'

'If not me, then who?' He yanked his hand out from under hers. 'I don't know if Ichiro had any other ties in this country. He told me it was his first trip to the U.S.'

Yet somehow, AnnaLise thought, he ended up in Sutherton. A nice small town, yes, but she couldn't fathom it as the debut destination for most foreign tourists.

'I didn't see him at Sal's last night,' AnnaLise said. 'Did he truly plan on coming or did you tell Sheree that to…?'

'Get her off my back?' Bobby shook his head. 'No. Ichiro said he'd come later, after you and I had a chance to catch up.'

'Ohh,' AnnaLise said, feeling badly, 'I'm sorry. He certainly could have joined us.'

'I told him that, but he said—' Bobby cracked a grin for the first time since AnnaLise had broken the news— 'that my "occupation" was good, because he had something else to do.'

Like what, AnnaLise wondered. Taking a swim? Going for a boat ride? Hiking the lake trail? At that time of night, who knew?

'Could you tell…' Bobby hesitated. 'I mean, do they know how long he'd been in the water?'

'I didn't really see…anything.' Talk about your uncomfortable conversation. As a reporter, AnnaLise was used to asking the hard questions. She certainly should be able to do a better job of answering them.

Regroup, girl. Bobby deserves to know as much as you do. Or, admittedly in this case, as little. 'I was in the parking lot when they pulled the body…pulled Ichiro from the water, so I couldn't really see anything beyond stick figures. I did talk to Nicole, who was today's runner on the boat. She saw something in the water as they approached the north launch after making their rounds with newspapers and alerted Cap'n Bob.'

The reporter was editing herself, leaving out the fact that the body had apparently been dragged a ways by some extrusion from the hull of the mailboat. 'Cap'n Bob started having heart palpitations, literally, so Nicole sat him down, told the tourists to stay put and jumped off to get help.'

'Nicole. The Goldstein girl, correct?' Mrs B said. 'Very impressive composure for someone so young. Such a pity she has no aspirations beyond the University of the Mountain.'

Bobby, who hadn't had the grades to get into U of M, and AnnaLise, who hadn't had the money, just looked at her.

Mrs B spread her hands. 'What?'

AnnaLise turned back to Bobby. 'Dr Stanton was there, but only to treat Cap'n Bob. The medical examiner was arriving and Chuck needed to talk to him, so I thought the only way I could help was to ride the short distance back here and let you know what'd happened.'

'And very considerate of you, Little One,' Mrs B said. 'Especially given that we were holding lunch.'

Bobby appeared too upset to respond to his mother's insensitivity. Or maybe he'd just gotten used to it. 'I suppose the police will be able to track down Ichiro's family from his passport.'

'Just hope he did not carry it with him,' Mrs B said.

This time AnnaLise ignored her. 'I'm sure there'll be papers in his apartment, especially since he was planning to stay and open a business here. Besides, what about the ancestry project you told us about?'

'Oh, of course,' Bobby said. 'His DNA will be on file and the results he's received should have a home address for him.'

'DNA,' Mrs B said, shaking her head. 'AnnaLise's mother was telling me about that. An invasion of privacy, in my opinion.'

'It's entirely voluntary,' AnnaLise pointed out. 'Your DNA profile becomes part of a database, where it can be compared and contrasted with others in the future.'

'So long-lost relatives can appear on your doorstep,' said Mrs B. 'Feet planted, but with their hands out.'

'Except maybe to give, not to receive,' AnnaLise said. 'Look at Kathleen.'

Mrs B tick-tocked her head, left-right-left. 'Kathleen whom?'

AnnaLise didn't mention it should be 'who', not 'whom'. Unless, of course, you changed the syntax so it became 'to whom are you referring?' Or, better yet, 'to which Kathleen…'

'Don't pretend you don't remember her, Ma,' Bobby blurted irritably. 'She practically lived here during high school.'

'Of course. The Tullifinny girl,' Mrs B said tightly. 'Given she rejected you, I thought you might not want to be reminded.'

'I'm not the one who likes to bury the past.'

'I *buried* your father, Bobby, and if I prefer not to talk about what I have lost—'

'Fine, fine,' Bobby said, holding up his hands. 'Don't.'

Mother and son glared at each other.

AnnaLise cleared her throat. 'I'm sorry. I didn't mean to reopen old wounds.'

'Not at all, dear. Now I believe you were talking about Kathleen—' she threw a look at Bobby— 'and someone giving, not receiving?'

'Yes,' AnnaLise said uncomfortably. 'And unexpected relatives. Apparently Rance Smoaks's mother left him a fair amount of money.'

That stopped Mrs B in her elitist tracks. 'What? That… inebriate?'

AnnaLise nodded. 'Sheree Pepper called the amount "a bundle".'

'One point six million dollars, to be exact,' Bobby said. 'A life insurance policy that Nanney Estill had forgotten about. When she died last month, Rance became a millionaire overnight.'

'Just last month?' AnnaLise asked. 'Did he get to spend any of it?'

'If there's any justice left in this world, only on the Jim Beam bottle he was emptying when he died,' Bobby said. 'Other than that, Kathleen gets it all.'

'Well, she certainly earned it,' AnnaLise said. 'Whatever did she see in him?'

'Power,' Mrs B said. 'Powerful men are immensely attractive.'

Like…Dickens Hart?

Bobby was looking at his mother. 'Rance Smoaks was a bully and a drunk.'

'But chief of police at the time,' AnnaLise said. 'Good-looking, too, back then.'

'Please,' Bobby said. 'You're not telling me you were "attracted", too.'

'No, I—'

'Star-fucker.'

Bobby and AnnaLise turned to Mrs B.

She actually blushed. 'Sorry, but that *is* what they call people who want to be with someone only because they are a celebrity or person of note.'

'I've heard the phrase,' AnnaLise said, well aware that she herself could be accused of 'star-fucking'. At least until two weeks ago.

'Movie actor, famous author, star football player,' Mrs B prattled on, 'it doesn't matter. The woman is so impressed by the guy's reputation that she forgets he probably still leaves the toilet seat up and his underwear on the floor. All she sees is the glory.'

'Glory? What glory?' Bobby demanded. 'Hot shit high-school quarterback turned lukewarm college prospect?'

AnnaLise added, 'Turned cold-blooded abuser.'

'Why did she stay?' Mrs B seemed distressed at both the distasteful subject and the inconvenience of someone being abused.

Bobby shook his head. 'I asked Kathleen, but your guess is as good as mine.'

AnnaLise nodded. 'I've talked to a lot of victims and there's no one answer to that. In Kathleen's case, at least, it turned out to be a blessing in disguise—not that I would suggest it.'

'Suggest what?' Bobby's mother asked. 'You are simply not making yourself clear, dear. One wonders what is being taught in schools these days.'

No need to worry about Mrs B—she was back to normal.

'Suggest,' said AnnaLise through clenched teeth, 'that anybody should stay in an abusive situation. In Kathleen's case, it happens she didn't divorce him before he died and, therefore…'

'Therefore,' Bobby took over, 'she'll inherit *his* inheritance. If they'd gotten divorced, it would have gone to his heirs. In this case, probably some second-cousin twice-removed.'

'Instead, Rance is removed,' AnnaLise mused. 'And it took just "once".'

Silence, and AnnaLise realized both Bobby and his mother were staring at her in horror. 'Not that I'm saying anything of the sort happened, of course.'

'Of course,' Bobby said, with a head tilt toward his mother for AnnaLise's benefit.

'Anyway,' AnnaLise continued, trying to oblige with a change of subjects, 'we were talking about DNA?'

'An abomination,' Mrs B thundered.

Whoops. Wrong subject. 'I—'

'Yet another way of controlling people,' Mrs B continued as Bobby turned a scathing look on AnnaLise. 'That *Big Brothers* movie was prophetic.'

'Big brother, singular,' Bobby corrected. 'But the film was actually *1984*.'

'When?'

'Not when, what.'

'What?'

'The movies, both versions.'

Mrs B was struggling to regain ground. 'Fine. I shall take your word on the date, Bobby, as well as the fact that Richard Burton's last picture was *Big Brother*. Singular.'

'For the last time, Ma,' Bobby said testily. '*1984*.'

AnnaLise stepped in before he knocked his mother's block off. 'The title of the book was *1984*, Mrs B, written by George Orwell in the year 1949. The movie you saw with Richard Burton was released during the year 1984.'

'And called…*1984*?'

'Correct.'

'Huh. Hardly a coincidence, I would suspect.'

'No, actually Orwell's widow—'

'Will you two stop it!' Bobby exploded. 'Big Brother isn't watching and so what if he is? We put everything online anyway—what we do, where we go, what we think. Apparently we don't value our privacy all that much if we're the ones who give it away.'

Mrs B looked hurt. 'Now, Bobby, there is no need to raise your—'

Bobby kept going. 'I, for one, think the ancestry projects are a great idea. In fact, I sent in my own DNA swipe about a week ago.'

'Bobby, you had no right to do that without consulting me!' Mrs B roared. 'Our family is no one else's business.'

If AnnaLise had any further doubt that Mama was right and Bobby was Dickens Hart's son, it evaporated.

'Jesus, Ma, do you ever think about anyone other than yourself? It's like you're wearing blinders. Self-imposed blinders.'

'That is quite enough, young man.' Mrs B gave him a little shove so she could get up off the chaise. 'Your friend's dying is no reason to be rude. AnnaLise, if you will excuse me?'

AnnaLise nodded and Mrs B took her leave, tip-tapping her kitten-heeled sandals over the bridge and toward the house.

Bobby shook his head. 'Aw, geez. I'm going to pay for that.'

AnnaLise decided it wasn't the best time to point out that if Bobby didn't still live with his mother, he wouldn't have to worry so much about what she thought. Though, arguably, the miles of separation didn't stop Daisy and Mama from attempting to kibitz in AnnaLise's city life. AnnaLise's solution was to tell them the parts she believed would make them happy, and keep the rest to herself. Which didn't always make *her* happy.

'I wish I knew what Ichiro had planned last night,' Bobby was saying. 'Then maybe we'd know if he got to do it or something happened to him on the way.'

'Did Ichiro drink?' As Dr Stanton had said, it was the obvious question to ask in a Sutherton drowning.

'Very little. And he was coming to Sal's, so I doubt he'd get half-stoked in preparation.'

The former reporter was fighting the urge to ask questions. And losing. 'Could Ichiro swim?'

'Honestly, Annie? I'm not sure. We never talked about it. Or, for that matter, the cause of his limp. Ichiro is—was—one of those rare people more interested in other people than himself.' Bobby's tone implied: unlike my mother.

'Which is why you can't be expected to know where his family is. He never told you.'

Hanging his head. 'The man could be married with five kids, for all I know.'

'I doubt it, or he wouldn't have suddenly decided to stay here and open a restaurant.'

Which, when AnnaLise thought about it, was still more than a little odd in and of itself. How many Japanese tourists entering the United States go directly to the mountains of North Carolina on vacation and decide to open a sushi restaurant?

Only one, to her knowledge.

And he was dead.

MAMA'S, WHEN ANNALISE finally got there, was abuzz with the news. Even in Sutherton, drownings on consecutive days got people's attention. Especially when the second body was discovered by vacationers who were more than eager to share their experience.

'Stuck right there on the mailboat, not three feet from where I was sitting,' a plump bottle-blonde woman in white capris was saying to Daisy at the cash register. 'Imagine. If I'd glanced down, I would have seen…' A shiver with a little too much delight in it, despite the following 'Eeww.'

'You have to wonder how long he was there,' a gray-haired version of the woman said. 'When you think about it, we could have latched onto him anywhere along the route.' A matching shiver from her.

'Hitch-hiker,' Daisy said as the women left the counter.

'Hitch-hiker' was what Daisy and Mama had dubbed ants who crawled onto a car's windshield before you pulled out, then rode with you 'a-ways'.

AnnaLise didn't like to think of the nice man she'd met as a doomed bug. 'You do know who it was, right?'

'That Ee-CHEER-oh—Bobby's friend—is what they're saying.' Mama had come up behind her with a stack of dirty dishes.

'EE-chir-oh,' AnnaLise corrected automatically, though she wasn't sure why she bothered anymore. 'And yes. I was at the post office when they docked.'

'With him still attached?' Mama asked. 'Must have been a mess.' As she spoke she was scraping the remains of a waffle special off the top plate and into a garbage bin.

'Was the chief there?' Daisy asked.

'Yup,' AnnaLise said, before adding wearily, 'and yes, I know he's gay. He told me last night.'

Daisy was breaking open a roll of quarters to put in the change drawer. 'You didn't know? I was just going to tell you he called this morning, early, to ask if you'd be at the parade tomorrow.'

'Wouldn't miss it,' AnnaLise said. 'I'll call him later.'

'Thought you said you saw him at the launch,' Mama said, stacking the dirty plate. 'You should've told him then.'

'Chuck was there, but we didn't talk. He was a little busy.'

'I suppose.' Daisy slid the cash drawer closed. 'Oh, and Dickens Hart called, too.'

'What's that pervert want?' Mama demanded. 'You stay away from him, you hear, AnnieLeeze?'

'Yes, Mama.' Amazing how elastic apron strings can be. From Sutherton to Wisconsin and back. Boing, boing, boing.

'AnnaLise is working for "the pervert",' Daisy said. 'And don't you utter a word, Phyllis. I've already said it all.'

Enough. 'Hart's hired me to write his memoirs.'

Now Mama looked really disgusted. 'It'll be all lies, you know. And you watch that man. He'll—'

'He'll give me his notes,' AnnaLise said. 'And journals, whatever. When I'm safely back in Wisconsin, I'll read them and put them into narrative form. At worst, he'll pay me scads of money upfront even if the book's never published.'

'And at best,' Daisy said, giving Mama the evil eye for some reason, 'he'll lie his way to a best-seller and Oprah will out him.'

'Oprah?' asked AnnaLise, now puzzled.

'Like that James Frey and his supposed memoir, *A Million Little Pieces*,' Daisy said. 'Once she found out he'd made up a lot of it, Oprah had Frey on the show and told him just what she thought.'

'She sure did,' Mama agreed, coming around the counter to sit on the stool where Daisy had been when Anna-Lise arrived. 'That Oprah is one amazing woman. She don't take crap from nobody.'

'Nobody,' Daisy echoed. 'Now there's someone I'd vote…'

And off they went on another adventure through Mama-in-Daisyland.

Relieved their collective attention had been deflected from her, AnnaLise pulled out the cellphone she'd picked up after stopping home to shower.

Dickens Hart answered on the third ring, as AnnaLise

could have predicted. Men like Hart didn't answer on the first ring. Doing so wouldn't send the right message—which was, in their minds: I'm busier and more important than whoever you are.

'Hart.'

'Dickens,' AnnaLise said crisply. 'This is AnnaLise Griggs returning your call.'

'Ms Griggs.' Putting the employee in her place for using his first name. 'If you're available, I thought this afternoon would be a good time for you to pick up the papers I mentioned. And we can talk about my book.'

'Certainly. I can be there in fifteen minutes.'

'An hour would be more convenient.'

AnnaLise bet it would. She checked her watch. 'Three o'clock—' she waited for him to make 'agreeable' noises on the other end and then added— 'but I'm afraid I have an appointment at four.'

'Well, that'll hardly give me time to outline what I expect—'

'We'll be in contact throughout the process, I'm sure'—a little white lie, along with the phantom appointment—'but I've found that it's preferable for me to look through the material first and then tell you how I plan to proceed.'

'Well, I—'

'The publishing industry is different than your world, Dickens. It's best to let someone knowledgeable guide you through the minefield.'

A cough. 'Of course. Today at three will be fine.' He clicked off.

'And next time,' AnnaLise said to her phone, 'answer my call on the first ring.'

'WELL, HERE WE ARE,' Dickens Hart said, ushering AnnaLise into the room he'd just referred to as his 'archives'.

AnnaLise had arrived at one minute to three. From the outside, the place had the feel of a Low Country mansion transplanted from manicured, undulating lawns to the High Country. Beautiful, but out of place.

Hart—the perfect country squire in a camel's hair blazer over a vermilion dress shirt and cavalry twill slacks—swung open the door to the archive/office and stepped aside.

AnnaLise thought, I'm not charging enough.

Piled in neat stacks on guest chairs and the floor in front of his desk were thirty or forty bound journals. 'Diligent. One a year?'

'At first. Then I got a computer.' He handed her a brown accordion file.

'What's this?' AnnaLise slipped the anchored band from around the file and opened the flap.

'Floppy disks. I started with five-and-a-quarter-inchers, then went to three-and-a-half. You'll probably have to get them converted. Oh, and CDs and a couple of DVDs. They store more, you know.'

Unfortunately, she did.

'And, most recently…' Hart moved to his desk and scrabbled through the drawer, coming up with a handful of USB flash drives. He dropped them into the open accordion folder as AnnaLise watched, speechless. 'Each one is labeled by month and year.'

Holy mother of God.

'I…' It came out as a squeak so she took a breath. 'I've been journaling for years, Dickens, but you clearly have me beat. I'm impressed.'

Nauseated, certainly, but grudgingly impressed as well.

'Thank you.' Hart had opened another drawer of his desk and pulled out a checkbook. Not the kind that fits into a purse. No, this one was big like an old-fashioned ledger. He swung open the front cover and looked up. 'I think half at signing and half at delivery of the manuscript is customary?'

Damned if AnnaLise knew, but it sounded good. 'That would be fine, but we haven't actually signed anything. Don't you want to have a contract drawn up?'

'Certainly.' Hart was scrawling on the second perforated check from the top, the first having presumably been written and torn out to be given to some lucky tradesman. Or indentured servant.

He finished with a flourish and held out the check. 'But, in the meantime…'

She took it, waiting for the thunderclap that would signal the irrevocable transfer of her soul. Holy shit. Fifty-thousand dollars. Could you even cash a personal check that big?

A child of technology and plastic, AnnaLise's paychecks were direct-deposited to her account and she paid bills electronically. The journalist's only exposure to paper checks was when the box from the bank arrived in the mail, and she stuck it in the top drawer of her desk.

'Would you prefer certified?'

At Hart's words, AnnaLise looked up from the check, startled. 'No, no, this will be fine.' A weak grin. 'I know where to find you, after all.'

She folded the check in half and, after just a moment's hesitation, slipped it into the zippered side pocket of her purse instead of her jeans' pocket. Bad form to have to ask Hart for another because AnnaLise's mother had washed her pants.

As she set the bag aside, AnnaLise searched for an intelligent question to ask Hart, who was waiting expectantly.

'You've obviously been keeping diaries and journals for

years. What made you decide to write your memoirs—or have them written—now?'

It was a good reporter-type question, and AnnaLise was rewarded with an approving nod.

'My parents died in an automobile accident when I was in my twenties.' Hart settled into his desk chair and signaled her to take one of the guest seats.

AnnaLise moved a stack of journals and complied.

'Back then, I was preoccupied with my own life and getting White Tail started' —not to mention getting significant 'tail' himself, from all accounts— 'and it wasn't until Mother and Father were gone that I realized I knew nothing about my family. Where we came from, even how my parents met. Nor do I know of any living relatives.'

The man projected genuine regret. He looked up, meeting AnnaLise's eyes. 'I swore that I would put all this into a readable form, so I wouldn't do that to my *own* children.'

Since Hart didn't have any kids he owned up to, it seemed a pretty moot point. But, ask and ye shall find out. Sometimes.

'Which…children are those, Dickens?'

'My,' Hart said, leaning back in his chair, 'you are a straight-shooter, aren't you?'

'It helps in my profession.'

'Then I think I've chosen the right person to write my memoirs.' He rocked forward in his chair and stood. 'Let me get my man to help you with these.'

His 'man' was about sixty-five, with a grizzled mustache and a military bearing, introduced as Boozer Bacchus. After AnnaLise packed the journals into boxes, Bacchus hefted each box onto his shoulder, wrapped a tattooed bicep around it and carried it down to the Mitsubishi where AnnaLise arranged them. Tight, but she managed to fit all the journals in the trunk and backseat of the little convertible.

Thank God for the information age, she thought. It could have been much worse. Dropping the envelope with the external storage disks and drives onto the passenger seat, she turned to say goodbye to Hart, who had followed Bacchus and her down on their last trip.

Hart had removed his camel's hair jacket, apparently in a show of solidarity with the people actually doing the work. 'Best you put the top up,' he suggested. 'Otherwise you could lose half of these resources to the wind.'

And still have more than AnnaLise would ever be able—or motivated—to read. 'Should I start with any particular year? Perhaps the one you opened White Tail?'

'No, no. You'd miss my travels and my early formative period. And those, in their own way, are the most fascinating parts of a fascinating life.'

Gag me with a silver spoon. 'It's an awful lot of material for one book,' AnnaLise said as she swung open her car door.

'Then maybe we'll make it into a trilogy,' Hart said, closing her door. 'Like *The Lord of the Rings*.'

More like *The Lord of the Bed Springs*, AnnaLise thought as she backed up in order to head nose-first down the driveway, under Hart's watchful eye.

Or maybe…*Star Bores*?

AnnaLise giggled. Better yet, *The Silence of the Glands*.

AnnaLise kept giggling and, seemingly pleased by her cheerfulness in beginning his project, Dickens Hart waved and turned back toward the house. Putting her car into gear, AnnaLise stepped on the gas.

Just as, behind her, two shots rang out.

ELEVEN

'WHAT THE HELL IS going on around here?' AnnaLise demanded. 'First Rance Smoaks, then Ichiro Katou, and now Dickens Hart? Did somebody put out a contract on people with unusual names?'

Boozer Bacchus scratched his head. 'Sure hope not.'

The two were standing side-by-side, arms crossed, watching as Hart was treated by EMTs. Two patrol cars were also on the scene, dome lights rotating, but so far the chief himself hadn't arrived.

'Sorry, Boozer,' AnnaLise said. 'I didn't…'

'No need to be sorry,' he said without looking at her. 'My mama knew right enough what I was in for when she named me.'

AnnaLise glanced uncertainly toward him. 'Your real name is…Boozer?'

'Family tradition.'

'Oh.' Eyes front.

'I'm Boozer Bacchus the Third.'

She cleared her throat. 'Has a nice ring to it.'

'Thanks.' Still watching the EMTs. 'You know what I can't figure out?'

'What?'

'There's been a mess of people threatened to kill 'ol Dickens over the years, but this is the first time somebody's actually gone and tried it.'

Now Bacchus turned an unblinking stare at her. 'Why would that be, do you think?'

'Luck?' AnnaLise wasn't sure whose luck or whether it was good or bad, but it was pretty much all she could think to say.

Bacchus just shrugged and went back to watching.

A third patrol car arrived.

'You're Lorraine's girl, aren't you?'

AnnaLise was startled by not only the out-of-the-blue question, but at Bacchus's use of Daisy's given name. 'You know my mother?'

'Sure do. Her—and most of the folks around—worked at the White Tail one time or the other, though there's them that like to forget Dickens Hart was the reason they got a decent start in life.'

It was a new way of looking at the place. And the man. 'I guess that's true,' AnnaLise said. 'My mother and Mama—I mean, Phyllis Balisteri. Even Mrs Bradenham—'

'Ema Sikes Bradenham,' Bacchus snorted. 'What an uppity piece of work that woman is. She's one of them who don't give the boss his due.'

What Mrs B did or didn't give 'the boss' wasn't something AnnaLise felt she should weigh in on

No matter, Bacchus didn't give her the chance: 'Now your ma, on the other hand, was always just plain nice to everybody.' Bacchus looked AnnaLise up and down. 'You don't take after her much, excepting you're short, too. Both pretty, though.'

Bacchus chin-gestured toward the EMTs. 'I better go make sure those medics don't fuck something up.'

Hart, upper arm heavily bandaged, was now being lifted onto a gurney. Enroute to the ambulance, Bacchus passed Chief Greystone. The two men stopped and spoke briefly, then each continued on his way—employee to employer, Chuck to AnnaLise.

'In a novel, I'd ask why you keep showing up at the scene of shootings. And drownings.'

'I did miss Mrs Bradenham's bloodletting earlier this week,' AnnaLise pointed out.

'Nobody can be everywhere.' Chuck seemed out of sorts.

'Are you OK?' AnnaLise asked. 'You seem a little... touchy.'

'Touchy? Let's see: first, my predecessor-in-office-cum-town-drunk is found dead drunk—as in, dead and drunk—in the lake with a bullet wound. Then a Japanese visitor drowns, but with a contusion to his temple. Now...this.'

'Ichiro hit his head as he fell into the water?'

'Can't tell you what I don't know,' Chuck snapped. 'Katou's in autopsy. I'll send you a full report with photos, OK?'

Ouch.

Chuck drew in a deep breath. 'Sorry, Lise. I don't mean to take this out on you. I was with Bobby when this last call came in and...well, you know how this town is. Everybody's got an opinion about how I should do my job.'

AnnaLise didn't want to get in the middle of a disagreement between her two friends, who just happened to be the town mayor and police chief of same.

She took advantage of an audible groan from Hart, who was jostled while being loaded into the ambulance, to ask, 'So what do you think? Hunting accident?'

'Ordinarily, more like "poaching" accident.' Chuck shook his head. 'Yahoos can't wait a couple of days for a legal season to start.'

'Lucky for Dickens. If that was an arrow rather than a bullet, it could have been worse.'

'"Dickens"? Since when are you and the great bene-
factor so friendly?'

Come to think of it, AnnaLise couldn't remember anyone referring to the man as 'Dickens'. It was usually Hart.
Or Mr Hart. Or occasionally, 'that pervert'.

'I'm practicing,' AnnaLise said. '*Dickens* hired me to
write his memoirs and I wanted to set the ground rules
right away. I'm his collaborator, not his subordinate.'

'Write his memoirs? You really want to spend that kind
of time with that kind of lech?'

Oh, yeah, and 'lech'.

'Hart…Dickens has been keeping journals for years.'
She hooked a thumb toward the overloaded Mitsubishi.
'I'm taking them with me.'

'All the way back to Wisconsin?' He walked around
the car. 'You're going to bottom out.'

'The car rides low-slung naturally, but you're right.
Maybe I should ship the boxes back. And charge Dickens.' She was only half-kidding.

Chuck raised his hand in a stop sign while he conferred
with one of his officers holding a plastic evidence bag.

When the woman had left, he said, 'While you're going
through all those papers, keep an eye out for someone who
might have wanted to kill him.'

'Meaning you don't buy this as even a poaching accident?'

He pointed to the closing rear doors of the ambulance.
'The man's wearing a blaze-red shirt—'

'Vermilion,' AnnaLise interjected. 'Kenneth Cole
makes one, but this…'

Chuck looked skyward.

'What?' AnnaLise protested. 'It's still deep red, just
with an orangish—'

'Lise?' Chuck interrupted. 'I know I'm gay, but please don't talk to me about this crap. It freaks me out.'

'Oh,' she said, sheepishly. 'Sorry. Go ahead.'

'Thank you. I was saying that with Hart wearing a blaze-*vermilion* shirt, he's not likely to have been mistaken for a deer, even with the tan pants.' A warning look toward AnnaLise. 'Besides, that officer I just talked with found a shell casing at the edge of the woods. Which tells me somebody was laying in wait.'

'Lying in wait,' AnnaLise corrected reflexively.

Chuck gave her the look she deserved.

'Sorry.' Now *beyond* sheepish. 'But are you serious? Someone actually aimed for Hart?'

'Dickens.' His turn to correct her. 'And, yes. Or the shooter isn't worth a damn and aimed for you and got Hart instead. Either way—' he leaned over and kissed her on the top of the head—'I have work to do.'

'Chuck?' AnnaLise called as he walked away.

Over his shoulder he replied, 'Yes?'

'You're not serious, are you? I mean, you don't honestly think someone meant to shoot me.'

'Of course not. I was just…' Then he stopped and turned back around. 'Why? Is there a reason you think it's possible?'

'Me? Don't be silly.' When Chuck hesitated she waved him on. 'Go. Solve crime. Fight evil.'

Chuck grinned and continued walking while AnnaLise moved to her car. There was no one who wanted to hurt her…at least so far as she knew. Nothing she'd written could possibly have offended someone here. All her bylines were in a Wisconsin newspaper. Sutherton, no matter how broadened its horizons, was unlikely to carry a publication so far removed from High Country.

AnnaLise looked at the cluster of uniforms examining the ground at the edge of the woods.

Nah, no one would want to hurt her.

Right?

PULLING PAST HER mother's parked car, AnnaLise stopped her own loaded-down Mitsubishi nose-on-sidewalk in front of the old garage on Second Street that the Griggs shared with an even older neighbor, Mrs Peebly.

Daisy had left her cream-colored Chrysler on the street so AnnaLise could take the garage. Given Hart's 'load', it worked out perfectly. AnnaLise wouldn't have to empty out her Mitsubishi only to have to repack when she left Tuesday morning for the long drive back.

Slipping the gear shift into park, AnnaLise climbed out and went to lift the closer of the two heavy, traditional wooden garage doors. There was no electric-opener on either, despite AnnaLise's repeated suggestions that both Daisy and Mrs Peebly would benefit.

'You know there's no electricity in that old hulk, AnnaLise,' Daisy would say.

'Whatcha going to do? Run an extension cord?' From Mrs Peebly.

Cue raucous laughter. Times two.

While it was true that adding electrical service to the free-standing garage wouldn't be cheap, not only would an automatic opener be a real convenience, but an overhead light was nearly a necessity. The dome-shaped, battery-operated closet light Daisy had found in a dollar store was hung on a nail between the doors and, despite its adver-tised promise to 'push-on/push-off', the thing was per-petually dead as…well, a doornail.

Thankfully, as AnnaLise steadied the door at its apex, the late-day light was still slanting in the single window of the cinder block rear wall. Through it, AnnaLise could see the patch of lawn where she had played as a child and over which Daisy still hung laundry to dry. The pale pink and blue flowered sheets billowing on the clothesline were the ones from her old room.

Smiling at the prospect of sleeping on fresh, air-dried linen tonight, AnnaLise turned and nearly collided with a shrunken woman of about ninety leaning on a walker.

'Mrs Peebly, I'm so sorry,' AnnaLise said, her hands coming up to keep the aluminum-framed walker vertical.

'Don't you worry, AnnaLise,' their neighbor said, bouncing the contraption up and down a couple of times, 'this thing ain't going nowhere.'

Nor was Mrs Peebly, at least anytime soon, if free will had anything to do with it. Larry Peebly had wanted his elderly mother to move in with him for years, but the old woman's eyes still burned with intelligence and, so long as her body held up, she had voiced every intention of staying in her own home.

The walker, though, was a new and somewhat worrying sign. And it tickled something at the back of AnnaLise's mind.

She hugged Mrs Peebly, careful not to crush fragile bones. 'I'm so glad to see you. You're well, I hope?'

Again, the older woman picked up the walker and for a moment AnnaLise thought she was going to press it overhead like a barbell, tennis-ball-covered aluminum feet pointing skyward.

'Aside from this thing, I'm doing just fine, thank you very much.'

'You don't seem to be having balance problems,' AnnaLise said, smiling.

'I'm not. Doc said this is "pro-phy-lac-tic".' She intoned the syllables like they amounted to a dirty word.

'He probably means it in the sense of "preventative",' AnnaLise said. 'Not, umm…'

'Hell, I know *she* don't mean it's a rubber,' Mrs Peebly said, emphasis on the gender of the physician involved. 'You kids think you're the only ones who keep up?'

Properly chastised at her presumptive use of the male pronoun, AnnaLise opened her mouth to answer the rest of the indictment, but Mrs Peebly was on a roll. 'And every last one of you ought to be grateful we *didn't* have all the contraceptive paraphernalia that's out there nowadays. Otherwise, half your generation wouldn't even be here.'

Bested again, AnnaLise held up her hands in surrender. 'Then count me grateful. But back to you—you're all right? You didn't fall or anything?'

'Not yet, knock on aluminum.' Mrs Peebly was leaning down, one hand on the walker, the other reaching for the door handle of her garage door, a twin to the one AnnaLise had just raised.

'Stop!'

Startled, Mrs Peebly looked up, back still bent and now twisted at the waist like the center strip of a pretzel.

'Sorry,' AnnaLise said. 'I meant, let me get that for you.'

The moment she had the door high enough for Mrs Peebly to fit under, the woman pushed a button on her key fob and crab-walked to a black Cadillac that answered 'tweet-tweet'.

Another brain tickle.

'You lock your car when it's inside the garage?' Typical some places, but rare to unheard-of in Sutherton, at least from AnnaLise's experience.

'You sound like your mother. "You're too trusting, Daisy", I say to her. "You ain't lived near as long as I have. Nor seen what I seen."'

'Daisy doesn't listen?'

''Course not.' Mrs Peebly tried the passenger door and, when it didn't open, pushed on her key fob again. 'Though we wouldn't have to lock our cars, if these old garage doors still locked. They need fixing.'

AnnaLise saw her wedge. 'They *need* replacing. New doors and electronic openers.'

'Waste of money,' Mrs Peebly said. 'But I have to admit I'm getting mighty tired of ruining my umbrellas.' She gestured toward the wall next to the door.

'Umbrellas?' Sure enough, AnnaLise saw a green and white golf umbrella resting there on a mangled metal tip. 'What happened to it?'

'Got bent, that's what. You think it's easy getting it through that track nice and snug?'

AnnaLise looked at the vertical track assembly and then the door itself overhead.

'Ohh, I see,' she said as light—though dim and battery-operated—finally dawned. 'The metal bar that slid through the track to secure the door is missing, so you're replacing it with…an umbrella?'

'I am, and Daisy would be wise to do likewise. I even offered to buy her the equipment. But your mother, if you don't mind me saying, is obstinate as a mule. During the day, I don't even bother locking up no more. What good does it do, if her side is wide open?'

A point, but: 'If you *both*…lock them from the inside, how do either of you get out?'

'I'm not too proud to admit—' Mrs Peebly deposited the walker on the seat— 'that question did arise.'

She slammed the door closed and turned. 'Now do you plan on moving that noisy foreign car of yours anytime soon? I need to buy my groceries and you're encroaching on my garage apron.'

Torn between saying, 'Yes, ma'am' and offering to shop for her elderly neighbor, AnnaLise chose the answer that wouldn't get her run over or hit with an idle umbrella. 'Yes, ma'am.'

She pulled her car into the right side of the garage while Mrs Peebly backed out the left. Leaving the Mitsubishi, she signaled the elderly woman that she'd close both garage doors.

'I'm not making any promises about "locking" them, though,' she said under her breath.

Ignoring the umbrella, AnnaLise crossed to the other side of her neighbor's door where a frayed rope hung. The ropes, one attached to each door, allowed Mrs Peebly and Daisy—and AnnaLise, for that matter—to get the door started on its downward journey without having to stand on their tippy-toes.

Though 'tippy-toe' might not be beyond Mrs Peebly's abilities, even now.

AnnaLise lowered the one door and was about to do the same with Daisy's when the brain tickle finally scratched itself. The result was two promises that AnnaLise intended to keep before she returned to Wisconsin. One: arrange for the garage to be wired for electricity, with automatic openers installed. Two: ask Chief Chuck Greystone if Ichiro Katou's cane had been found.

TWELVE

'I COMPLETELY FORGOT about the cane,' Bobby Bradenham said.

'I did, too,' AnnaLise said. 'It was only when I saw Mrs Peebly's walker that it occurred to me.'

The two friends were sitting at Daisy's kitchen table just as they had throughout their school days. The only difference was that margaritas had replaced Cokes and they weren't even pretending to do homework.

AnnaLise gestured toward a blank white wall. 'Weird not having a door there, isn't it?'

Prior to Daisy's retirement, a connection between the kitchen and the then-grocery made it easy for AnnaLise's mother to move from apartment to cash register whenever the cowbell on the outer door signaled a market customer. Many a meal was interrupted in the Griggs household because someone else needed a loaf of bread or a gallon of milk to take home to theirs.

While convenient, it did make for an unconventional living space. The Second Street apartment entrance opened directly into the eat-in kitchen where AnnaLise and Bobby sat. A tiny parlor completed the Griggses' portion at street-level, a staircase leading to the second floor's two bedrooms and one bath.

'Don't tell me,' Bobby said. 'You miss the market? You hated having to jump up every five minutes to wait on someone when your mom wasn't around.'

'It was a good way of life,' AnnaLise said nostalgically.

'Are you kidding?' Bobby exclaimed. 'Not only did you complain, but you told people you lived in the back room of a store.'

'I did,' AnnaLise protested. 'Only now it's the back room of a nightclub.'

'But,' Bobby said, looking a little sad, 'AnnaLise doesn't live here anymore.'

'I know.' She stared at Bobby for a moment before mentally shaking herself. 'Sorry. What were we talking about?'

'You asked Chuck whether Ichiro's cane had been found. What did he say?'

'He thanked me and hung up.' AnnaLise rose to replenish their drinks from the blender on the counter.

Standing, she saw James Duende's tousled dark hair pass by the window, the rest of him hidden by the shutters Daisy'd installed to provide privacy against Second Street's sidewalk. AnnaLise hadn't had a chance to speak with Sheree's boarder at Sal's, so she hoped he'd be at tomorrow's parade. Sutherton could use all the good-looking men it could get. Dickens Hart was old, Chuck was gay, and Bobby was...well, his mother's son.

'Interesting,' Bobby said.

'What?'

'Chuck just "thanking" you.'

For some reason, his tone made AnnaLise a little uncomfortable. And defensive of Chuck, who shouldn't need her defending. 'I had the impression he was busy, probably with the shooting at Dickens Hart's place.'

'Or, Chuck's embarrassed he hadn't thought about the cane himself.' Again, the mildly critical tone, but seemingly no real concern from the mayor over the shooting of, arguably, his town's leading citizen. At least in that one citizen's mind.

Whose future was now tied to her own. 'Have you heard any updates on Hart's condition?'

'Bullet in the fatty part of the arm,' Bobby said distractedly. 'He'll be fine, but he's kicking up a huge fuss. Demanding an investigation, like he's the only one who's ever been shot around here.'

Silly man. This was, after all, Sutherton.

'However, look here,' Bobby continued. 'You're absolutely right. If Ichiro was unsteady because of his leg and toppled into the water, where's the cane?'

'Presumably somewhere in the lake or, alternatively, on the bank where he fell in,' AnnaLise said. 'You told me at your...at Bradenham that you didn't know what was wrong with his leg. His left one, correct?'

'Right.'

AnnaLise looked at him.

'Correct,' Bobby amended. 'And the short answer is, I still don't know. Ichiro never made a big deal about the gimp himself, so I didn't want to, either. After a while I didn't even notice the cane. It was just...I don't know, part of him?'

'But since I'd just met Ichiro, I hadn't known him long enough to see past it like you, or maybe even Chuck, could have.'

Bobby said, 'Did he tell you that apparently I was the last one to see Ichiro alive?'

'No, he didn't. When was that?'

'You were there,' Bobby said. 'You and your mother. At Hart's Landing, remember?'

'Oh, of course.' AnnaLise was remembering Katou at his window, holding the giant cotton swab and laughing down at them. Daisy and she departed then, but Bobby had stayed on. 'So how did you leave it with him?'

'Ichiro?' Bobby gave her a strange look. 'Like I told you, we made plans to meet at Sal's.'

'After he did…something.'

'Correct.'

'But we don't know what.' AnnaLise said it almost to herself.

'We may never know.' Bobby looked at the wall clock over the sink. It was in the shape of an apple. 'I'd better go or I'll be late for dinner.'

'If I had a dime for every time you said that,' Anna-Lise said, getting up to follow him to the door.

'The more things change, the more they stay the same,' Bobby said.

A cliché, but AnnaLise knew that very little had changed for Bobby. Still living in his mother's house at, what, the age of twenty-nine?

Bobby continued, 'Ma will kill me if dinner—'

'Gets cold,' AnnaLise finished, stepping out onto the sidewalk after him. 'But I think you're probably safe this time. Look.' She pointed to the Mercedes parked at the corner. 'Isn't that your mother's car?'

'It…is. Now where in the world would she be?' Bobby seemed nonplussed that Mrs B wasn't home making their dinner.

'Maybe she decided to eat out,' AnnaLise said mildly.

'But what about…?' Seeing the grin on his friend's face, he stopped. 'OK, you're right. I'm still a mama's boy.'

'And spoiled rotten. C'mon, let's go see if "Ma" is at Mama's.'

A closed sign hung crookedly on one of the doors of Torch. 'Not open on Sunday, I see. I'm surprised Tucker didn't want to take advantage of the holiday weekend.'

'He was serving this morning,' Bobby said, 'for the

after-church coffee crowd, but I think he realized soon after his Grand Opening that people don't go out on Sunday night in Sutherton.'

'Tell Mama that.' AnnaLise pointed to the cars filling nearly every space in front of her place. Visible through the big window was a line at the cash register waiting to pay Mama, and another, for Daisy to seat them.

'This is different, though. Mama Philomena's is an institution. Sure hope if Ma is there, she's already seated.' Bobby seemed to be weighing the inconvenience of his mother not cooking for him with the convenience of her already having snagged a table where he could join her.

'Seated where?' his mother's voice asked from AnnaLise's blind side. 'And have I not asked you repeatedly not to call me that?'

'Ma…Mother,' Bobby said, turning. 'I didn't know you were there.'

'Obviously.' She turned to AnnaLise with a smile. 'I *should* be waiting dinner for him, while he is dilly-dallying with you, Little One.'

'Just like old times,' AnnaLise said, a tad too brightly. There was nothing like going home to make you feel like a kid again. And not always in a good way. 'Did you eat at Mama's?'

'Oh, heaven's no,' Mrs B said, dismissing the idea with a wave of her hand. 'Such a madhouse. I glanced in the window and saw dear Lorraine trying to deal with that queue. I knew it was hopeless.'

As she spoke, developer David Sabatino came storming out the door of Mama's, wife and kids scurrying after him. 'Thirty-minute wait,' he was muttering. 'Who do they think they are?'

'New Yorkers,' Mrs Bradenham said, shaking her head. 'So impatient.' She turned to Bobby. 'Pizza night?'

'Sounds good,' he said, his face lighting up. 'Want to join us, AnnaLise?'

'Thanks, but no.' She restrained a shudder and hooked a thumb toward the restaurant's door. 'I'd best eat here if I know what's good for me.'

She loved Bobby, but 'pizza night' at the Bradenham Mansion sounded like a scene out of *Psycho*. Bobby and 'Ma' enjoying a 'slice' at their dining-room table, while AnnaLise lay sprawled and naked in the shower down the hall, tomato sauce and pepperoni grease slowly... circling...the...drain.

Still smiling at the thought as she entered Mama's, AnnaLise managed to conveniently ignore the fact that she, too, was dining with Mother tonight.

Both of them, actually.

'DID YOU LEAVE the garage door open?' Daisy asked AnnaLise.

The daughter paused with her key in the front door of the Griggses' apartment. It was just after ten. 'No. I closed our side after I parked and motioned to Mrs Peebly that I'd get hers as well. I thought about leaving her side open, so she wouldn't have to get out of the car again when she got back, but I figured our neighbor would have my hide.'

'I swear that woman is losing it. She probably locked her side when she came home and walked out mine, forgetting to close it,' Daisy said, pulling up at Mrs Peebly's garage door unsuccessfully. 'Sure enough.'

AnnaLise, who had followed her mother over from Mama's, peered into the garage. 'I don't know how either of you can see anything.' She felt for the plastic globe hanging on the wall. Amazingly, the light went on, albeit dimly. 'Hey, you replaced the battery,' she said.

'From five years ago? Of course I did,' Daisy said. 'Just because you're gone, you think things don't get done?'

'Honestly? Yes. But it's not just batteries. It's the whole town. I can't believe how much has changed.'

'Life goes on,' Daisy said, moving into the shadowy garage. 'People get sick, grow old.' She turned back toward AnnaLise and the headlights of a car turning the corner reflected in her eyes. 'Even die.'

The combination of the words and her mother's catlike pupils gave AnnaLise goose bumps. 'Don't say that,' she said, rubbing at her arms.

Daisy laughed. 'What's wrong—somebody step on your grave?'

'I don't like this…dank cave,' AnnaLise said. 'I'm putting in electricity and garage door openers, whether you and Mrs Peebly like it or not.'

'You're such a fraidy-cat,' Daisy said. 'I bet you haven't been down in our cellar since middle school.'

The very definition of dank.

'Elementary,' AnnaLise said, a little hurt. Daisy rarely made fun of her daughter's fears. 'And calling that crawl space under the old market a cellar is being overly generous.'

'About three feet of headroom, generous?' Daisy suggested with a smile.

'More like four. Even in third grade, I couldn't stand up in it, and Bobby, even less so. But don't change the subject. I left Scotty the Electrician a message. Said we wanted proper doors and locks, with remote controls.'

She gestured toward the umbrella Mrs Peebly had jammed into the track in place of the now-defunct metal lock bar. The umbrella had partially opened and hung there by its beak like some colossal green and white bird.

'I told her it was a silly idea,' Daisy said, shaking her head.

'And why an umbrella?' AnnaLise nodded toward a black wooden dowel that must have been hidden behind Mrs Peebly's umbrella earlier. 'This would work better.' *Any*thing would work better.

AnnaLise nudged the dowel with her toe, accidentally tipping it away from the wall. Not until she lunged to grab hold did she realize the thing was polished, not rough. It also sported a brass knob on one end.

A sticky knob, at that.

THIRTEEN

AMONG ALL HOLIDAYS secular and sacred, Labor Day has stood above all others in Sutherton.

'We should just call it Get-the-Hell-Out Day,' Sheree Pepper said, quoting herself. Again.

'Does have a nice ring to it.' AnnaLise waved to Mayor Bobby Bradenham, sitting in the parade's lead vehicle, an apple-red Chrysler Sebring convertible.

Bobby returned the gesture with a suitably mayoral smile plastered on his face. Every once in a while, he'd pick someone out and give him or her a thumbs-up.

'Bobby doesn't even register us.' AnnaLise was standing with Sheree on the beach side of Main Street, across from Mama's.

'It's the huge throng,' her friend said dryly. 'Who mostly have no idea who he is.' She shouted, 'Go home!', not to Bobby, but to the crowd on the sidelines.

'Fine attitude for someone whose livelihood depends on tourism,' AnnaLise said. 'Besides, the banner in front does read "Mayor".'

'Yeah, and the doors say "Courtesy of Sutherton Mountain Chrysler/Jeep". For all we know, the cheering is because they think he's a car dealer in a flashy convertible.'

For the umpteenth time, AnnaLise obsessively wiped her right hand on her sundress, like she could rub away the sensation of congealing blood on Ichiro Katou's cane.

She hadn't told Sheree about the discovery the night before. Hell, AnnaLise was proud of the fact that she'd picked up the phone—only after washing her hands, of course—and called Chuck. Every fiber of her being told Daisy's daughter to get rid of the thing—so clearly the murder weapon.

Because, of course, Katou had been murdered. Hit on the head with his own cane and then plunged into the lake.

But…how had the thing gotten into the Griggses' garage?

Across the street, Mama and Daisy were perched on chairs from inside the restaurant, closed for the holiday. Daisy seemed utterly unaffected by what had happened.

Even when it happened.

In contrast, AnnaLise had panicked, remembering all those old movies where the idiot good-guy picks up the smoking gun or bloody knife—or, in this case, sticky cane—and gets blamed for the crime.

Which was ridiculous, certainly. Chuck would never think that. Could never.

Unless AnnaLise tried to get rid of the cane. Hid it, like someone had planted it in the garage. A game of Hot Potato. Here you take it. No, *you* take it.

So she'd called him.

Chuck had arrived in street clothes, accompanied by two uniformed deputies and a crime-scene investigator. God knows what the neighbors thought was going on, but so far no one had mentioned anything. At least, that had reached AnnaLise's ears.

After ten on the eve of the big Labor Day celebration. Maybe they'd all gone to bed early in preparation.

Bed. AnnaLise had finally gotten there at about one a.m. and though the fresh, air-dried sheets had been lovely, she couldn't quiet the questions rattling around in her head.

Had the cane been there earlier, when she was talking to Mrs Peebly? AnnaLise couldn't be sure, especially since the thing would have been obscured by her neighbor's umbrella.

When Chuck asked the same question, AnnaLise suggested he talk to Mrs Peebly, who might have noticed it either then or when she removed the umbrella to 'lock' her side of the garage.

The first of five emergency vehicles—a fire engine—drew even with Sheree and AnnaLise. Along with the high school marching band, assorted kids pulling wagons or riding bikes and a couple of trailered boats, they would constitute the parade.

The ladder truck hit its air horn and AnnaLise, despite her 'police-beat' experience, jumped, hand leaping to her heart.

A concerned look from Sheree. 'As I was saying, he's just gone. Paid up until the end of September, but—'

AnnaLise tuned back in. 'Are you talking about James Duende?'

Her friend's eyes narrowed even further. 'Who the hell else have we been talking about? I think Daisy's beginning to rub off on you.'

'I saw him last night.'

'Jim?' Sheree asked. 'Where?'

'He passed by my mother's kitchen window,' AnnaLise said. 'Bobby and I had been sitting at the table when I stood up to get the pitcher of margaritas and there was James, on Second Street.'

'You had margaritas and didn't invite me?' Sheree seemed more concerned about the social slight than the abrupt disappearance of her guest. And, presumably, lover.

'It was just spur of the moment,' AnnaLise said truthfully. 'With Ichiro's death and all, I thought Bobby might want to talk.'

'How very sensitive of you,' Sheree sniffed, not appeased.

'But now Duende is missing? Are you sure?' Anna-Lise raised her voice to be heard over the whoop-whoop siren of an ambulance and accompanying applause of the onlookers.

Sheree shrugged. 'All I can tell you is that he didn't sleep in his bed last night.'

'And exactly how would you know?'

Genetically incapable of embarrassment, Sheree just smiled. 'Why, when I went to clean his room, of course. Whatever else were you thinking?'

'Nada,' AnnaLise said as the emergency vehicle passed, leaving a clear view of the street. Parade components were kept generously spaced, lest the event last less than even the ten total minutes allotted.

On the other side of the street, Mama and Daisy had been joined by Chuck.

AnnaLise hadn't seen him approach, so she assumed he'd come from around the corner on Second Street. Mrs Peebly's house had been dark last night, and the chief, rather than wake the nonagenarian, said he planned to speak to her that next—meaning, this—morning.

Apparently, he had.

'Excuse me,' AnnaLise said to Sheree. 'I need to talk with Chuck about something.'

Waiting out a four-wheeled cotton-candy vendor, AnnaLise nevertheless looked both ways before crossing the street.

'Parade comes from only one direction, you know.' Bobby Bradenham was behind her.

'It's the pedestrians that can't be trusted,' AnnaLise said. 'What did you do, go AWOL? The parade's not over.'

'It is if you're in the lead car. Four blocks of smiling and waving and your duty is done.'

AnnaLise hesitated. She'd initially thought the fewer people who knew where the cane had been found, the better, but Chuck's presence here meant the truth was going to come out, and soon. Best that Bobby hear it from her.

'Listen,' she said, stopping short of where Chuck stood talking to Mama and Daisy in their chairs. 'I haven't mentioned it to Sheree or anyone else this morning, but I found Ichiro's cane last night.'

'You did?' Bobby seemed astonished. 'Where?'

AnnaLise swallowed. 'My mother's garage.'

'Your...' He glanced at the threesome and whispered, 'Did you report it?'

'Of course,' AnnaLise said. 'I mean, I had to, right?'

'Right,' Bobby said. 'Was the...was it...hidden?'

'Call it semi-plain sight.' She had to admit confiding in someone—other than Chuck, of course—felt good.

'Semi-plain sight?' Bobby asked.

'Leaning against the wall inside, by the door jamb. The thing was behind an umbrella, so I don't know how long it had been there.'

'What'd she say?'

Bobby was speaking so quietly, AnnaLise wasn't sure she'd heard him correctly. 'She?'

'Daisy.' He looked at AnnaLise's blank face. 'Your mother.'

'I *know* who Daisy is.' Recalling Sheree's recent comment on 'rubbing off', AnnaLise's voice rose against her will. 'Are you insinuating my mother put it there?'

'Shh.' Bobby held up his hands to quiet her and glanced around. 'I don't know any more than you just told me.'

'That's right. You don't,' AnnaLise said angrily, then considerably softened. 'So why are you jumping to conclusions?'

'I'm not,' Bobby said, 'but…'

'It's Mrs Peebly's garage, too, after all, and nobody's blaming her. Maybe she found the cane and put it in the garage, thinking it might come in handy some day. Instead of her walker.'

'Pretty optimistic of her, at age ninety.'

'But a spry ninety,' AnnaLise said stubbornly.

'Enough to be hiking around the lake?' As AnnaLise tried to turn away, Bobby grabbed her arm. 'I'm sorry, but ever—'

'Ever since I got here all hell has broken loose?' AnnaLise completed for him. 'Believe me, I'm very aware.' She shook off his hand.

'Not just since you got here. Even before.'

She could feel rage rising in her. So much for the joy of 'confiding'. 'You're talking about the blood drive. You're saying that was the first "incident".'

He nodded tightly.

'You are wrong, you hear me?' If they were the same height, she'd have been in his face. As it was, AnnaLise had to settle for being around his breastplate. 'Daisy had nothing to do with any of this, Bobby. The accident with your mother was just that, an accident. Leave. Daisy. Alone.' She punctuated each word with her index finger.

Point made, if not necessarily taken, AnnaLise Griggs turned away and collided with the chief of police.

'FOR THE LAST TIME,' Chuck said. 'I'm not targeting your mother.'

The three old schoolmates were sitting in Chuck's office, the parade mercifully having ended a few minutes earlier.

'Bobby here said you were.' Or would. Or should. AnnaLise was still being stubborn, mostly because she felt bewildered by how angry she'd become. *And* at one—or two—of her oldest, dearest friends.

The closer of which was now the mayor of her hometown, sitting in the chair next to her and across the desk from the chief.

'I did not,' Bobby said. 'I merely asked—'

'Enough, already,' Chuck thundered. 'This is why law enforcement in a small town is such a pain in the ass. Everyone's a buttinsky.'

Now both Bobby and AnnaLise looked at him.

'I'm just saying.' The chief centered a piece of paper on the desk in front of him. 'So here's what we know and, I should add, this is all—or will be—public knowledge.'

He raised his thumb. 'One, there was blood on the cane belonging to Ichiro Katou.'

Bobby flinched.

'Two.' Index finger. 'Mrs Peebly is absolutely positive…' AnnaLise leaned forward.

'…that she's not sure if the cane was there or not when she put her car away yesterday.'

A released breath AnnaLise hadn't realized she'd been holding. 'Maybe Mrs Peebly's covering for someone.'

'If only,' Chuck said. 'When I knocked on your neighbor's door this morning, all she was wearing was her nightgown. A diaphanous nightgown. Any cover-up would have been much appreciated, believe me.'

'Diaphanous, huh?' AnnaLise said. 'Who says you don't talk fashion?'

Chuck's glare made it very clear who said it. And what his job was.

Properly put in her place, AnnaLise said, 'I was saying to Bobby that maybe Mrs Peebly—'

A knock on the door interrupted her, and a nervous officer stuck his head in. 'Chief, there's—'

A manicured hand swept him out of the way and Bobby's mother swept in. Daisy and Mama were close behind.

'May I ask what is going on here?' Mrs B demanded.

'To be frank?' Chuck remained seated. 'No.'

Mrs B hesitated, though whether it was because she didn't understand the sentence structure or wasn't used to being told no, wasn't clear.

Mama took advantage of the opening. 'AnnieLeeze, have they arrested you?'

'Arrested me?' AnnaLise leaped to her feet. 'Wherever did you—'

'Girl, the whole town's talking,' Mama said. 'That the chief here came out from seeing Mrs Peebly and then up and took you and Bobby into custody.'

'I did not,' Chuck said, rising now, too, if slowly.

Meanwhile, Daisy had somehow slipped into AnnaLise's seat. 'Told you so,' she said, folding her arms and crossing her legs.

'Bobby and I were merely having a…discussion,' AnnaLise said.

'Looked more like a fight from where we were sitting,' Mama put in. 'Ain't that right, Daisy?'

'Yes, ma'am.' AnnaLise's mother was busy looking around the office.

Mrs B seemed to have gotten a second wind. 'What are you doing about all this, Chief? I understand an assault weapon was found in Lorraine's garage.'

'Assault weapon?' AnnaLise squeaked. 'It's a cane, not an AK-47. Besides, our garage is unlocked. Anybody could have put anything in there.'

'Just what are you insinuating?'

'Me? What about you?' AnnaLise and Bobby's mother were toe-to-toe now.

'Do not use that tone with me, missy.'

'Ma…' Bobby got up, too.

'And you, do not "ma" me, child.'

'Child?' Daisy cupped her hand over her mouth like a kid caught telling secrets. 'But he's…old.'

'You stay out of this, Lorry,' Mrs B snapped. 'Mind your own business.'

Daisy twisted to face the woman, tears springing to her eyes. 'Don't you dare yell at me, Ema Sikes. I am just trying to help.'

Mrs B's mouth dropped open in astonishment as she realized what AnnaLise knew the moment she saw tears in her mother's eyes.

Daisy Griggs—the adult version—did not cry. Not even when her young husband had died. But apparently Lorraine 'Lorry' Kuchenbacher still could. And did.

FOURTEEN

'WHAT ARE YOU going to do?'

Bobby and AnnaLise had returned to the Griggses' kitchen. And also to being friends.

'I don't know.' She walked over to glance up the stairs to where Mama and Daisy, now seemingly back to normal, were watching television in one of the two bedrooms.

'What I *do* know,' AnnaLise said, sitting back down and drumming her fingers on the table, 'is that I can't leave tomorrow like I planned.'

'Are you going to bite my head off if I tell you I'm glad? I've missed you.' He raised his hands as if to ward her off. 'Platonically, I mean.'

'I've missed you, too,' AnnaLise said. 'And I'm sorry I yelled at you. I'd forgotten what it's like to have a friend without limits on what you can tell him.'

She stared off into the distance for a moment and then met his eyes. 'Especially things you've been afraid to tell yourself.'

Bobby covered her hand with his, probably to quiet the drumming. 'Saying something out loud makes it real, remember? That's what we always thought as kids, at least.'

'Which is why we never 'fessed up, even to each other, about breaking Mrs Peebly's window.'

Bobby nodded. 'I looked at you and you looked at me.'

'Then we ran away as fast as we could and hid in the crawl space under the market.'

He nodded again. 'And got stuck down there.'

'Three hours, and not one word was spoken about that window.'

'Until now.'

Silence.

'Bobby, I *hate* that crawl space.' AnnaLise gave his hand a squeeze before pulling away her own.

'So say it.'

'Say what? That we broke Mrs Peebly's window? There, it's been said.' She stood up to open the refrigerator door. 'You want something to drink?'

'No. And that window's not what I'm talking about and you know it.'

AnnaLise turned, can of Diet Coke in her hand. She held it out to him like a wireless microphone. 'So tell me, Mayor Bradenham. What things do *you* think I'm not admitting to myself?'

He took the can away and set it on the table, but that didn't stop AnnaLise.

'Let's see.' She plopped into her chair and popped the top on the soda. 'How about that I thought I was crazy in love with a married man in Wisconsin who, as it turns out, is pretty crazy himself?'

Bobby's eyes widened.

'That when I came to my senses and ended it, he apparently wasn't listening, because he keeps texting and calling.'

She lifted the cellphone which had been face down next to her hand. It showed nineteen incoming messages. AnnaLise slammed it back onto the tabletop.

'Have you contacted the police up there?' Bobby asked, reaching out to cover her hand again.

'The police?' AnnaLise wanted to laugh. 'Now *that* would be a little awkward. He's the district attorney. Besides, he hasn't been threatening. He just—' she shrugged— 'wants me back.'

'Can't blame him for that.' The smile on Bobby's face invited her to smile back.

She tried. 'I'm sorry to unload like this, Bobby. It's just…' She pulled back her hand once more and looked skyward, blinking back tears. 'This is my fault. I had an affair with a married man. A high-powered one at that, so—'

'So you've been keeping this all bottled up inside you.'

AnnaLise bit her lip. 'Who could I tell?'

'Me, Annie,' Bobby said. 'You can always tell me.'

She studied his face. It wasn't—wouldn't ever be—that of a lover, but Bobby was her best friend. How could she have forgotten that?

'I know. And now I have and, buddy—' a nervous laugh— 'aren't *you* sorry?'

'Never. What can I do?'

'You've already done it.' AnnaLise drew in a deep, amazingly cleansing breath, then let it out. 'Thank you.'

'Anytime.'

'The real question for me now is…Daisy'

'There's something very wrong,' Bobby said. 'You do know that, right?'

'Hell, I knew—or feared—*that* when I decided to come back here. Alzheimer's, dementia—I've been trying to convince myself otherwise, but…' She shrugged.

'Listen, Annie. I don't blame you for being afraid. That spell in Chuck's office was…'

'Creepy,' AnnaLise finished for him. 'And you're right, I am scared. Scared for Daisy and—I'm so ashamed—but I'm scared for me, too. Despite everything that's haywire with my life up north, I don't want to stay in Sutherton for the rest of it.'

Now she put her hand out to him. 'I'm sorry, Bobby, but I don't.'

'Not to worry. I'm the mayor and sometimes *I* don't want to be here.'

'But you are.' AnnaLise shook her head. 'You're a good person, Bobby. Me? I'm selfish and self-absorbed—the prodigal daughter—what kind of caregiver does that combination make?'

'Human, Annie. Forgive yourself.'

She mustered the ghost of a smile. 'First you want me to talk to myself, now you want me to forgive myself? What is this? Do-it-yourself confessional?'

He grinned back. 'You're not Catholic. What do you know about repentance and absolution?'

'Not much, but I'm aces on guilt. You Catholics don't have anything on us Lutherans when it comes to that.'

When Bobby let that lie, AnnaLise squared her shoulders. 'OK, first thing I'm going to do is get Daisy in to see Dr Stanton. Tomorrow. Second, I'm going to contact my boss at the paper and tell her I need to take some personal leave. Then…'

'*Then* you'll go on from there,' Bobby said. 'No need to make any further decisions right now, and you've got a lot of good friends here to help you with future ones.'

'Right.' AnnaLise picked up her cellphone and moved toward her computer.

'And one more thing?'

She turned. 'Yes?'

'Don't you dare underestimate yourself, Annie. You *can* take care of Daisy. No matter what.'

AnnaLise closed both eyes, tears now really threatening to fall. 'How can you possibly know that, when even I don't?'

'Because you already are.' Bobby's voice was low. 'And you always have, ever since the day your daddy died.'

AnnaLise Griggs began to sob, then shudder, until she felt Bobby Bradenham's hands clamp on her shoulders. First gently, then more strongly, helping his friend keep herself together while she allowed herself the first full-body cry since the age of five.

Crying for a father she'd barely known, and a childhood she knew was past.

WORDS. YOU CAN place them on the page or on the wind, but can you ever take them back?

Though that was precisely what AnnaLise had considered doing with both Dickens Hart's check and archived memories as she'd toted the boxes out of her car and up the staircase, on each trip barely clearing her father's old gun cabinet that stood on the landing to the upper level.

Stairs safely negotiated, AnnaLise had dropped the boxes in her bedroom. She couldn't see the bed or dresser past all Hart's crap, but AnnaLise did feel better when the stevedoring was done.

Accomplishment can do that for a person.

She and Dr Stanton had finally connected by phone and Daisy was to see him in his office at nine a.m., Tuesday. The next morning.

AnnaLise also emailed her boss, Jan, to ask for the coming week off or, failing that, whatever the union rules provided as a temporary leave of absence. No reply yet, of course, but at least AnnaLise had gotten the ball rolling. Put the request—OK, the *need*—into words. The upside of Bobby's and her belief that if you said things out loud, they became real.

Jan and the newspaper could say either yes or no. But, whichever, AnnaLise was prepared to deal with it. Especially since she had—thanks to the stacks around her—the equivalent of two years of severance, if her Wisconsin employer decided to pull her proverbial plug.

AnnaLise sat cross-legged on her bedroom floor, surrounded by the boxes relating to the years of Hart's life that she thought might be the more—or, at least, somewhat more—interesting.

'If I have to read his elementary school diaries,' she said aloud, 'I'll crowbar the lock off Dad's gun cabinet and just blow my brains out.'

AnnaLise pawed through the boxes until she found the volume she was looking for: 1981. The year of Bobby Bradenham's birth. Was he Dickens Hart's son? The answer, AnnaLise thought as she put her hand on the bound journal, could be inside. She felt more than a little surge of excitement. Intrusive? Perhaps. But the question intrigued AnnaLise and with everything else going on right now, she needed some diversion. Failing a trashy celebrity magazine, this was likely to be as close as she'd get.

'AnnaLise?' Daisy's voice echoing off the stairwell walls.

The journalist struggled to her feet, lower spine jibing her for sitting hunched over so long. Oh, to be age twelve again, when body parts seemed perfectly lubricated against each other and synchronized to create a smooth, silent machine.

And she wasn't even thirty yet.

AnnaLise opened the door and called down to her mother on the first floor. 'Yes, Daisy?'

'The chief is here.'

Uh-oh. 'For me?'

'No, for me.'

It took a second for AnnaLise to realize her mother was kidding. 'Can you send him up?'

When Chuck Greystone stepped into her bedroom, he looked around. 'The décor is a little different than I remember.'

'Granted, corrugated cardboard wasn't the new black then. But not to worry, my 'N Sync bedspread is still in the closet.'

'What a relief,' Chuck said, moving a box to sit on the bed. 'I loved that thing.'

'I know you did,' AnnaLise said, resuming her position on the floor. 'I should have known a guy who shared my taste in music was too good to be true.'

'You can be forgiven,' Chuck said. 'I sure didn't know, either.'

He waved toward the boxes. 'Moving in or out?'

'Still to be determined. But for now I'm rooming with *Dickens Hart—The Untold Story*.'

'You have my sympathies.'

She shrugged. 'Maybe I'll find him interesting.'

'Not as interesting as he finds himself. The man's left town, you know.'

Huh? 'No, I didn't. Because of the shooting?' One measly flesh wound? Sutherton folk were usually made of sterner stock. Hell, Mrs B had lost a bucket of blood and she kept on ticking. Not that AnnaLise was going to remind Chuck of the incident guided by Daisy's own hand.

'He's convinced some disgruntled current investor has targeted him.'

'Maybe not such a bad guess,' AnnaLise said. 'Ichiro did say Hart's Landing was underwater.'

'He did?' Chuck asked, suddenly more than mildly engaged. 'When was this?'

'Saturday afternoon. Daisy and I wanted to take a look at the new development and saw Ichiro there.'

'Bobby told me he'd seen you. Was he or anybody else around when Katou mentioned this?'

'Just Joy Tamarack, but she already knew. In fact, Ichiro found out by accidentally eavesdropping on her, Hart, and I think this David Sabatino.' AnnaLise looked at Chuck curiously. 'Why do you ask?'

A shrug. 'Hart's not talking about it, as you might expect. He's afraid if potential *new* investors hear, they'll turn tail and run, leaving the current investors holding the bag. And blaming him.'

'It makes some sense, I suppose. But why does Dickens think somebody already in the fold is mad enough to take a potshot at him?'

'Guilty conscience would be my guess. If you're asking what someone might gain by shooting him, it gets kind of twisty.'

'How about pure and intense self-gratification?'

'Hey,' Chuck said with a grin. 'I don't rule anything out.' His face changed. 'Listen, I need to talk with you about the Katou case. Your mother, too.'

'OK.' AnnaLise got back onto her feet. 'Did you want to talk to Daisy after me, or should I go get her now?'

'No, I mean I want to talk to you about...your mother.'

Reflexively AnnaLise crossed her arms into a defensive posture. 'What about Daisy?'

Chuck moved another stack of journals and patted the bed next to him. 'How about sitting down? I'm not the enemy here, Lise.'

'I know that.'

Problem was, she didn't know who—or what—was. But AnnaLise sat. 'Listen, if you checked for fingerprints on the cane, you know that Daisy didn't touch it.'

Even as AnnaLise's words hit the air, she was praying they would come true.

'You're right,' Chuck said, and AnnaLise let out her breath. 'In fact, the only fingerprints on it were yours.'

Well, that wasn't good, on two counts. 'So somebody wiped it.'

'Correct.'

AnnaLise was thinking furiously. Someone strikes Ichiro in the head with his own cane, then cleans the thing and finally hides it in the Griggses' garage.

But why? 'Do you have a cause of death yet?' she asked.

'Drowning,' Chuck said. 'Mr Katou was alive when he hit the water.'

'But unconscious?'

'Presumably. Or he couldn't swim, maybe on account of the bum hip.'

Hip, *not* leg. 'Have you been able to contact his family?' AnnaLise asked.

'We're working on it,' Chuck said. 'The closest relatives seem to be Mr Katou's grandparents, who raised him, but his grandmother died a few years back and his grandfather just months ago.'

'Maybe Ichiro had been taking care of his grandfather and now he was free to see the world.' In the still unlikely form of Sutherton, North Carolina.

'Using any inheritance to open a sushi restaurant in the High Country?' The irony of chosen locale apparently hadn't been lost on Chuck either.

'No wife or kids?'

'Nope.'

'Well, that's good.' She saw Chuck cock his head at her. 'I mean, Ichiro's not leaving a family behind, one that depended on him.'

Chuck shrugged. 'Family comes in many forms, but so far as we can tell, he also wasn't in a serious relationship.'

AnnaLise was quiet.

Chuck cleared his throat. 'I hate to ask this, but I need some...whereabouts. On Saturday—after you met Bobby Bradenham and Ichiro Katou on the island—where did Daisy and you go?'

AnnaLise swallowed hard. She knew he had to ask, but it nevertheless stung a bit. 'You know where I was— Sal's. Daisy went to Torch.'

'What time?' Chuck pulled a notepad from his jacket pocket.

'We had dinner at Mama's.' Not exactly a revelation. 'Then Daisy walked down the block to Torch and I crossed the street to Sal's. When I sat down for Frat Pack it was seven-thirty.'

Chuck was writing. 'Good. Now I know you left Sal's at eleven when it closed. Did you go right home?'

'No,' AnnaLise said. 'I went to Torch, made sure Daisy was OK. Don't you remember? I asked you if you wanted to come.'

Chuck looked up. 'Just because I came out, Lise, doesn't mean I want to sit through an evening of show tunes any more than I did before. Maybe you should have asked Bobby.'

'By the time you turned me down, he'd already left.'

'So you got to Torch just after eleven and joined Daisy?'

No hesitation. 'Yes.'

More writing. 'Until when?'

'One-thirty. I remember seeing the time on my alarm clock as I was going to bed.'

AnnaLise pointed toward the clock on her nightstand, only to find it obscured by notebooks.

Chuck moved them. 'Ahh, T-Rex lives. The alarm still work?'

'Don't know, I haven't needed it.' She reached for the

clock with the face of a dinosaur. She pushed a button and got a reverberating 'ROARRRRRR'.

'Yup.'

Chuck took it. 'You were a child of—to put it charitably—eclectic tastes.'

'I like to think so.' She smiled brightly and stood. 'Any other questions?'

'Nope, that should do it.' Chuck tucked the notebook back into his pocket and followed AnnaLise downstairs.

'I'm going to be here for a few more days, as it turns out,' she said on the bottom step. 'Maybe lunch?'

'Dinner would be better. I never know when something *else* is going to blow up.'

'I hear you.' She turned at the front door. 'At least the Smoaks case is easy. You even have somebody in custody.'

'Palooka, the idiot. Or, as I should call him, Stewart Chapel. Not a bad guy, but his new best friend is whichever yahoo last bought him a round. He and Rance each had blood-alcohols of nearly triple the legal limit.'

AnnaLise opened the door and they both stepped out onto the sidewalk. To their right was the garage. 'That cane was planted, Chuck. You have to know that. Daisy and I had no reason to hurt Ichiro—we liked him, even though we also hardly knew him.'

'You and everybody else, it seems.' He was studying the sidewalk between them.

AnnaLise looked down and saw a large black ant.

Chuck stepped on it.

'Why'd you do that?' AnnaLise protested.

'Carpenter ant. You may have an infestation.'

'But they don't *eat* wood like termites. They just tunnel into it and build their nests.'

Living with Daisy, AnnaLise had been the one to deal with bugs—usually by picking them up gingerly in a paper towel and relocating them. Outside. Where neither mother nor daughter had any problem with them.

'You're right,' Chuck said. 'Which *only* means you have structural posts and beams that might look like Swiss cheese. You should check.'

'Check,' AnnaLise said, making a giant check-mark in the air with her index finger.

Chuck hesitated. 'Listen, I should have asked earlier, but how's your mom doing?'

'Fine. Why?' AnnaLise had been fairly certain that Chuck was oblivious to Daisy's momentary regression in his office.

'Somebody mentioned she's having…problems. And beyond the mistake at the blood drive.'

'Honestly? Daisy does seem forgetful,' AnnaLise admitted. 'I've made an appointment with Dr Stanton. Might be a vitamin deficiency.'

That was her story and she was sticking to it.

Chuck met her eyes and AnnaLise looked down. 'Oh, look. He's going to help his friend.'

A second ant was levering the wounded one onto his own back.

'More like helping himself,' Chuck said, turning toward the parked patrol car with what AnnaLise had learned on the police beat in Wisconsin was a 'cop laugh.'

'Huh?'

'Waste not, want not.' Chuck opened the car door. 'Carpenter ants got into recycling long before man began walking this earth of ours.'

'I don't…recycling?'

'Your "helper" is taking his sidewalk-kill friend back to the nest for a snack, kind of a cannibal kabob.'

AnnaLise swallowed her 'eewww' and stomped both insects flat.

FIFTEEN

Monday, Sept. 6, 9:46 p.m.

Yet another new message from Ben. He has to 'see' me, as soon as I return. Honestly, the man's next campaign slogan should be, 'I can have my wife, and meet you, too.' (As sanitized for general audiences, of course.)

AG

ANTS MIGHT EAT THEIR PALS, but did they also lie to them? Because AnnaLise had. She'd told Chuck that she'd met Daisy at Torch by eleven on Saturday night. In truth, that's when AnnaLise got there. Only, she hadn't seen her mother until nearly midnight.

Now it was Tuesday, the morning after Labor Day, and AnnaLise was standing in front of Torch once again, hoping to snag another 'what's-the-point' latte before taking Daisy to Dr Stanton's office for her mother's nine o'clock appointment.

The sign on Torch's door read: Open 7:30 a.m. Anna-Lise checked her watch, recalculated to Eastern time and settled in for a three-minute wait.

When she'd arrived on Saturday night, the first thing she'd done was find Tucker in the packed place to congratulate him. 'Looks like you have a hit on your hands.'

All the tables were filled and Tucker's 'chanteuse' was onstage singing 'Some Enchanted Evening'.

'She's wonderful,' AnnaLise said, spotting a few openings at the raised counters on three walls facing the talent. 'I'd never have recognized this place as our old deli.'

'Your mom says the same thing.' Tucker gestured for AnnaLise to take one of the few elevated stools. 'Can I get you something?'

AnnaLise'd had enough to drink at Sal's, but felt obligated to order something. Which is the classic way hangover stories start. 'Do you have anything for after-dinner?'

'Well, I have no personal knowledge of it, of course, being too young to drink and all,' he replied with an impish grin, 'but I'm told my bartender makes a mean espresso martini—calls it the Midnight Espresso.'

And so, the die was cast. AnnaLise had just finished the sinful concoction, served in a glass rimmed with chocolate syrup and biscotti crumbs, when Daisy finally showed up.

'Where have you been?' Daughter to mother.

'At our house, of course,' Daisy said. 'Did you think I would come here right from dinner? Who in the world goes to a nightclub at seven thirty?'

'Me, apparently. But then my clubs, if Sal's can be described as such, close at eleven.' AnnaLise looked down at the sweet dregs in her glass. 'Can we go home?'

'Don't be silly.' Daisy hiked herself up onto the next stool. 'I just got here.' She signaled for drinks and the rest evolved into, and remained, the already-reported blur.

The sound of a latch turning and the heavy door pushed open. Back to current reality.

'Morning,' greeted the barista who'd made AnnaLise's latte on Friday. 'Give me just a sec, and I'll be right with you.'

'No hurry,' AnnaLise said, settling down at the counter where she and Daisy had sat. 'I'll have a latte when you're ready.'

'Large decaf, non-fat, no-foam, and with a Splenda, right?'

'Wow, great memory. But this time use the high-test, not the unleaded. I need all the boost I can get.'

'High…test?'

'Caffeine. All the cup will hold.'

'You got it.'

While the barista worked behind the espresso machine, AnnaLise tried to relax. Her jaw was aching from clenching her teeth, a sure sign of tension.

Five days ago, AnnaLise had been getting ready to go to the courthouse, unaware—if not exactly blissfully so—of the telephone call she would get once there.

Daisy was 'not right', Mama had said. That seemed the tip of the iceberg now. Could Chuck, or anyone else for that matter, honestly believe AnnaLise's mother would brain a sweet Japanese visitor, clean his cane of fingerprints, but not DNA-laden blood, and then absent-mindedly stick the murder weapon in her own garage?

Ridiculous. But then, so was the incident at the blood drive.

'Is there anything else I can get you?' The barista was beside her. AnnaLise hadn't even registered her approach.

'Oh, I'm sorry,' AnnaLise said, looking at the latte. 'I meant to ask for a to-go cup.'

'Not a problem. Are you heading home this morning?'

Home. Define that, please. 'Not yet,' AnnaLise said. 'My mother has a doctor's appointment.'

'Ahh.' The barista carefully poured the latte in a cardboard cup and capped it. 'How is Daisy doing?'

It wasn't the question but the tone that made Anna-

Lise look up sharply, credit card in hand. 'Fine. Why do you ask?'

The woman flushed. 'No reason.'

AnnaLise put out her hand as the woman turned away. 'I'm sorry. I didn't mean to snap at you, but I need to know. Have you noticed Daisy being odd, or…unwell?'

'Just…' The door opened and the barista looked up to see who had come in behind AnnaLise before she answered. 'Just not acting like herself.'

'Morning,' Tucker Stanton's voice said. 'Who are we talking about?'

AnnaLise turned, wondering why she hadn't thought to speak to him about her mother. After all, besides Mama's, Torch was where the subject of concern had been spending most of her time. 'Good morning, Tucker. We're talking about Daisy.'

The barista, caught by her boss talking about a customer, squirmed. 'I was just saying AnnaLise's mother has seemed…a little under the weather once or twice.'

'Cuckoo for Cocoa Puffs is the way I would have put it,' Tucker said. 'But like my wonderful barista here says, just a couple times.'

Well if that was his attitude, at least Tucker wasn't likely to discipline his employee for her more tactful characterization.

'Did it last long?' AnnaLise picked up her latte and followed the younger Stanton to the stage.

'Nope, just a flash.' Tucker began gathering sheet music from the music stand used on Saturday night. 'More like she was tripping, actually.'

'My mother doesn't do drugs,' AnnaLise said.

'Hey, I'm not saying they aren't prescription. Maybe she just needs her meds adjusted.'

'Uh-unh,' AnnaLise said. 'No drugs, prescription or otherwise. Daisy doesn't even like to swallow an aspirin.'

'Well, then I don't know,' Tucker said, raising the lid of the piano bench. 'Has she seen my dad?'

'Appointment this morning,' AnnaLise said. 'I should have gotten her there sooner.'

'Sooner? Didn't you just arrive Saturday?'

'True, though it seems a lifetime ago.'

'No kidding, huh?' Tucker had put the sheet music in the bench and now eased the lid down. 'Sutherton really outdid itself this weekend, crazy-wise. I hear Ichiro's bloody cane was found in your garage.'

'You heard right,' AnnaLise said.

Tucker read something from her expression. 'Hey, you're not afraid that Daisy…'

'No, no. Of course not,' AnnaLise said, though that was precisely what she feared. 'She'd have no reason to hurt Ichiro.'

Unless, of course, he reminded her of somebody else. Someone from the past she'd been slipping into of late. Someone…

'You know,' Tucker said slowly, 'I honestly hadn't thought of it, but you and your mother must be suspects. At least, technically speaking.'

AnnaLise gulped.

He said, 'Has the chief talked to you?'

'Well, yes,' said AnnaLise. 'But…'

'You both have alibis?'

'I do. And Daisy—well, I sort of told Chuck she was here.'

'But she wasn't,' Tucker protested. The barista's head turned toward them and he lowered his voice. 'From what I hear, Ichiro died before midnight.'

AnnaLise hadn't heard that, but it didn't surprise her.

Something—or, more precisely, somebody—had kept the man from meeting Bobby at Sal's at ten p.m. How long before ten seemed anybody's guess.

Tucker continued, 'And we both know that Daisy didn't arrive until after the singer started her third set.'

'Has Chuck asked you?'

'No.'

'So we don't have a problem, am I right?' AnnaLise raised her eyebrows at him.

'Right.' Tucker studied AnnaLise's face. 'But just so we're straight, if Chuck puts the question, I'm going to have to tell him the truth.'

'Of course. I wouldn't have it any other way.'

And Chuck would ask eventually, AnnaLise knew. Especially if no other possibilities—or suspects—arose.

'I know your dad owns the condo Ichiro rented,' AnnaLise said. 'Any chance you'd have a key?'

'Do you think I'm going nuts?'

They were en route to Dr Stanton's office at University Hospital in AnnaLise's little convertible with the farting muffler.

'No,' AnnaLise said, glancing quickly at her mother in the passenger seat. 'Do you?'

'Honestly? I don't know.' Daisy was looking straight ahead. 'I do know that I'm scared.'

'Don't…' AnnaLise changed her mind. If mother could be honest, then daughter needed to do the same. 'Let me start over. I'm scared, too.' She touched Daisy's shoulder. 'But we'll figure it out. Together, OK?'

'Now you sound like Phyllis,' Daisy complained, though AnnaLise could hear a smile coming through her voice.

'I know,' AnnaLise said, turning into the hospital's

entrance. She bypassed the emergency and outpatient entrances and turned into the parking lot that serviced the professional building where Dr Stanton's office was. 'And I'm right, just like Mama always is.'

'Or thinks she is,' Daisy said.

The smile was still there when they got out of the car, which AnnaLise took to be a good sign. 'You saw Dr Stanton after the blood-drive accident, right? What did he do then?'

'A physical exam first, then he wanted me to tell him what day it was, to count backwards from twenty. That kind of thing.'

'And you could?'

'I don't recall.'

AnnaLise's mouth dropped open.

'Oh, God,' Daisy said. 'I was kidding. I passed all his tests with flying colors.'

Then why had Dr Stanton, according to Mama, stated that Daisy 'wasn't right' in the head?

AnnaLise had an opportunity to ask the horse's mouth that question while Daisy was having blood drawn in another room.

'Your mother appeared disoriented when she and I spoke last week,' Dr Stanton said from the other side of his office desk. 'Phyllis was there as well and she may have misinterpreted something I said.'

AnnaLise felt an irrational sense of reprieve. Irrational, because she herself had seen disturbing signs in her mother. Reprieve, because human nature is what it is.

She forced herself to press the issue. 'I've witnessed two episodes just this weekend, where my mother...' AnnaLise was searching for a word. 'Reverted?'

Dr Stanton's eyes narrowed. 'To?'

'Her youth. The first, she acted like my dad was still

alive. The second, she seemed to be just out of high school, though I'm less sure of that one.'

'What do you mean?'

AnnaLise shifted uncomfortably in the 'patient' chair. 'It was more her speech patterns and, well, she cried.'

'Cried?' Dr Stanton didn't understand, but AnnaLise lost the chance to explain when Daisy rejoined them.

'Good, you're back.' Dr Stanton waved her into the chair next to AnnaLise. 'So, let's talk about where we go from here.'

He opened a folder on his desk. 'We've covered the physical exam and we should have the results of the blood work and other labs in a few days. If that all checks out, I'd suggest a neurologist.'

AnnaLise blanched, but Daisy was nodding. 'I think that's a good idea. And maybe a psychiatrist or psychologist?'

'I'd like to hear from the neurologist first.'

AnnaLise, open-mouthed, was looking at her mother.

'What?' Daisy said. 'You don't think I know how to research stuff on the Internet?'

Dr Stanton laughed and stood to shake hands with both of them. 'Recognizing the problem, along with wanting to address it, constitutes a very good start.'

'Thanks for your time, doctor,' AnnaLise said. 'I'm sure you have a long day ahead of you.'

'No, though not for any pleasant reason,' Jackson Stanton said, holding the door to the waiting room open for them to pass through. 'I'm leaving at noon to attend Rance Smoaks's funeral.'

RANCE SMOAKS MIGHT HAVE been universally despised, but what small town doesn't love a potentially toxic funeral?

And Sutherton loved Kathleen Smoaks, as well, so 'planting Rance' made for a double celebration.

The widow stood in the vestibule between the chapel portion of the church, where the service had just been concluded, and Fellowship Hall, where lunch was about to be served.

'I didn't know the guy well,' Joy Tamarack said to AnnaLise as the two waited in line in front of Daisy and Mama to pay their respects. 'But there doesn't seem to be a whole lot of mourning at his funeral.'

'Let's just say to know the deceased was to hate him,' AnnaLise said over the general chatter and frivolity that surrounded them.

'If you didn't like him, why are *you* here?' Joy asked.

'Because I've known Kathleen for a long time and wanted to support her.' This despite the fact that, until Dr Stanton mentioned it, AnnaLise had completely forgotten about the funeral.

'Looks like the young widow's got lots of support.' Joy craned her neck to see around Bobby's mother in front of them. 'In fact, I think she was just high-fived.'

Joy held up her hands. 'Not that I'm criticizing. If the man was an ass, good riddance, I say.'

'Amen,' Daisy intoned from behind them and a half-dozen people around the vestibule echoed it, though not for the same reason. Mama exchanged looks with AnnaLise and shrugged.

An older gentleman, who had been talking with Kathleen, moved away, taking five family members with him, and suddenly Mrs Bradenham was at the front of the receiving line.

Kathleen Smoaks was about five foot seven, with honey-colored locks trailing past her shoulder. She'd always reminded AnnaLise of a Barbie doll, but with non-synthetic hair.

'Kathleen,' Mrs B was saying as the two air-kissed. 'I am so sorry to see you again under these circumstances.'

'Bullshit,' Sheree, who'd been standing with the widow, said in AnnaLise's ear. 'That shrew hated seeing Kathleen under any circumstances. Thought she wasn't good enough for Bobby.'

'Nobody was.' Especially AnnaLise, way back when. Gradually, though, Bobby's mother had seen that AnnaLise and Bobby really were 'just friends' and laid off her, at least.

'A mama's boy, then?' Joy said. 'I wondered why he's still single.'

'My opinion?' Sheree nodded toward Kathleen as Mrs B moved on. 'Bobby never stopped loving the one who got away.'

SIXTEEN

ANNALISE DIDN'T SEE Bobby Bradenham until she and Daisy, Mama and Joy Tamarack were sitting down to eat in Fellowship Hall. He came over to say hello, but was promptly flagged down by Sheree Pepper at the next table with Kathleen Smoaks.

'Interesting,' Joy said with a nod toward the neighboring clump. 'I mean if what Sheree was saying about Bobby and—'

'Sheree Pepper?' Daisy said, jumping into the conversation by shattering its context and shifting its drift. 'Bobby should watch out for her. That girl was loose all through school, remember, AnnaLise?'

Friend glanced at friend, not ten feet away, and stammered, 'I…uhhh…no…'

Joy laughed. 'It's a stage we girls go through, Daisy. You know what people used to say about me?'

'No, what?' Daisy responded eagerly.

'That wherever I went, I spread…Joy.'

'BUT IT'S TRUE,' Sheree said, later that night.

'That I spread 'em?' Joy asked. She was sprawled on her back on the inn's living-room floor, a half-filled margarita glass balanced on her flat stomach.

'Well, yes. I'm certain of that, too,' Sheree said. 'But I meant what Daisy said. Everyone thought I was a slut in high school, even though I was practically a virgin.'

Practically.

'True or not,' AnnaLise said sternly, 'it's not like Daisy to blurt out something like that.'

'Maybe not,' Sheree said. 'But it is what it is.'

'Stupid expression,' Chuck said. It was his night off and he was taking advantage of it, stretched out on the floral couch. '"It is what it is." What's "it", anyway?'

He leaned over for his glass on the coffee table and nearly slid off the couch. AnnaLise pushed the margarita closer to him. She was on the floor, back against the couch and Sheree was sitting in the red chair, feet tucked under her.

'What is it? And it is what?' Sheree intoned, Zen-like.

'It's sort of like, I am what I am and that's all what I am,' Joy offered.

'Popeye, the Sailor Man!' Chuck sang out and, having sat up heroically to take a sip of margarita, collapsed back into the couch.

'Aww, geez,' AnnaLise said. 'And we didn't even do drugs in our youth, so we can't blame this conversation on burnout or flashback.'

'Speak for yourself,' Joy said, executing an ab crunch while still—incredibly—balancing her margarita.

An intake of breath from Sheree, released as Joy—and liquid-filled glass—settled back onto the rug. 'Doing drugs and spreading joy. Were you the bad-ass you'd like us to believe?'

'You want the truth?'

AnnaLise was looking at Joy upside down, so she scooted around so she could see her face in normal orientation. 'Yes, please.'

'No.' Joy sat up, simultaneously lifting the glass carefully and putting it on the coffee table.

'Umm, no what?' Chuck asked sleepily. Apparently his role tonight as inquisitor was less than grand.

'No, I wasn't a bad-ass. Worst thing I ever smoked was cigarettes, which is *not* recommended for an athlete. I play the bad girl because I was always a jock and when you're a female one, people tend to think—'

'You're a lesbian,' Sheree finished. 'No offense,' to Chuck.

'None taken.' His eyes were closed.

AnnaLise rolled hers and turned back to Joy. 'So how did you end up married to Dickens Hart?'

'I told y'all that he hired me to run the fitness center at the White Tail Spa, didn't I?'

'Y'all?' Sheree repeated. 'Aren't you from Brooklyn?'

'Where'd you get that idea? I'm from Indiana. *Southern* Indiana. Now, may I continue?'

'Certainly,' Sheree said. 'But, to reprise, I think what AnnaLise meant was that if you're truly not a slut, you clearly aren't Dickens's type.'

Joy looked at AnnaLise.

AnnaLise shrugged. 'I think Sheree meant more summarize than reprise, but…yeah, I guess that's where I was eventually going.'

'Hah. Well, then, good question,' Joy said. 'But surprisingly, Dickens is an honorable guy in his own, self-involved way. Not quite the pig you might think.'

'How much of a pig is he?' Chuck, suddenly seeming alert.

'Not enough for me to shoot at him, if that's what you're wondering.' She retrieved her glass from the low table. 'If I were you, I'd be looking at the people who've been investing in Hart's Landing.'

Apparently, all gloves were now off when it came to keeping the development's financial issues quiet.

'Hart's Landing?' Sheree asked. 'Why? Is there a problem?'

AnnaLise realized her friend had no way of knowing

the development was underwater. And wouldn't be terribly crushed by the news, given that she'd feared rentals there would become competition for her inn.

Joy shrugged. 'Just Dickens and his partner over-promising, then under-delivering. I wouldn't want to be in a room with them when the construction loan comes due.'

'Speaking of David Sabatino—what about him?' AnnaLise asked Chuck. 'Would he have a reason to shoot Hart?'

The eyes stayed closed. 'Only if their partnership agreement stipulates that Hart's half-interest goes to the survivor in the partnership instead of the decedent's personal heirs,' Chuck said. 'Besides, half of noth—'

'Heirs?' Joy interrupted. 'And exactly how is that devil in the details defined?'

Chuck shrugged. 'Depends on whether Hart has a will or not. If he dies intestate, his estate would be divided amongst his children or their descendants. Assuming he didn't have children, you'd move on to his parents, then siblings, etc.'

'Sounds like *ex*-wives are pretty far down the list,' AnnaLise said. 'And even then, there are two others ahead of you.'

'No ex-wives need apply,' Chuck said, 'unless there were children from the union. Then Hart's ex might be able to glum something.'

'I think you mean "glom",' said AnnaLise. 'Like "glom onto something". Unless you're talking "plumb", as in "plumb the depths".'

The other three turned to look at her.

'Sorry,' AnnaLise said meekly. 'The reporter in me.'

'More like the pain in the ass, in you,' Joy growled.

Sheree turned to Chuck. 'What about Bobby?'

'What about him?'

'You don't know?' she asked, looking eager to spread the word. 'From what I hear, Hart sold Mrs B that place for peanuts back in the Eighties. She has no visible means of support, so how's she keeping it up?'

'I don't know,' Chuck said. 'I assumed she had family money or that Bobby's father, the guy that died in the car crash, was loaded.'

'Bobby's father may have money,' Sheree said, 'but I bet you'll find no evidence he died in a car crash.'

'Cryptic doesn't suit you,' Joy barked, looking upset. 'Are you saying Dickens and that Bradenham woman… what's her first name?'

'Ema,' AnnaLise supplied. 'E-M-A.'

'That Dickens and 'Ema, E-M-A, Bradenham,' Joy said, 'did the dirty and Bobby was the result?'

'Ema Bradenham?' Chuck repeated, seeming to find the thought troubling. 'But she's…old.'

AnnaLise rolled her eyes. 'So is Dickens Hart. Sixty-eight, according to his journals.'

'Journals?' Sheree asked. 'Why do you—'

'AnnaLise is right,' Joy interrupted, glaring at Chuck. 'Ema Bradenham has to be at least a full decade younger than Dickens.'

'But if she *was* older, what's the big deal?' AnnaLise demanded, her voice rising. 'Guys "do" younger women all the time and nobody seems to have a problem with it. In fact, it's a badge of honor.'

AnnaLise stopped, realizing all three had again swiveled toward her.

She cleared her throat. 'I'm just saying.'

'Hey, no need to get mad,' said Joy, shaking her head. 'You're preaching to the choir here, girl.'

'Amen,' Sheree said under her breath, earning a glare from Joy.

Chuck held up his hands. 'Don't anybody look at me. I don't even have a filly in this race.'

Everybody laughed, awkward moment evaporated.

Having supervised the refreshment of drinks, Sheree changed the subject back to Dickens Hart. 'Any relationship he could have had with Bobby's mother would have been well before you came on the scene, Joy.'

'1981,' AnnaLise supplied, grateful—and not a little surprised—by Sheree's tact.

'Fourteen years before, then,' Joy said. 'Dickens was fifty-three when we met, and God knows he hadn't been exactly celibate. And if he knew Bobby was his son, Dickens would have taken care of him. That's what I meant about him being oddly honorable.'

'Then shouldn't he be "taking care" of a gaggle of "Bobbies" and "Robertas"?' Sheree asked, her sensitivity reservoir apparently drained for the day. 'As you said, the man's never been known to keep it in his pants. And not just around the Fawns of White Tail Lodge.'

'Yeah,' conceded Joy, 'but, in or out of his pants, Dickens was shooting blanks.'

AnnaLise couldn't believe her ears. All this talk of Bobby being a 'little Dickens' and the man was… 'Sterile? Like from mumps or something?'

Joy laughed. 'Nah, he had himself clipped.'

'Ahh, a vasectomy,' AnnaLise said, wondering if she'd find any mention of the procedure in Hart's journals. *Dear Diary: Today I got my weenie snipped.*

'Do you know when?' Sheree asked Joy.

'Before I came on the scene. The early Eighties sounds about right.'

'So he learned from his mistake,' Sheree said. 'No offense to Bobby.'

'Or me, I guess,' Joy said.

Uh-oh, AnnaLise thought. Maybe Joy's biological clock isn't so different than that of her sorority sisters, no matter what the Frat Pack leader might maintain.

'It's not a mistake, it's a baby,' Chuck intoned, not so soberly. He swung his legs off the couch.

'Where are you going?' AnnaLise asked.

'Gotta get a good night's sleep,' he said, rising to full height. 'Tomorrow I need to talk to a man about a will. And a partnership agreement.'

ANNALISE LEFT HER CAR at Sheree's inn and walked home, since the five-block distance didn't warrant risking a DUI or worse, hurting herself or someone else.

It was well after eleven, so Sal's was closed and the only sign of life—or even light—on Main Street was the glow coming from Torch.

Speaking of illumination, AnnaLise loved Chuck dearly, but she was starting to think he might not be the brightest bulb on the tree. Hadn't he thought to check the partnership agreement and ask Hart about his heirs? After all, 'who benefits from this crime' was always the first question TV cops asked themselves.

Then again, the chief was smart enough to lie there on the couch, maybe feigning a near stupor while quietly absorbing local gossip that might advance the investigation of his case.

Or now, *cases*.

It didn't surprise AnnaLise that Chuck seemed as unaware of the rumor regarding Bobby's paternity as AnnaLise had been. All of them, including Bobby, so far as she knew, had hook-line-and-sinker believed that Bobby's father died in an accident involving a car he had been driving and in which the infant Bobby and his mother had been riding. And spared.

Now, seemingly out of the blue, there was all this speculation. Maybe Bobby had said it best: people shared the most intimate details of their lives online, not to mention on television. Maybe that trend had desensitized us to the point that we were willing to open old wounds, talk about things long hidden?

Or maybe Phyllis 'Mama' Balisteri was just really good at starting rumors and Sheree Pepper at repeating them.

Whatever, AnnaLise was just as happy to have Chuck investigating Dickens Hart's heirs, since that would distract him from Ichiro Katou's murder. And, more to the point, Daisy's alibi, or lack thereof.

Tucker had promised not to volunteer the fact that Daisy—contrary to what AnnaLise had assured Chuck—hadn't arrived at Torch until after midnight the evening Ichiro died.

Unless the police chief asked, of course, and the fact he was busy with Hart—a higher profile, if still-breathing victim—might give AnnaLise the time she needed to dig up an alternative suspect in Ichiro's death.

Tucker, to her surprise, also had been happy to affirmatively help her. 'Hey, Daisy's my bud and, besides, I'm psyched to work with an investigative reporter.'

Ahh, youth. They'd made an appointment to meet outside Ichiro's apartment at ten the next morning, the young man with a key to same.

Not wanting to encourage questions from her eager apprentice that she couldn't answer—for example, what AnnaLise hoped to find in Ichiro's rooms—she avoided Torch's entrance, instead crossing Second Street diagonally to get to Daisy's front door.

Her mother's car wasn't parked anywhere in sight—unusual, considering the hour. AnnaLise had her house key in its lock when she noticed a muted glow coming from the garage. Daisy must have put her car away for the night and forgotten to turn off the now-faithful light.

AnnaLise returned her key to a pocket and moved toward the garage. No wonder the lamp's always out. 'Batteries don't last forever, Daisy.'

However, as AnnaLise reached down to grasp the door handle, the light went off.

'*Y voila*. What did I say?' AnnaLise yanked the handle with the angry strength of the consistently confirmed. The door slid up, but the light from the street lamp above revealed no sign of Daisy's cream-colored Chrysler.

Stepping in, AnnaLise reached for the light, finding and then pushing it.

And 'on' the little dome came.

AnnaLise pulled her hand away like the thing was scorching hot and took a convulsive step backwards, instinctively wanting to be out of this particular cave.

The groan of ancient wood caused her to look up, just in time to see the overhead door come crashing down. The clatter of something metallic on the concrete was the last thing she registered.

SEVENTEEN

'OUCH!'

AnnaLise opened her eyes. 'Ouch?' she asked, looking up at Dr Jackson Stanton.

'Sorry.' The doctor was gingerly lowering himself to the sidewalk, presumably to examine her. 'My knees have hurt ever since I ran the Piedmont marathon.'

Amazing how people who've accomplished admittedly impressive things like a marathon manage to drop the fact into casual conversation. Even at the most unlikely moments.

Say, for example, after you've been pounded like a carpet tack into concrete by your mother's rogue garage door.

'Are you OK, AnnaLise?' Daisy asked.

'Does she *look* OK?' Mrs Peebly asked. 'A garage door just fell on her head.'

'I think it got me…more in the shoulder.' AnnaLise struggled to sit up.

As the doctor helped her, Mrs Peebly peered down at AnnaLise, a hairy but bleached chin resting on the frame of her aluminum walker. The woman was amazing flexible for a ninety-something. Hell, she was lithe for a twenty-something.

Especially one who had run into a door. Or vice versa.

'See, Daisy?' Mrs Peebly was now shaking a finger. 'I told you these doors should be kept locked.'

'For the last time,' Mother Griggs said, 'you can't jam both doors shut from the inside and still get out yourself.'

AnnaLise decided that particular horse had been beaten to death. With umbrellas.

'I am buying you new doors,' she said, slowly but firmly, as the doctor examined her shoulder, 'with real locks, lights and a modern opener.'

Mrs Peebly winced. 'These old wooden ones weigh a ton.'

'Forgive me,' Dr Stanton said, 'but more like a hundred, hundred-fifty pounds.'

'I was speaking figuratively,' Mrs Peebly replied. 'And, besides, nobody likes know-it-alls.' She shot a look at AnnaLise.

AnnaLise ignored it and glanced around. The street was still dark and, with the exception of herself, the two older women and the doctor, it seemed deserted.

'How'd you all get here?' she asked. AnnaLise didn't think she'd lost consciousness, but the blow certainly had left her disoriented, struggling to focus.

'It was me who found you,' Mrs Peebly said proudly. 'I was just turning off my television set after *Hondo*.'

'From the novel by Louis L'Amour,' AnnaLise said. She might be disoriented, but she was still a writer.

'And starring John Wayne and Geraldine Page,' Dr Stanton said. 'Not to mention Ward Bond, pre-*Wagon Train*. Great movie.'

Apparently Tucker's 'classic-television' apple didn't fall far from his father's 'classic-movie' tree.

Mrs Peebly looked pleased. Daisy, on the other hand, said, 'Don't encourage her,' but AnnaLise wasn't sure if that was directed at daughter or neighbor.

Stay on the beam, even if it's wavering a little. 'So you turned off your TV,' AnnaLise reminded Mrs Peebly, 'and...'

'And,' the elderly woman took up, 'I heard a clang, like

somebody'd dropped something, and then a bang. I knew right away it was the garage door again, but this time it sounded different. Like it was muffled. Or maybe padded.'

'By me and my shoulder, as it turns out,' AnnaLise said. 'One more step, and I would have been clear before the door came slamming down.'

'Maybe you should work out more,' Mrs Peebly said. 'That explosive, out-of-the-blocks reaction doesn't come as naturally to some people as it does to me.'

Daisy ignored her. 'She called, probably wanting to scold me...'

'It was late, Daisy,' Mrs Peebly protested. 'You oughta know better than to make that kind of noise.'

'The late hour doesn't stop you from blasting those movies of yours,' Daisy said. 'Besides, it wasn't me. It was AnnaLise, remember?'

'Oh. Right.'

'Your car's not in the garage,' AnnaLise said to Daisy. 'Where is it?'

'On the street.'

'Where?' The doctor's car blocked the driveway apron, but there was no sign of Daisy's vehicle.

'Around the corner,' said AnnaLise's mother.

'In the angle parking on Main Street?' Daughter tried to get her head around that. 'But you hate backing out into traffic.'

'Honestly, AnnaLise.' Daisy glanced at Dr Stanton, embarrassed. 'You make me sound like I'm ninety. Oh, no offense, Mrs Peebly.'

'Some taken.'

Daisy shrugged. 'Anyway, AnnaLise, you're being silly. Next thing you'll be saying is I don't like to make left turns.'

'You don't.'

'Neither do I,' Dr Stanton said. 'You're taking your life in your hands even trying that during tourist season.'

'And when is it *not* tourist season?' Daisy said, spreading her hands. The two laughed.

AnnaLise's mother and Dr Stanton? Could it be?

'Stop making moon eyes over there,' Mrs Peebly groused. 'Like I said, when I heard you drop the door, AnnaLise, I called your mother.'

'I was asleep,' Daisy said, 'but the telephone woke me up. When I realized you weren't home—'

'We both hightailed it down here to the garage,' Mrs Peebly said triumphantly, 'and there you were, laid out like a deer carcass on this very ground.'

'So they called me,' Dr Stanton said, getting to his feet with a grin, but also another 'Ouch'.

'I know, I know,' AnnaLise said. 'Running injury. Marathon.' Dr Stanton's grin grew wider. 'Give me your right hand and I'll help you up.'

She did and he eased her to a standing position, her left arm lagging a bit behind the exercise.

'Sore, but no sharp pain,' AnnaLise said, rubbing at the joint gingerly. 'The shoulder doesn't feel dislocated.'

'It's not,' Dr Stanton confirmed. 'But I'm pretty sure you do have a slight separation. I want you to ice it for fifteen minutes each hour for the next four. Then stop by the office tomorrow and we'll do a quick X-ray to make sure you haven't cracked anything. I think you'll be fine, though.'

'Does she need a sling?' Mrs Peebles asked. 'I have just the thing. The sheet from Larry's crib.'

'Larry's nearly seventy,' Daisy pointed out, 'and you still have his *crib*?'

'Never know,' Mrs Peebly said, lifting up her walker

to get it past a rough spot. 'He likes 'em young. I could be a grandmother yet.'

It was as though AnnaLise had fallen asleep during the cougar discussion at the inn earlier and awakened to the same one, but with a very different set of characters. *Through the Looking Glass* kind of different, where the seventy-year-old Larry was a cradle-robber and Daisy, a cougar. Kind of.

'I don't think a sling will be necessary,' Stanton, the younger 'stud', said as he opened his car door. 'But if letting the arm hang at your side hurts...'

'I'll elevate it,' AnnaLise said quickly. Her own childhood sheets having been emblazoned with Smurfs, she couldn't imagine what baby sheets, circa 1930, sported. Coats of arms? Mastodons and sabre-toothed tigers?

Given the circumstances, though, no need to find out. Daisy was bound to have a spare pillowcase.

'I DON'T UNDERSTAND,' AnnaLise said. 'Why can't we get this to work?' Her left shoulder was starting to ache as she held up the elbow for Daisy to tie a knot at the neck.

'I told you, the pillowcase isn't big enough. You should have taken Baby Larry's crib sheet.'

AnnaLise shuddered, causing Daisy to once again lose her grip. 'I think not. Besides, this has to work. I always used pillowcases as slings back when I was pretending to have a broken arm.'

'And sitting on the stool next to the cash register at Mama's, trolling for sympathy.'

'And candy. Don't forget the candy,' AnnaLise mumbled over the cloth corner she was trying to hold in her teeth.

'You were six,' Daisy said. 'The pillowcases didn't get smaller, you just got bigger.'

There was that.

AnnaLise let the pillow case drop. 'OK. This option is kaput.'

Daisy picked up the pillow they'd stripped the case from. 'Why don't you rest your elbow on this. At least it'll cushion the weight from your shoulder.'

Daisy put the pillow on the arm of AnnaLise's chair and gently placed her daughter's elbow on it. Then she dragged over the ottoman for AnnaLise's feet.

'Thank you, Mommy,' AnnaLise said. It was nearly three a.m.

'Your whole childhood, you never called me mommy, except when you were hurt.' Daisy was sitting on the couch across from her. 'Or trying to get away with something.'

'Untrue,' AnnaLise said, letting her eyes drift closed.

'So,' she heard Daisy say, 'when we lifted the garage door off you, your car wasn't inside.'

AnnaLise kept her eyes closed. 'Left it at the inn,' she mumbled. 'I was…drinking.'

'So…?'

'Hmm?'

'Then why were you going into the garage, at all?'

AnnaLise's eyes sprang open.

Two hours later, they'd given up on sleep.

'Should I make some coffee?' Daisy asked.

'Please.' AnnaLise took the plastic bag of partially melted ice cubes off her shoulder. 'Can you take this, too?'

'I'll put it in the freezer,' Daisy said. 'You have to use it again in forty-five minutes, anyway.'

'Then drape it over a loaf of bread, so it'll be formed more to my shoulder than the freezer shelf.' AnnaLise didn't suggest swapping out the cubes for new ones because Daisy's old refrigerator didn't have an icemaker. Her freezer, like everything else in Sutherton, worked at its own pace.

'Gotcha.' Daisy let the freezer compartment door slap shut before removing a bag of ground coffee from the refrigerator and closing that, as well.

'You really shouldn't store ground coffee in the fridge,' AnnaLise said.

'OK,' said Daisy, measuring out the grounds and then returning the bag to the refrigerator anyway. She flipped on the ancient Mr Coffee machine and came back to sit down. 'Are you going to tell Chuck?'

'That you ignore me or that you keep ground coffee in the refrigerator?'

'AnnaLise Marie Griggs, you know perfectly well I'm talking about the attack on you.'

Hearing the words laid out there like that made AnnaLise uneasy. 'I didn't imagine anything, right? The light couldn't have gone out on its own?'

'And then slammed the garage door down on you?' Daisy asked. 'I think you give that light way too much credit. After all, I bought the thing from the dollar store.'

'Which is just my point. Maybe the battery died. Or there was a loose connection or something.'

'And when you tried again, it worked? Anything's possible, of course, but did you push the light once or twice?'

'Once, I think. Why?'

'Well, if the thing went out on its own, wouldn't you have had to push *twice*? Once to turn it off and once again for on?'

AnnaLise, even dog-tired, had to admire her mother's reasoning. 'I guess so, but I honestly don't know what's inside the gadget. I just know that when you push, the light should go on. Or off.'

'And when you raise the garage door, it should stay up, too.'

'Unless you don't push all the way up. Then the wooden bastard can come slamming down.'

'Please, AnnaLise, no profanity. But, as you said two hours ago,' Daisy continued, suddenly sounding weary, 'that should have happened right away. Not after you stepped in and turned on the light.'

'But that's just the point, the light went on. If somebody was inside, why didn't I see them?'

'AnnaLise, this is your story, not mine.'

'It's not a story,' she said stubbornly. AnnaLise tried to cross her arms, but that hurt enough that she settled for just jutting out her bottom lip. 'Everything I told you—and Mrs Peebly and the doc—actually happened.'

'*I* believe you,' Daisy said. 'Though I'm not sure… you do.'

AnnaLise settled back miserably in her chair. 'I just don't want to start an uproar and then have it turn out I was wrong, especially stupid wrong. How in the world do people take the witness stand and testify under oath to something that happened in the past? I can barely remember what I did an hour ago.'

'Wait 'til you're my age,' Daisy said.

Mother and daughter looked at each other, hanging in the air between them the thought that whatever was happening to the older woman could also befall the younger.

AnnaLise struggled to say something—anything—to lighten the mood.

Daisy held up her hand. 'This isn't hereditary, Anna-Lise. My grandmother was "sharp as a tack", as my mother used to say. And she was the same. It's…it's just…me.'

For the second time since AnnaLise's arrival, Daisy looked like she was going to cry. In this case, though, the speaker wasn't a young Lorraine drifting up from the past. This was AnnaLise's mother, Daisy. Present tense, but also present and understandably tense.

'It's going to be all right, Daisy,' AnnaLise said, climbing out of her chair in a seven-count movement to sit on the arm of the other's chair. 'I swear.'

'I won't have you cussing, young lady.' Daisy blinked back her tears with an embarrassed smile. 'I'm sure things will work themselves out.'

AnnaLise leaned over to give her mother a one-armed hug. 'I know.'

'Only...'

AnnaLise pulled back to look at her mother. 'Yes?'

Daisy's eyes were closed, her head bowed. 'Only...I don't want to forget.'

'Of course, you don't.' AnnaLise squeezed her hand.

'There are people who want nothing *but* to forget. People who have had such pain in their lives, that remembering is unbearable. But for me...even the day your father died, I treasure.'

'The day Daddy...?'

'Do you know why?' The blue eyes opened.

AnnaLise's own eyes were welling, primed by the Labor Day waterworks. That was the problem with tears. You let them out once and...

She shook her head. 'Why?'

'Because you, practically still a baby, stood in the center of that waiting room, your little fists clenched, and said just what you said today.'

'What did I say?'

'You said, "It's going to be all right, Daisy".' AnnaLise's mother cocked her head and smiled. 'And you know what?'

'What?' The tears were rolling down AnnaLise's cheeks.

It wasn't the way she recalled that awful day, but Daisy's memories, however fragile or suspect, were what mattered now.

'You were right.' Daisy picked up the discarded pillow case and dabbed AnnaLise's tears. 'Just five years old and damned if you weren't right.'

AnnaLise Marie Griggs laughed—just a different form of release—and caught her mother's hand. 'Hey, no cussing!'

EIGHTEEN

Mama's opened at 6:30 a.m., so AnnaLise and Daisy stepped onto their sidewalk at 6:29. A minute to lock the door and round the corner and they'd arrive just as Mama unlocked hers. Assuming she was on time. Mama could be…well, 'capricious' might be putting it mildly.

'Wait,' AnnaLise said. 'Let's check the garage.'

'We'll be late,' Daisy protested. 'And Wednesday is Coffee Time.'

'Every morning is coffee time as far as I'm concerned,' AnnaLise said, turning right toward the garage instead of left toward Main Street. 'I want to see if that light really is working.'

'And if the door stays up, too?'

'Exactly.'

AnnaLise gave the door a tug with her good arm and the thing rolled to the roof perfectly. And stayed there, too. 'Huh.'

'Try the light,' Daisy urged. 'That cake goes fast. Sometimes people even buy a whole one, which I think is a lot of nerve. They should order ahead.'

'Cake?' AnnaLise said. 'What cake?'

An exasperated look. 'Coffee Time, of course. I told you.' A refocusing. 'Now, try the damn light.'

'Patience, Mother Griggs. That must be some cake, if it induces cussing.' But AnnaLise pushed the light. On.

And the thing stayed on. She pulled the plastic dome off the nail and shook it. 'Not even a flicker.'

Daisy nodded. 'I was right. You were viciously attacked. Now let's get some cake before the thundering herd eats it all.'

'You are a very odd woman,' AnnaLise said, replacing the light and turning it off before lowering the door. 'Has anyone ever mentioned that to you?'

'Daily, though mostly you, when you lived at home here.' Daisy was leading the way around the corner and down the block to Mama's. 'See? I told you. Look at all the cars.'

AnnaLise looked. An old Chevy Suburban and an SUV towing a trailered waverunner. The SUV had angled in and then nosed back out, so the whole thing took up three parking spaces and resembled a vehicular boomerang.

'Two. I think your cake is safe.'

'Three,' Daisy said pointing.

'That one's yours.'

'Oh. Well, hurry anyway. Phyllis is turning over the sign.'

AnnaLise checked her watch. Six thirty-seven and, better late than never, Mama was indeed flipping 'Closed' to 'Open'.

A man of about forty hopped out of the SUV and pulled at her door impatiently. When it didn't open, he pounded on the plate glass with the side of his fist and gestured for Mama to turn the deadbolt.

With a sweeping motion of her right hand, she indicated the man should step back. He did. One step.

Another sweep. And another step.

Framed in the door, Mama put her hands on her hips and cocked her head toward his improperly parked vehicle, which would earn Mr Impatience at least one ticket if Mama decided to call the police.

He took two more paces back.

Skirting the man, Daisy put her hand on the door handle. Mama snapped the lock so the door would open. AnnaLise caught it with her uninjured arm as Daisy entered.

'I wouldn't pound on the glass again if I were you,' she told the man. 'Mama really doesn't like it.' She threw a look over her shoulder at the trailer arrangement. 'Or personal watercraft.'

He bristled. 'Well, then, your Mama can just kiss my—'

The scent of fresh-baked coffee cake wafted through the open door.

Ahh, yes. Coffee Time. The aroma of cinnamon, bananas, cream cheese and vanilla evoked the memory the cake's name hadn't. And a very tasty memory, it was.

The illegal parker got one sniff and made a verbal U-turn. 'Cook. Mama should kiss the cook.' He followed AnnaLise and sucked in a lungful. 'What is that?'

'Coffee cake.'

'And don't even think about ordering a whole one,' Daisy interjected. Then to Mama: 'AnnaLise hurt herself, so four pieces, please, Phyllis. We'll eat two here.'

Hoping that meant one apiece, AnnaLise took a booth.

'What happened to you?' Mama asked, lovingly laying a piece of cake in front of her while steadfastly ignoring Mr Impatience.

The poor sucker, properly chastised, stood quietly at the cash register.

'She was attacked in my garage,' Daisy said, sliding onto the bench across from AnnaLise.

The head of the guy at the register jerked around and Mama gave him a mind-your-own-business look. He did.

The interplay reminded AnnaLise of James Duende, Sheree's 'boarder'. Who really was the man living over the dining room? The first time AnnaLise had laid eyes on him had been here at Mama's and now, according to Sheree, Jim was gone.

Could his disappearance have anything to do with the recent attacks? And if so, was he perpetrator or…another victim?

'Some lunatic sent the door slamming down on AnnaLise's head,' Daisy was saying. 'She barely escaped.'

'Good thing our girl is quick,' Mama said, sitting down next to her lifelong friend. 'Bet the fellow wasn't counting on that.'

'I don't know if it was a fellow,' AnnaLise said, forking a piece of cake into her mouth. Still warm and topped with cinnamon and sugar pecans. Heaven. 'I didn't see him. Or her.'

'You didn't?' Phyllis asked. 'Pretty small garage.'

'That seemed strange to me, too,' Daisy said to Mama. 'Do you think she might have amnesia?'

'Amnesia of the *shoulder*?' AnnaLise raised her elbow and was rewarded by a twinge from the higher joint. After meeting Tucker at ten, she had to remember to run by his father's office for that X-ray.

'We don't know,' Daisy said. 'Maybe you hit your head when you fell.'

Phyllis added, 'Or the trauma just scared the memory out of you.'

'Important thing is you'll recover,' Daisy said.

'And finger the guy,' from Phyllis.

Daisy and Mama were starting to sound like an old married couple, finishing each other's thoughts in spoken sentences.

AnnaLise had a thought or two of her own: 'I wondered, too, why I didn't see whoever,'—*whomever*?— 'was in the garage. But he or she must have been in the corner, up against the wall.'

'And pulled the door down with the rope,' Daisy said, hand over mouth.

'Whyever *did* you put that rope there?' Phyllis demanded.

'Because I'm too short to reach otherwise,' Daisy said. 'I pull to get it going and step out of the garage before the door comes roaring down.'

'Just like it did on AnnieLeez.'

'Exactly.'

The two mother figures nodded at each other solemnly.

The chime on the door sounded and the three women turned to see Kathleen Smoaks enter, looking like she hadn't slept. Which put her in the same category as AnnaLise herself and her mother. Daughter swiped at a crusted mustard stain on the leg of the navy sweats she'd pulled on when Daisy had dangled the idea of breakfast at Mama's.

'Kathleen, you poor thing,' Phyllis said, getting up. 'What can I get you?'

The guy at the cash register raised his hand. 'A coffee, to go?'

'Do you mind?' Mama demanded. 'This woman's husband was buried yesterday.'

He shut his mouth, turned on his heel, and just exited. Daisy rolled her eyes. 'Cretin.'

Kathleen laughed. 'You both are too much. AnnaLise, you're lucky to have such joyful people in your life.'

Joyful was one thing. Totally whacked was another. Still, AnnaLise had to agree with the overall sentiment. She *was* lucky. 'Join us, Kathleen?'

'Well, maybe for just a moment,' she said, taking Mama's vacated spot next to Daisy. 'I'd planned to pick something up and take it on to the office, but…'

Kathleen worked at Sutherton Real Estate, which handled lakeside properties. She headed the rental division.

'That realty can't spare you for a while?' Mama asked, approaching the table with a coffee pot. 'They should be ashamed of themselves.'

Kathleen turned over the heavy white mug in front of her, so Mama could pour. 'Oh, you can't blame *them*. It's me. I need to be around…people.'

Daisy touched her hand. 'How are you sleeping, dear? You look awful.'

Just what every woman wants to hear, but the observation was right on the mark.

'Pretty well, honestly. Until last night.' She gave Daisy's hand a squeeze and then picked up her coffee. 'I know y'all are aware that Rance was not an easy person.'

'Rance Smoaks was an asshole.'

AnnaLise looked at her mother.

Daisy shrugged. 'Well, he was.'

Phyllis cocked her head. 'She's right, you know.'

Of course, Daisy was right, both about Kathleen looking awful and Rance being an asshole. Everybody *knew* Daisy was right.

But was Daisy…'right'? Such candor wasn't her usual way.

Kathleen didn't seem bothered. She pointed at AnnaLise, who was massaging her shoulder. 'What's wrong? Sleep funny?'

'A garage door fell—' AnnaLise started.

'She was attacked,' Daisy said. It seemed to be her new favorite word. 'Right there on my property.'

'Oh, dear,' Kathleen said, visibly upset. 'Whatever is going on here in Sutherton?'

Kathleen had always struck AnnaLise as someone who had her head screwed on right. Except for a blind spot, and it was a monumental one: Rance Smoaks.

May he rest. In pieces.

'It is odd, isn't it? All of these—' AnnaLise made finger quotes— '"accidents", I mean.'

Kathleen, if anything, looked more upset. Almost like she was going to cry.

AnnaLise hastened to clarify. 'Though Rance's death, of course, was truly an accident.'

The other woman burst into tears.

'What in the world did you say to her?' Mama asked, scurrying over with a big square of cake, her answer to any unhappy situation. She eased the plate in front of Kathleen and Daisy placed a fork in the widow's hand.

'Eat,' they implored in unison.

Kathleen looked at AnnaLise.

'They're not going to quit until you do, and besides, the cake is great.'

Kathleen sniffled. 'Is it, is it…Coffee Time?' she managed.

'Yes, ma'am,' from Daisy and Mama.

Kathleen dug into the sinfully moist cake topped with cinnamon. And she didn't sit back until the square was gone. 'Thanks, that helped. Really.'

'Always does,' said Phyllis, sweeping the empty plate away with a long-suffering attitude that screamed, 'Why would anyone doubt me?'

'I'm sorry,' AnnaLise said to Kathleen. 'I didn't mean to imply that there was anything suspicious about Rance's death.' She leaned forward. 'In fact, it's the one "purely" accidental death in these last few days.'

'If you don't count Daisy de-blooding Ema Bradenham,' Mama said from behind the cash register.

'But that didn't result in a death,' Daisy protested.

'Neither did Dickens Hart's getting himself shot, Daisy, but…'

AnnaLise tapped Kathleen on the arm and they leaned

forward across the table so they could hear each other over—or in this case, under—the older women's discussion.

'Anyway,' AnnaLise said. 'I'm sorry.'

'Don't be,' Kathleen said, an unexpected touch of venom entering her voice. 'Turns out, you're right.'

'Right?' AnnaLise whispered.

'It wasn't an'—matching exaggerated finger quotes—'"accident".'

AnnaLise sat back as though she'd been slapped across her face. 'You're kidding.'

'Believe me,' Kathleen said, following suit, 'I didn't stay up all night enjoying the joke.'

'What joke?' Daisy asked.

'Somebody has a joke?' from Phyllis. 'I heard a good one the other day. Now just let me think on it.' She tapped a finger to her temple.

AnnaLise had learned from experience that it didn't pay to keep things from her two mothers. 'Kathleen was just…'

She looked toward the young widow and Kathleen took it from there. 'The chief came by last night to tell me that Rance's shooting…wasn't an accident.'

'Joe Palooka did in Rance on purpose?' Daisy gasped.

'No,' Kathleen said. 'That's just the point. The police lab says the bullet that killed Rance came from a deer rifle. Joe and Rance were both just plinking bottles with pistols.'

'A poacher, then?' AnnaLise asked. 'According to Chuck, Dickens Hart was shot by a deer rifle, too.'

'Not just "a" deer rifle,' Kathleen Smoaks said, eyes now clear and a little hard. 'The *same* deer rifle.'

NINETEEN

'THE BULLETISTICS CAME BACK?' Phyllis Balisteri was a faithful fan of *CSI* shows, if not a reliable learner from them.

'Ballistics,' AnnaLise corrected.

'I don't know the specifics,' Kathleen said. 'All I was told is that Rance and Dickens Hart were shot with the same gun.'

Now AnnaLise understood Kathleen's sleeplessness. The widow—the newly enriched widow—would naturally become the prime suspect in her scumball husband's killing. But given the ballistics convergence between the two shootings, would she also be implicated as Hart's assailant? Or, again given the convergence, exonerated of both?

'It doesn't make sense,' AnnaLise said. 'What possible connection could there be between Rance Smoaks and Dickens Hart?'

'Hold on,' Daisy said, 'that sounds—'

'No, she's right,' Kathleen said. 'Rance was a mean, out-of-work drunk and Hart is a rich, successful—'

'Egomaniac,' AnnaLise supplied. 'Maybe that's what they had in common.'

'Big heads?' Mama looked at Daisy and they both giggled.

If synchronized eye-rolling were an Olympic event, the two younger women would have received medals.

'Their *egos*.' Kathleen glanced up at the clock. Swinging her legs out of the booth, she dug a five-dollar bill from her bag. 'Thanks for the cake and conversation.'

'Feel better?' Mama said, taking the five to the cash register.

'Not so much, but also not your fault.' Kathleen Smoaks went out the door.

'Nice girl, but a pretty undeveloped sense of humor,' Daisy said as she and AnnaLise got up to leave as well.

Then Mother Griggs looked around. 'Phyllis? Did you cut us two more pieces of Coffee Time?'

'Of course not. What if there's somebody wanting to buy them in the meantime?'

'You'd sell our cake right out from under us?' Daisy protested.

'You'd ask me to turn away a paying customer?'

'I'm a customer, too,' Daisy pointed out.

'But not paying.'

'Only because you won't let us,' AnnaLise said. 'We'd be happy to…'

As if on cue, the door chimed and Mrs Bradenham swept in. '*Please* tell me you still have a cake.'

'A whole one?' Mama said, taking aluminum foil off a pan big enough to hold the aforementioned entire cake— but now, of course, minus three large squares. 'How many times have I told you, Eee-mah? For a whole cake, you got to call ahead of time. Otherwise it's not fair to my other—'

'I apologize, Phyllis, but I am entertaining a few people for tea this afternoon, and I simply *must* have one of your cakes.' Mrs B was stripping a bill out of her wallet as she spoke.

'Sorry, Ema,' Daisy said, approaching the counter, 'but I'm afraid that cake's already been spoken for.'

Stand-off at the 'I'm OK, You're *Not*' Corral.

'How about a compromise?' AnnaLise, as Intervening

Adult, suggested. 'Daisy will purchase—' with a look to-ward Mama— 'one piece and Mrs B can buy the rest.'

'Which reminds me,' Mrs B said. 'I dearly hope Lor-raine can come to my little party.'

She turned to Daisy. 'Tell me you will, please? It has been far too long, and I promise plenty of goodies.'

'Goodies?' Daisy said it like *Sesame Street*'s Cookie Monster says, 'Cookies'. The only thing missing was furry blue paws clapping together.

AnnaLise knew all was lost, cakewise. The only thing she could hope for was leftovers from the 'tea'. Unless Mrs B...

'And I am so sorry I cannot include you, Little One,' Bobby's mother said to AnnaLise, 'but it will be just we old gals.' Tee-hee.

Us old gals. Tee-hee that.

Mrs B turned to Mama. 'I know you need to be here, Phyllis, tending to your business. I so admire that quality in you. Now, if you will just wrap up my cake?'

She slapped a one-hundred-dollar bill on the glass-topped counter.

As the door closed behind Mrs B, Mama held the bill up to the light, flexing and straightening it like a flag in the wind. 'Give my regards to the "old gals" this after-noon, Daisy. Me and Ben Franklin here, we'll be having a little party of our own.'

It was barely eight a.m. on the kitchen wall clock when Daisy and her mother returned home.

'I don't have to meet Tucker until ten,' AnnaLise said, 'so I think I'll start going through Hart's journals. Maybe I can find something that'll shed some light on who might have wanted to kill him.'

'Or still wants to see him dead. I have to say I don't pic-

ture Kathleen killing anyone, even her lowlife husband.'
Daisy set her handbag on the kitchen table.

AnnaLise looked at it. 'They say you shouldn't put
purses on tables. The leather picks up all sorts of bacteria.
You know, from public restrooms and restaurants, where
you set them on the floor.'

'I'd like to be there when you suggest to Phyllis that her
floor is dirty,' Daisy said, leaving the purse where it was.

'One fray I think I'll avoid, thank you very much.'

'Good decision,' Daisy said, dumping out the coffee
she'd made hours ago. 'Speaking of staying out of things,
please don't get involved in whatever is going on here. Just
let the police handle it.'

'I'm sure Chuck is very capable,' AnnaLise said, 'but
you know me. Poking around is what I do for a living.'

'Well, then, when exactly are you going to go back and
do it?' Daisy was looking firm, unusually so for her. She
set down the rinsed pot. 'I thought this was supposed to
be only a weekend visit.'

Honesty is universally touted as the best policy, though
in AnnaLise's experience that always hadn't been the case.
'I asked my newspaper for a temporary leave of absence.'

'Because of me?' Daisy's arms were defiantly crossed
in front of her breasts.

'Originally.' AnnaLise shrugged her good shoulder.
'Now maybe I'm eligible for temporary disability.'

'You're lucky it's not permanent. You could have been
badly hurt. I think you should go back to Wisconsin and
your life there.'

'While I still have it? Is that what you mean?'

'You have to admit, everything was fine until you rode
back into Sutherton.'

Ouch. Though AnnaLise's mother—while patently unfair—was right, if you discounted her starring role in Mrs B's near exsanguination.

'So what are you saying, Daisy? That I'm the cause of Rance Smoaks and Dickens Hart being shot? Then what about Ichiro Katou? I didn't even know the man until four days ago.'

'Yet the cane that hit him was found in our garage.'

'In *your* garage, and by *me*.'

'Yes, by you. And don't tell me you didn't suspect that I put it there.'

Daisy had her on that one. 'Maybe at first. You have been suffering…spells, you know.'

'I'm forgetful, not homicidal.' Daisy picked up a dish towel, looked at it and then threw it back toward the counter. The towel hit the edge and slipped to the floor. AnnaLise picked the thing up, waving it like a red-striped flag of surrender.

'Truce, please? I don't think you hurt anyone, Daisy. But you can't possibly believe I did, either.'

'I don't.'

'Then why are you so angry at me?'

'Because I want you to be safe. I want you to go home to Wisconsin and mind your own business.'

'Sutherton *is* my home, Daisy. And back in Wisconsin, I'd still be a police-beat reporter and therefore not minding my own business. Besides,' AnnaLise was relenting a little, 'I'm not going anywhere until I know that everything's OK here. That this mess is all figured out.'

AnnaLise swung away toward the stairs, wondering why she was espousing exactly the opposite of what she'd told Bobby just two days earlier. Now angrily declaring Sutherton home and swearing her allegiance—not just to Daisy, but to the whole damned town and all its current, major problems?

The Prodigal Daughter, halfway up the steps, needed to have her head examined.

'Well, then, let's do it.' Daisy's words stopped AnnaLise, not so much for what she said, but for the tone in which she said it. Calm. Measured. Almost…resolved.

AnnaLise turned. 'Do what?'

'Let's sort this all out, so you can go back north where you belong.'

'How can we do that? You know something I haven't been told?'

'Lots.' Daisy shrugged. 'Mostly not very interesting or important. But you know the right questions to ask and I'm thinking maybe if we put our heads together, some sense can be made of these goings on.'

This was a Daisy that AnnaLise wasn't accustomed to. Her mother tended toward follower—of Mama, even of AnnaLise—not leader. But maybe she was turning over a new leaf. Or just really, in her heart of hearts, wanted AnnaLise long gone and hard to find.

Daughter took one step down to sit on the landing next to the gun cabinet. She looked at her mother through the spindles of the railing. '*Oookay*. So where do we start?'

'Well, like people said—' Daisy was now leaning against the cupboard— 'I don't see Kathleen killing Rance. With Joe Palooka right there, she'd have to shoot her husband in cold blood and then fool Joe into thinking he'd done it himself.'

'Not so high a bar, given how much both men had drunk, but I agree. Besides, why wouldn't Kathleen have put Rance out of her misery years ago?'

'The inheritance, maybe?' Daisy said. 'Remember that Nanney Estill died just a month ago. With Rance gone, Kathleen wouldn't have to worry about him drinking their money away. She could start over—maybe even with Bobby Bradenham.'

AnnaLise shifted uncomfortably. 'You think he still has a thing for her? And vice versa?'

'What I think is that each human believes there's a soulmate awaiting them somewhere in the world. Bobby's fixated on Kathleen as his. That's why he never married anybody else.'

And just maybe some influence from his mother, as well.

'Like Daddy was your soulmate.' AnnaLise said it off-handedly, the way you ask someone how they are and just expect them to say 'fine'.

She wasn't prepared for Daisy to look up at her in surprise, then turn away. 'Timothy Griggs was a very good man.'

'But you *did* love him?' The question was out of AnnaLise's mouth reflexively, like she was back on the beat in Wisconsin, putting questions to strangers. Now, though, the reporter was intruding on her own mother, a completely different emotional vector.

Truth to tell, AnnaLise had been so young when her father died that she could barely recall life before the hospitals and the waiting rooms. And what she did 'remember' was probably highly subject to nostalgic embroidery.

Being hoisted onto her father's shoulders to place the star atop the Christmas tree. Did AnnaLise actually remember the moment or had she concocted an internal video to expand the photo in the family album?

Tim Griggs crooning a song to Daisy in the middle of Sal's Taproom. Fact, or a scene from some movie, with her father and mother substituted for the actors performing the leading roles?

'Yes, I loved Tim,' Daisy said, meeting AnnaLise's eyes. 'It just seems like such a long time ago.'

'I know.' Silly, but AnnaLise's world was righted. Her personal love life could be as ambivalent as…well, it currently was, but she wanted an ironclad fairy tale for her parents, living or dead. To know that Joanie really *did* love Chachi.

AnnaLise smiled.

'What?' Daisy asked.

'Just thinking about an old TV show,' AnnaLise said. 'Hey, did you ever tell me about any uncles?'

Daisy looked heavenward. 'No. You have no Uncle Jesse or Auntie Em, or Cousin It, either. You just spent way too much time in front of the television, adopting imaginary family as your own.'

'Well, I certainly didn't have any *real* relatives to play with.'

They both laughed.

'Nope, but you did have real friends. At first, only Bobby Bradenham. Then, when you got a little older, Sheree and Chuck. You were—and remain—very lucky in your friendships.'

AnnaLise couldn't dispute that. 'Speaking of Bobby, I'm worried about him. If he *is* in love with Kathleen, as you believe, that gives him a motive for killing Rance Smoaks.'

'Using the same gun that wounded Dickens Hart?'

'Well, that's just the problem. Or one of them, at least,' AnnaLise said, warming to her subject. 'If Bobby turns out to be Hart's potential heir, it'll look to the police like Bobby had a pretty good reason to kill Hart, too.'

'Another inheritance? That would mean you have a mighty greedy friend.'

Daisy was right: Bobby gets the money and the girl. And the girl's money to boot.

AnnaLise decided to change tacks. 'Let's look at this from the police point of view.'

'And by that, you mean Chuck's?'

'Yeah. Weird having both the chief of police and the primary suspect as friends.'

'Probably even worse for them,' Daisy said.

There was that. 'You know what I don't understand? I've known Bobby for more than twenty years and always thought his father was killed in a car accident. Now, all of a sudden, people are talking about his being "a little Dickens", as Mama so delicately put it.'

'You can't rely on everything Phyllis says.'

'But I heard it from Sheree, as well. And who knows what Bobby has picked up on.' A thought struck. 'Maybe that's why he was interested in doing a DNA test like Ichiro Katou did.'

A slight cloud across Daisy's face. 'Didn't you tell me that paternity testing is different from this grand, "world-wide" kind?'

'True,' AnnaLise admitted. 'To prove paternity you'd have to have samples from both people.'

'Samples?'

AnnaLise slipped her right hand through the railing, using her thumbnail to click flaking paint off a spindle. 'Like the scrapings from inside your cheek.'

Daisy gazed up at her. 'Or the blood from a shooting?'

TWENTY

'DOESN'T THAT SORT of put the cart before the horse?'

'My point exactly,' said Daisy.

AnnaLise had come down from her encampment on the staircase landing and was sitting at the kitchen table with her mother.

Which didn't mean she understood the woman. 'And what "point" is that?' AnnaLise asked.

'Look, Bobby wouldn't shoot his maybe father in order to get proof that he was his *real* father. Even if he was.'

Well, that certainly clarified things.

'Besides,' Daisy continued, 'in North Carolina, an illegitimate child can't claim any portion of a parent's estate unless the parent acknowledges that child prior to the parent's death.'

AnnaLise's jaw dropped. 'How in the world do you know these things?'

'You're not the only one who watches television, you know. I just prefer cable access and news. Educational programming that broadens the mind.'

Well, lah-dee-dah. 'But assuming Hart knows Bobby is—'

'*If* he is—'

'AnnaLise started over. 'Assuming Bobby is Hart's son, Dickens may already have a will naming Bobby as his heir. And, by now, Chuck should know about that.' AnnaLise glided her mother's purse away from her and picked up her own cellphone.

'You're just going to call the chief of police and ask him?' Daisy seemed stunned at her daughter's directness.

'Of course.' AnnaLise punched up Chuck Greystone's official number. 'You'd be surprised how much law enforcement will tell you. A lot of it's public information available on the department's daily blotter, anyway.'

Daisy began to say something, but AnnaLise cut her off. 'Ugh. Just his voicemail. I'll try him later.'

The cell beeped as she went to put it down. 'Battery's dying,' AnnaLise said, waving it off.

But Daisy wasn't paying any attention to the phone. 'You know, maybe we're bothering about the wrong thing.'

'What do you mean?' AnnaLise asked. 'You don't think Hart's will is important?'

'Maybe, maybe not. But isn't the real question what *Bobby* knows? Does he believe—or at least, suspect— Dickens Hart is his real father? Because, if not, none of the rest of this matters.'

Daisy was right. Maybe a confused mind throws a stronger beam of light into darker corners. AnnaLise picked up her cell again.

'I thought your phone was dead,' Daisy said. 'Besides, are you sure you want to talk with him about this over the telephone?'

'Good point.' AnnaLise plugged her phone into its charger and checked her watch. 'I have just enough time to get dressed and meet Tucker at Ichiro Katou's apartment.'

'What do you expect to find there?' Daisy asked as AnnaLise got up from the table.

'I'm not sure. Maybe some connection between Dickens Hart and Ichiro. Who knows,' she teased, 'maybe he's a "little Dickens", too.'

'You really do enjoy digging up all this dirt, don't you?'

Startled by her mother's tone, AnnaLise laughed, trying to recapture their earlier mood. 'C'mon, Daisy—you say that like it's a bad thing.'

But mother was standing—or sitting—her new ground. 'You just be careful, AnnaLise Marie Griggs,' she called from the table as her daughter mounted the stairs to change. 'Sometimes secrets are kept for good reason.'

DAISY'S WORDS WERE echoing in AnnaLise's head as she retrieved her car from the inn and drove toward Hart's Landing.

Her mother knew something—something that she wasn't prepared to share with AnnaLise. All of the doubts that had been set aside by Daisy's cogent conversation in the kitchen came rushing back. The Daisy who had discussed the shootings of Rance Smoaks and Dickens Hart was the old Daisy. Hell, *better* than the old Daisy.

AnnaLise's mother had ably laid out possible motives, including those for Bobby Bradenham and young Widow Smoaks. Then, when AnnaLise said she was meeting Tucker at Ichiro's apartment, Daisy'd done a 180—telling her it might be best to just leave things alone.

Almost like Bobby and Kathleen were a diversion, designed to keep AnnaLise off the trail of the real perpetrator. But why?

The obvious choice—Daisy as stone-killer—didn't merit thinking about. Still, as AnnaLise left the house, she'd paused on the landing to give the door of the cabinet that housed her father's old deer rifles a half-hearted tug.

Locked. But how much weight did that carry if Daisy still had the key in a drawer in her bedroom? Had she ever fired guns? Most locals had, almost a rite of passage in the High Country. Though, come to think of it, knowing how to swim would seem a requisite of lakeside life, and Daisy couldn't do that.

AnnaLise felt sick. Sick to be thinking such things about her own mother. Even sicker to be wishing the crimes on innocent friends, instead.

The more you looked at it, in fact, the sicker the whole scenario had become.

Daisy Griggs had no reason to shoot Rance Smoaks or Dickens Hart, AnnaLise told herself as she crossed the bridge to Hart's Landing and parked. And Ichiro Katou? How in the world did he fit in? Anywhere?

Tucker Stanton was waiting for AnnaLise at the door that had stymied her on the last visit. Not that it ended up mattering much. By that time, Katou was already dead.

'So, what are we looking for?' Tucker asked as he opened the lobby door and moved aside for her to enter.

'I'm not sure,' AnnaLise answered honestly. 'Maybe some sort of connection between Ichiro's death and the other events.'

'Events?' Tucker was unlocking one of the small mailboxes lined up on the facing wall. Very few label spaces had names on them.

'You know, the two shootings?' Could Tucker really be so dense? 'One fatal, one not?'

'Oh, yeah. Yeah, sorry.' The young man turned away, three white envelopes in his hand. 'I've been a little preoccupied with Torch.'

Apparently. 'What are those?' AnnaLise pointed at the mail.

'My dad asked me to check the mailbox.'

'Ichiro's? Anything interesting?'

Tucker started to hold out the letters, but then snatched them back. 'Hey, wait. Sharing these could be a federal crime, right?'

'For you to show me the envelopes that were in the mailbox for the condo you and your father own?'

'Well, when you put it that way.' He held them out again.

AnnaLise extended her hand to receive, but Tucker withdrew once more.

'Wait. Ichiro paid the rent. I think according to tenant law or whatever, that means he has the right to expect privacy.'

'Except he's dead.' AnnaLise grabbed the envelopes and read aloud, 'Resident, resident, current resident.' She handed them back. 'Fat lot of good that'll do us.'

Tucker shrugged and pushed a button between two sets of double doors.

AnnaLise looked up and around the lobby. 'An elevator?'

'It is a four-story building,' Tucker pointed out.

'I suppose.' After a minute: 'But would it kill people to walk? Get a little exercise?'

'Wow, what made you Miss Crabby today?' The doors opened and Tucker stepped into the car.

AnnaLise followed suit, torn between reacting to being called 'Miss Crabby' by someone a decade younger or acting like an adult.

She chose the latter because, after all, Tucker was doing her a favor. 'Sorry. I hurt my shoulder last night and didn't get much sleep.'

'What'd you do to it?'

The car stopped on the second floor. AnnaLise could have crawled up the stairs faster. 'Problem with my mother's garage door. Which is the condo Ichiro rented from your father?'

AnnaLise hoped not to get into another discussion of tenants' rights.

'That one,' Tucker said, pointing at the sign on the door that spelled out the word 'Three' in scripted, individual brass letters. No plain-Jane, Arabic numerals for the fabulous Hart's Landing, no siree.

AnnaLise knocked on the door.

'Who are you expecting?' Tucker asked, elbowing her aside and putting his key in the lock. 'A ghost?'

'I don't know,' AnnaLise said. 'It just seemed polite. Like knocking on a bathroom door when it's closed.'

'You knock on bathroom doors, too?' Tucker clicked open the deadbolt and stepped in. 'Or, close them in the first place?'

AnnaLise followed, thinking how glad she was that her life hadn't been burdened by brothers.

A so-called 'great room' combination of living, dining and kitchen awaited them as they stepped in. To the right was the living end, which had a planked floor and thick area rug between the couch and the fieldstone fireplace, surrounded by floor-to-ceiling windows.

'God,' AnnaLise said, gazing out across the lake toward Main Street. 'This place is beautiful. Can I live here?'

'Sure. Just pay our condo fees, taxes, and a little profit, and it's yours on a long-term lease.'

'Something tells me I can't afford any, much less all three.' Believing she was oriented, AnnaLise turned toward the kitchen at the opposite end of the room. Slate tile floor, beech cabinets, granite countertops and a breakfast nook looking north toward the mountains.

It was like AnnaLise had died and gone to heaven. But also an uncomfortable reminder of Ichiro, the dead man whose apartment she was coveting.

'This condo, my father's and mine are the only occupied units in the building—you can do the math on the monthly maintenance.'

'Well, somebody has to pay for the elevator and highfalutin' brass numbers,' AnnaLise said, catching sight of a desk tucked into a corner.

Tucker slid open the window over the table—the one Ichiro had talked to them through just three days earlier. Beginning in September, the Carolina mountains provided their own, natural air-conditioning.

'Exactly what are we looking for?' the doctor's son asked, turning. 'The police have probably already snapped up any smoking guns.'

'More like a smoking cane, in Ichiro's case,' AnnaLise said. 'But you're right, they would have taken anything obviously connected to his death. What I'm trying to do is link Ichiro to Dickens Hart and Rance Smoaks.'

'The trifecta: a Japanese guy, a rich guy and a drunk guy. That shouldn't be hard.'

'I sense sarcasm.' AnnaLise was sorting through a pile of maps and tourist information on the top of the desk.

'I would have said facetiousness,' Tucker said, 'but I'll bow to your greater mind-span as a wordsmith.'

'I just find facetiousness both kinder and gentler than sarcasm. But you're the one speaking, so you're the best judge of intent.'

'Perhaps I was trying for…ironic?'

'I think not.' AnnaLise set aside the Chamber of Commerce propaganda and opened a desk drawer.

'So you believe all three men were attacked by the same person? But two were shot and one…well, clubbed. I thought most killers stuck with the same weapon?'

Tucker seemed to be warming to the task, though going through the refrigerator probably wasn't going to help them much.

'On television,' said AnnaLise, 'but in real life? I don't know. Besides, we're not talking about a serial killer here.'

'Two people dead and another shot? What constitutes

"serial"?' Tucker had found a Diet Coke and was sitting on the couch.

'You have a point,' AnnaLise admitted, pulling out a stack of rubber-banded letters. 'But I guess I think of a serial killer as being random in the choice of victims even if consistent in the method. In this case, though, the attacker seems to take advantage of whatever's convenient.'

Like a garage door, for instance.

'What do you have there?' Tucker asked, using a hinged photo frame he'd picked up to gesture at the envelopes in her hand.

She waved the packet. 'Letters from home—in Japanese.'

'Go figure, him being Japanese and all.' He recited: 'Missives from Japan / To mountains one did carry / Til with leaves, he fell.'

'Beautiful, if sad,' AnnaLise said. 'That's haiku, right?' And this time rated PG, in contrast to the one accompanied with bongos she'd witnessed upon arrival at Torch.

'It is,' Tucker said. 'I really enjoy the form, though I have to "blue" up the lines to get any of our clientele to actually listen to the lyrics.'

'Take the blue out, and I'll listen anytime.' She held up the letters. 'I don't suppose you can read Japanese?'

'Not yet,' he said.

AnnaLise wouldn't underestimate him. 'What's with the frame?'

He brought it to her. 'Trade you.'

Tucker accepted the letters as AnnaLise examined the photos. The one to the left was of a gray-haired man— likely the grandfather—and a boy maybe ten or eleven, sporting a distinct resemblance to Ichiro. The photograph in the right side of the gold frame was older, its colors faded.

'Looks like an Asian June Cleaver,' Tucker said, cheating by looking over AnnaLise's shoulder.

The classic TV buff was right. Despite the fact the pretty woman pictured appeared to be Japanese, she was wearing the classic shirtwaist dress and string of pearls popularized by Barbara Billingsley in *Leave it to Beaver*. The sitcom had run in the late Fifties and early Sixties, overlapping with another Tucker favorite, *Dobie Gillis*.

This kid had to get out more.

'Probably Ichiro's mother,' AnnaLise said. 'Or maybe grandmother. It's hard to tell her age from the photo.' She held it out to him. 'Anything else?'

'Not that I saw.' Tucker was looking out the window he'd opened.

With a sigh, AnnaLise put the framed photos down and resumed her search of Ichiro's desk. Her head was halfway stuck in the lower file drawer when she heard a car door slam.

'Uh-oh,' Tucker said, sliding the window closed quietly just as Ichiro had done on Saturday, fearing he was 'overdropping'.

'Uh-oh, what? Who is it?' Digging through as rapidly as she could with one good arm, AnnaLise found the folder she wanted and pulled it out, suffering a paper cut in the process.

'Shit,' she said, as her blood dripped onto the other half dozen files in the cabinet.

'What?' Tucker asked.

'Manila folder-cut, damn it.' She sucked on her thumb to staunch the bleeding. 'But I asked you first—who's out there?'

'Jim Duende.' Tucker pointed at the droplets in the drawer. 'Aren't you worried about DNA?'

'I am, but not in the context you're talking about.'

'You mean you're not afraid they're going to…finger you?' He pointed at her paper cut.

'Cute, but it's my thumb.'

'Still a finger,' Tucker said defensively.

'Sorry, but I consider it a digit. The thumb opposes the fingers.'

'Oooh, I'm impressed.' Tucker raised his eyebrows. 'Now *that's* sarcasm.'

'Agreed. But, did you say Jim Duende is downstairs? Sheree told me he'd disappeared.'

'Nah, the guy was just off on assignment.'

'Assignment?' AnnaLise had gingerly picked up the file folder to show Tucker and now she stopped. 'He's a reporter?'

'More freelance writer. Hart wanted him to do his autobiography or some crap, but then the big guy changed his mind.'

'And hired me,' AnnaLise said.

'Hart hired…you? Why would he do that?'

AnnaLise's turn at defensive. 'I'm a good writer.'

'Sure you are,' Tucker said. 'But Jim is a big-time ghost-writer. That's what "duende" means in Spanish, by the way. Ghost.'

'I think the gist is more like "spirit".'

'Hey, Ms Know-it-all, will you lay off? I took high school Spanish, too. And a whole lot more recently than you did.'

AnnaLise couldn't argue with that. Or her being a pain in the ass, as Joy had put it. 'It is clever, though. Do you know what books he's ghosted?'

'No, but lots of them. For a bunch of famous people.'

Abandoning any hope of getting specifics from Tucker, AnnaLise held up the folder. 'You were talking about DNA. Look what I found.'

'"Genome"?'

'It's the name of the project, but it boils down to DNA testing.'

'Ichiro was doing that? Cool.' Tucker looked around. 'Where's the equipment?'

'He wasn't doing the actual lab work,' AnnaLise said. 'He had his own DNA tested as part of a worldwide project. Bobby Bradenham was doing the same.'

'And all that means…?' Tucker held out both hands, palms up.

'Well, I'm not sure,' AnnaLise said. 'I guess I'm hoping it'll tell us something.'

'What? You think they're related? Now *that* would be awesome. Maybe they're brothers and Bobby killed him so he wouldn't have to share some inheritance.'

'From Hart?' Geez, did everyone know about the 'little Dickens' rumor?

'Dickens Hart?' Tucker stared at AnnaLise, his eyes widening. 'Holy shit! Are you saying Bobby Bradenham is his love child?'

Tucker started a little dance—half-strut, half-beatnik. 'And Ichiro, too? Wow, I betcha Hart was in Japan. Hey, with all his money, why not? That is so cool. No, double cool. Maybe even triple cool. That's—'

'No, no,' AnnaLise said, waving her arms—or, at least, the good one. 'I didn't mean…'

A knock at the door. Tucker and AnnaLise looked at each other.

'Uh-oh,' Tucker said.

'You said that before,' AnnaLise whispered. 'Duende?'

Tucker shrugged. 'Probably. I know he asked my dad if it was OK for him to come by sometime and look around. I guess he wants to do an article.'

'An article?' AnnaLise squeaked. 'You mean for a magazine or newspaper?'

'Yeah, like I said, he freelances. Or else he's a stringer, now I'm not sure. For the *Times* or something.'

'The *Times*?' AnnaLise repeated. The *New York Times*? 'The last thing we need is him to find us poking around…'

'Don't worry,' Tucker said. 'He can't get in without a key and this—' he twirled one— 'is it.'

'Then how did Duende get into the lobby downstairs?' AnnaLise demanded. 'Your father would have more than one key.'

'So if the dude has a key, why would he knock?'

'He's being polite,' AnnaLise hissed. 'Like I was. And you're not. Is there another way out of this apartment?'

'Sure. Off the bedroom.'

As AnnaLise followed him, she heard a key clitter and turn the unit's deadbolt lock.

Tucker stealthily slid open the glass patio door in the bedroom and they stepped onto its deck.

'We're on the second floor,' AnnaLise said.

'Hello? Remember the elevator?' Tucker swung a leg over the railing.

'But I have a bum shoulder. And a file folder.' She held up the latter. What panic she was feeling was way out of proportion to the situation. So what if James Duende found them there? She'd tell him that…that she was looking at the apartment, maybe going to rent it. Sure, she'd…

'Hello? Is someone here?'

Tucker dropped over the deck rail.

'How's it going to look now?' AnnaLise whispered toward the ground. 'The real estate agent down there and me up here?'

'Real estate agent?' Tucker said, getting to his feet.

'Are you on crack? Jump, and I'll catch you!' He held out his arms.

'But my shoulder...'

Then she heard a second voice join the first in the condo behind her. 'What's wrong? Did you hear something?'

Chuck. As in Chief of Police Greystone.

In one impulsive movement, AnnaLise rolled up the folder, stuck it in the waistband of her pants and, bum wing forgotten, did a one-handed vault over the railing.

TWENTY-ONE

'Agghh.'

AnnaLise rolled off Tucker. 'Are you OK?'

He groaned.

'Truly,' she repeated. 'Are you hurt?'

Another groan, but at least this one was closer to a real word.

'I'm really, really sorry,' she said. 'Should I call your father? Or an ambulance?' Though, come to think of it, either would be impossible. AnnaLise had left her cellphone charging in Daisy's kitchen.

Happily, it didn't become an issue.

Tucker sat up partially, holding his chest. 'Just…trying…to catch…my breath. You knocked the…wind out of me.'

'I am so sorry,' AnnaLise said again. 'But I thought you were going to catch me.'

'And I thought you were going to drop straight down like I did, not launch yourself over the railing like some lunatic gymnastics chick.'

Tucker got to his feet, albeit unsteadily.

AnnaLise stood, too. 'I am so—'

'I know, I know. You're sorry.' He was checking his body parts for injuries. When he got to the back pocket of his jeans, he pulled out a crumpled packet. 'Here.'

AnnaLise took it and brushed off the dirt. 'Ichiro's letters? Why did you take them?' Perhaps he intended to learn Japanese quicker than AnnaLise had thought.

'I didn't mean to. I just stuck them in my pocket when I closed the kitchen window.'

'Which reminds me,' AnnaLise said. 'Your Coke is still sitting on the coffee table.' Probably making a ring, to add insult to injury.

'He'll think the can's been there forever.'

'They. Duende has Chief Greystone with him.'

'Huh.' Tucker rubbed the back of his head, then checked his hand for blood. 'Even so, my point stands. *They* will assume the Coke belonged to Ichiro.'

'Except that it's cold.'

'Oh.' Tucker was in full, re-trenching denial. 'Well, then, they won't know whose it is.'

'Unless they do a DNA check.'

His head jerked up. 'You think…'

'No, I don't,' AnnaLise said, letting him off the hook. 'Besides, you have a right to be there. If anything, it's my blood in the file drawer they'd worry about.'

'If anything,' Tucker echoed.

AnnaLise was looking at the building. The bedroom and therefore the deck off it faced the lake, just as the big windows in the living room did. That combination had the added advantage of situating the plumbing in the kitchen and bathroom back-to-back in the same wall to save contractor and maintenance costs.

All that meant nothing to AnnaLise against the fact that the layout had allowed them to land on the grassy slope leading to the water.

'Good thing that deck faces the back rather than the building entrance,' she said.

'You're not kidding,' Tucker said. 'If I'd been standing on that unforgiving sidewalk when you landed on me, they'd be scraping up Tucker Stanton with putty knives.'

AnnaLise ignored his use of third person. 'Did you know Chuck was coming with Duende?'

'Of course not,' Tucker said. 'I didn't even know Duende would be here now. Do you think I'd have let you into the apartment if I had? Come on, let's get out of here.'

AnnaLise waved for him to stay close to the building's footprint as they circled it, so neither Chuck Greystone nor James Duende could catch sight of them if either man happened to look out a window.

'The police chief and the freelancer,' she mulled as they walked. 'Sounds to me like Duende is interviewing Chuck for his story.'

'He couldn't do it at the station?' Tucker seemed to have lost his taste for investigation. Falling bodies, even live ones, could to that to a person, AnnaLise supposed.

'Maybe he's one of those "literary" types who need to soak up the atmosphere,' AnnaLise said.

She was thinking of her own bare-bones, fact-driven articles. The couple of times she'd tried to add a 'what if', 'why not', or 'how come' to the Who, What, When, Where, Why and How of news-reporting, she'd been shot down.

Ahh, but cheer up. Writing Dickens Hart memoirs would no doubt allow all sorts of license, literary—and literal—included.

TUCKER DECIDED TORCH needed his attention, though AnnaLise had a feeling it was his own injuries he'd be nursing.

She thanked him again and resisted the impulse to apologize yet again. As Tucker got gingerly into his jeep and drove away, she worked her own shoulder up and down.

'Huh?' she said. 'Feels better.' Earth—or Tucker Stanton—as chiropractor.

Need to visit the doctor's office empirically eliminated, AnnaLise walked to her Spyder, parked at the far end of the building. Glancing back, she saw Chuck exit the main entrance. She ducked around the corner, but he'd turned the other way, toward his patrol car.

AnnaLise waited until Chuck pulled out and then climbed into hers.

So James Duende was a writer. AnnaLise should have guessed it by all the red Flair marks he'd made on the newspaper that morning she'd seen him at Mama's. AnnaLise did the same thing when she read papers and magazines, underlining or circling story ideas and other items of interest in red, which didn't obscure the black type beneath it but would remind the 'Flairer' to clip.

It also explained his hanging out in the restaurant to listen. Again, looking for ideas, rumors—maybe even something that would help him land the job of writing Hart's memoir.

But Hart had given the job to AnnaLise instead of this supposedly big-time 'ghost'. Why?

There was the local angle, of course. As her new employer had said, AnnaLise was familiar with the people and places of Sutherton. She could bring a sense of heart and depth to the story that an outsider never could.

And Dickens Hart, despite everything negative you could say about him, was an intelligent, successful businessman. People like that had an eye for spotting untapped but applicable talent.

Hart said he'd read her stuff and been impressed. Was AnnaLise, despite not having the opportunity to flex her 'literary' muscles, truly that good? Or did Hart believe that AnnaLise would be more malleable than a seasoned professional? More willing to show her hometown—and, in Hart's mind, that hometown's hero—in a good light?

And, perhaps in the process, bury the skeletons he wanted to keep hidden.

If so, he was a bad judge of character. That should have become eminently clear to Hart when AnnaLise laid down the conditions of her employment.

So, again, why? Unless…unless AnnaLise had under-priced herself, despite her attempt to achieve just the di-ametric opposite.

Now that would *really* suck. She sat back in the Spy-der's driver seat, the wind taken out of her sails as thor-oughly as she'd full-body Heimliched it out of poor Tucker Stanton's lungs.

How much money did someone like James Duende get for a book?

AnnaLise didn't know, though she'd once met a writer at a cocktail party who claimed she made 'half a mill a book' to ghost the novels of a *New York Times* best-selling romance writer.

'But, shh—' manicured finger to Botoxed lips— 'don't tell anyone.'

Five hundred thousand dollars? And AnnaLise had settled for—hell, herself requested—a measly…

AnnaLise stopped. Talk about looking a gift horse in the mouth, as Mama would no doubt say. The Hart proj-ect would allow AnnaLise to try something she'd never done and, if she proved good enough at it, maybe some-day command that magnitude of fee.

AnnaLise started the car, still scolding herself. As she went to put the car into reverse, though, she paused.

Five hundred thousand dollars for just one romance novel? If true, then what the hell did the Kitty Kelleys of the world make? And even if James Duende wasn't in that pantheon, he certainly could make at least as much

off Dickens Hart as the egomaniac proved himself willing to pay a young, untried journalist.

Giving Duende reason to curry favor with said 'egomaniac' and motive to put the person threatening that
paycheck—our aforementioned 'young journalist'—out
of commission. Like by a heavy garage door rendering
her unable to type.

Suddenly, Chuck's flip comment about the shooter at
Dickens Hart's mansion not being 'worth a damn' didn't
seem so far off the mark.

Though the same couldn't be said for Duende, if he
indeed had been aiming for AnnaLise and nearly killed
his prospective patron by mistake.

ANNALISE ASSUMED she'd find Bobby Bradenham in the
mayor's office. A blessing, since questioning him at home
about his father in front of his mother was not high on the
reporter's wish list.

As she drove to Town Hall, AnnaLise shelved the possibility that Duende had targeted her, both by bullet and
garage door. Why?

Because that still left two other victims, both of them
dead. What possible motive—rival 'ghost' or not—could
James Duende have had for killing Ichiro Katou and
Rance Smoaks?

AnnaLise pulled into the town hall lot, shared by
Sutherton's police department. Presumably Chuck's patrol car was one of the two parked there, not a problem
now that AnnaLise could no longer be caught bleeding
on files or jumping from decks.

When she entered the municipal building, the buxom
strawberry blonde at the desk was a stranger.

'Hello, I'm AnnaLise Griggs. Is Melba Lee still working here?'

'Melba retired two years ago,' the blonde said. She stuck out her hand. 'I'm Judi, with an "i".'

'Good to meet you, Judi. Is Mayor Bradenham available?'

'Bobby sure is here, but Chief Chuck just went in with him. You mind waiting a sec?' She handed AnnaLise a 'visitor' pass, also something new.

AnnaLise alligator-clipped it to her blouse and sat down with a magazine.

One *Us* and two *People* later, AnnaLise was still waiting. She checked her watch. Nearly one. The six-thirty Coffee Time cake was seeming like fuel taken on an awfully long time ago. She got up to make sure Judi hadn't forgotten her, a chronic fear of AnnaLise's since the time she waited an hour in the exam room for her doctor, only to find everyone gone and the lights out when she'd finally emerged in her blue paper robe to check.

A chronic fear, not a cute one.

As AnnaLise approached the desk, the door to the office beyond opened and Chuck stalked out. AnnaLise raised her hand in greeting, but the chief of police barely nodded and kept on walking.

'Maybe this isn't the best time,' AnnaLise started to say to Judi.

Before the woman could answer, Bobby stuck his head around the door frame.

'AnnaLise? Did you want to see me?' If Chuck looked frustrated, Bobby looked defeated.

'Only if you have time,' AnnaLise said. 'I don't want to—'

'No, no,' Bobby said, sputtering and passing his hand over his face like he'd just surfaced from a deep dive. 'Come on in.' Bobby stepped aside to let her pass.

Judi threw her a 'good luck' look and AnnaLise preceded Bobby into his office.

'You remodeled,' she said, kind of missing the former dark wood and slight tang of mildew.

Bobby plopped himself into the chair behind his desk, elbows now on the blotter with eyes fixed there, too, but seemingly seeing nothing.

Then he looked up. 'What?'

'The renovations?'

'Oh, yeah. A year ago, give or take.'

'Bobby, what's wrong?' AnnaLise said softly. Whatever had just happened with Chuck, she didn't want to add to it now with questions about Dickens Hart.

'Wrong?' Bobby raised his eyes ceiling-ward and AnnaLise thought she saw the glitter of…tears? 'Let's see: for starters, Dickens Hart is my father and our chief thinks I might've tried to kill him for his money.'

Well, apparently that cat had fully wormed its way out of the proverbial bag. 'So, you didn't know?'

'Absolutely not.' Bobby's eyes narrowed. 'Why? Did you?'

AnnaLise tried to answer honestly. 'I heard a couple of rumors, but only over the past few days I've been back in Sutherton. Do you think it's true?'

'I guess the biological father should know, right?'

'Not as surely as the biological mother. I take it you haven't talked with her?'

'I started to call Ma as soon as Chuck left the office, but then decided this wasn't exactly a conversation appropriate for the telephone. Besides, she's having people over for tea.'

Yeah, right. Wouldn't want to distract Mum from logistical preparations with pesky questions like, 'Have you lied to me all my life?'

AnnaLise cleared her throat.

Bobby held up his hands. 'I know how stupid that sounds, believe me.'

'Well, stupid or not, it's probably better that you take some time to think before you confront Ema. What *had* she told you about your dad?'

'Pretty much what I said to you or anybody else who's ever asked. I practically had it memorized. Quote: "Your father was driving and another car crossed the center line and hit us straight on. I woke up four days later in the hospital with this—" she'd point at the scar on her temple— "and they told me your father was dead and already buried. Before I could start crying, they brought you in. So tiny, but miraculously without a scratch thanks to that infant seat. My miracle baby." Unquote.'

The mayor picked up a pen, then stared it down, seemingly at a loss for why he had it in his hand. 'Every time, exactly the same. Words, cadence, expressions on her face. I should have known it was a lie. Carefully rehearsed and perfectly repeated, but a lie nonetheless.' He slammed the pen back onto his desktop. 'I'll bet by now, even she believes it.'

'Maybe Ema didn't want you to be hurt,' AnnaLise said. 'You know, the gossip and all. Now, granted, it doesn't matter. But back then?'

'The person she didn't want hurt was herself. Mrs Bradenham. Probably even made up the name, or stole it from a next-door neighbor or some poor, pious shmuck who died in church. But no matter, Ma comes back pure as the driven snow—brave widow, single mother. Her reputation intact, she gets a big house as a bonus. Hart, he gets to keep his lifestyle. The even bigger money, the perpetual rotation of broads.

'But me?' Bobby looked up. 'What did I get?'

A pretty damned nice life to date, though AnnaLise had no intention of saying that. Bobby hadn't been judgmental during her emotional meltdown on Labor Day. The least she could do now was to give her friend equally unconditional love and support.

But again, Bobby seemed to read her mind. 'I know, Annie. I know I didn't exactly suffer. I lived in a nice house, went to a good school, had great—' he gestured to her— 'friends. Thing is—' his hand dropped— 'my entire life is built on a lie.'

'Not *your* life, Bobby. Hers.' AnnaLise came around the desk and leaned down to hug him, her shoulder still remarkably recovered. 'Everything about you is genuine and good.'

She tapped him on the forehead. 'Especially your taste in friends.'

The mayor mustered a smile. Then a shadow crossed his features. 'I didn't even tell you the worst. Rance Smoaks' shooting wasn't an accident.'

'So I heard,' AnnaLise said, settling on the edge of Bobby's mayoral desk. 'And apparently with the same gun used on…' The slightest pause. 'Dickens Hart.'

'Whatever you do,' Bobby said, 'don't start calling him my father.'

'Got it,' AnnaLise promised. 'So, Chuck thinks you shot Hart?'

'I'm the only one who benefits from his death.'

'What about his business partner—Sabatino?'

'Apparently their agreement stipulates that Hart's interest goes to any heirs, not the surviving partner.'

'And the only heir is you,' AnnaLise said.

'You got it.' Bobby was looking defeated.

'So does that mean you're supposed to have killed Rance Smoaks, too?'

'What the chief thinks and what he says are two different things. Chuck can be surprisingly wily.'

As AnnaLise had suspected when the chief 'nodded off' at Sheree's inn. 'So what is Chuck *saying*, at least?'

'First off, that he thought I had a right to know about Hart.'

'Which you do.'

'Agreed. But then he casually mentioned the will, in which Hart acknowledges me as his son and then leaves everything to…me.'

Even after all the gossipy speculation, AnnaLise was stunned. She couldn't imagine how Bobby must have felt at hearing those same words. 'Chuck probably wanted to see if you'd show surprise.'

'Well, I did. And he sure should've seen that.'

'Which is a positive for you on the motive front,' AnnaLise said, trying to be reassuring. 'What happened next?'

'Chuck did one of those pauses at the door—you know, a Lieutenant Columbo-like afterthought? Then he said, "Oh, by the way, both Rance Smoaks and Dickens Hart were shot by the same firearm. Quite the coincidence, eh?"'

'Again, looking for your reaction.'

'And again, I gave it to him. I was shocked.'

'Did Chuck say anything else?' The two men had certainly been together in the mayor's office long enough.

Bobby closed his eyes, then seeming to reach a decision, opened them. 'Only that he knew Kathleen Smoaks and I had been having an active affair for the better part of the last five years.'

AnnaLise felt her own eyes go round. 'And what did you say to that?'

'What do you think?' Bobby picked up the receiver

of his desk phone. 'I told friend Chuck, Chief of Police Greystone, to get the fuck out of my office so I could call my lawyer. And…' Tone softening. 'I'd appreciate your doing the same without the accompanying obscenity.'

TWENTY-TWO

ANNALISE HAD TRIED to say the right things before leaving Bobby Bradenham's office, but that usually requires knowing what those things are.

And, quite frankly, she was at a loss.

The evidence against Bobby might be circumstantial, but AnnaLise had seen prosecutors in Wisconsin build ironclad cases from less. The fact he was Sutherton's mayor might be all the more reason somebody would delight in—or benefit from—toppling him.

For that matter, all the more reason the whole shebang should be turned over to at least the county authorities, if not the state of North Carolina. Chuck, wily police chief or not, shouldn't be investigating a homicide in which his boss was a prime—hell, the *primary*—suspect.

AnnaLise found a parking spot on Main Street next to Tucker Stanton's jeep and right around the corner from her home. The majority of the summer folk—especially those with kids who needed to start school elsewhere—had already left. Most of the rest would head out sometime this month, leaving October largely to day-trippers or weekenders, coming to marvel at Sutherton's foliage turning colors on the trees.

As AnnaLise exited the car with Ichiro Katou's 'genome' file folder and personal letters, she could almost feel the town putting its collective feet up to relax until ski season arrived—snow willing—in late November. Mama's was relatively busy, but there were no lines of people waiting to pay or be seated. It seemed as though everybody was hanging out, catching up, moving on.

Passing Torch, AnnaLise again fought the impulse to drop in. A bad idea on two fronts. First, she'd gotten the distinct impression that Tucker preferred to get far away from the 'intrepid reporter's investigation', at least until he could walk without whimpering.

Second, she really wanted to discuss Bobby Bradenham's situation, but doing so with Tucker, a newcomer by Sutherton's let's-see-your-birth-certificate-and-your-daddy's-too standards, would feel like a betrayal of her old friend's confidence.

Talking to Daisy, on the other hand, wouldn't count. Family exemption and all. But, when AnnaLise unlocked the door, there was no sign of her mother.

'Hello?' she called out, dropping the folder and letters on the kitchen table.

AnnaLise went to the stairs and tried again. Still no answer. She eyed the gun cabinet on the landing. Daisy had always kept the key for it in her bedroom dresser. Now would be a perfect time to make sure all the guns were there.

Which begged the question, what if they weren't?

Prosecutor Ben Rosewood, a Gulf War vet, had once told AnnaLise he never asked any witness a question to which he didn't already know the answer. 'It's a minefield,' he'd said, 'and once the device blows up, you can't replant it. Only thing left is trying to deal with the aftermath.'

Words. The cat that won't go back into the bag. At least not without leaving you bloodied.

A 'bing' from the laptop she'd left on the end table by the couch gave her a momentary reprieve. 'Chicken,' she said to herself, crossing to the computer and tapping a key to bring up the screen.

One new message from her editor at the newspaper: 'I'm so sorry to hear about your mom. Stay for whatever you need to do, and I'll notify Human Resources we won't be seeing you before the end of the month. You and I can revisit your mother's situation then and go from there. Just keep me informed. All the best, Jan.'

Bosses didn't come any better. AnnaLise hoped she really would be back working for her by October 1.

She typed a quick thank-you reply. As AnnaLise hit 'send', a second message popped up, also from Jan: 'Forgot. Ben Rosewood has been calling. Are you working on a story I need to reassign or maybe delay?'

AnnaLise sighed. Time to bite the bullet. Or at least type it.

'No, but thanks. He's calling on a personal matter that I can handle from here.'

She hesitated, eyeing the words 'personal matter'. The overused phrase sounded like she was telling Jan, who'd been so kind on a very personal front, to mind her own business.

AnnaLise cursored back and changed 'personal' to 'non-news' and added, 'Don't worry, I'm not being arrested.' And, God help her, a winking smiley face. Yuck. Reading it over one last time, she changed 'I *can* handle from here' to 'I *will* handle from here' and pushed 'send'. Then she shut down the machine.

Like District Attorney Ben Rosewood, the gun cabinet wasn't going away. It was still standing there on the landing, insidiously whispering her name. Mocking her for being a weenie.

'Who says ignorance isn't bliss?' AnnaLise said aloud, willing herself to put the Wisconsin issues aside for now.

God knew, she had enough North Carolina ones to keep her busy.

If a rifle was missing, what would she do? Go to Chuck? Keep quiet and let the case against Bobby continue to build?

Neither struck her as acceptable.

But not knowing was even worse.

AnnaLise mounted the steps. 'Shaddup,' she said as she passed the cabinet toward Daisy's bedroom.

Light and airy. Yellow walls, white woodwork. The maple-framed bed was covered by a predominantly blue quilt with a subtle yellow thread that picked up the walls perfectly. AnnaLise moved to the matching maple dresser and slid open the top drawer.

Daisy, who could concededly out-drink her daughter, also had more 'intimate apparel' than AnnaLise. And, by all appearances, nice stuff. Steadfastly resisting the urge to check labels to see just *how* nice, AnnaLise slid her hand along the bottom of the drawer. She was rewarded in the right rear corner with what felt like a small key.

'What are you looking for?'

AnnaLise jumped, caught literally with her hand in the lingerie drawer.

She slipped the key into her other hand and then turned, holding up a bra. 'I didn't get a chance to wash clothes and wanted to borrow a bra. Where did you come from?'

'The bathroom.' The answer should have been evident, Daisy wearing a robe and her hair wrapped in a towel. 'What's wrong with the one you have on?'

AnnaLise looked down. 'The strap hurts my shoulder.'

'Well, the one you're holding is too small, even for me.' Daisy snatched the bra out of her daughter's hand.

AnnaLise hooked both thumbs in her jeans' pockets

and watched as her mother dropped the bra back into the drawer.

Digging around, Daisy finally pulled out a sapphire blue, lacy number. 'Try this.'

AnnaLise accepted the bra and did a quick eye-appraisal. 'A LaPerla push-up?'

'I'm fifty, AnnaLise, not dead.' Daisy closed the drawer and pulled out the one below it. 'Anything else you need? Panties?'

Afraid her mother was going to come up with a matching thong, AnnaLise shook her head. 'No. No, this is great. Thanks. Umm, you getting ready for the tea?'

'Yes, though I'm not really looking forward to it. I've never been to Ema's house, but I'm imagining an elaborate silver service and tiny lettuce sandwiches.'

'You've never been to Bradenham?' AnnaLise asked, flopping down on Daisy's bed to prolong her cover story. 'I thought you and Mrs B were old friends.'

'We've known each other a long time, but we haven't been what I'd call "friends" for years. More like acquaintances with some history.'

'That's too bad. Did you have a falling out?' AnnaLise was trying to think back.

'Not really, just sort of drifted apart.' Daisy had the closet door open and was sorting through her dress hangers, selecting first one, then another, and so on.

'Because Ema Bradenham went away and got married?'

Daisy's hand froze. Then: 'Well, yes. I suppose.'

'"You suppose" that's why you drifted apart or "you suppose" she got married?'

No answer.

But then, AnnaLise hadn't really expected one. 'That's a bit much, don't you think?'

Daisy turned, a sequinned little black dress in her hand. 'What?'

'The LBD.' AnnaLise gestured toward the sequinned number. 'It's too dressy for afternoon tea.'

'I know that.' Daisy put the hanger back on the rod.

AnnaLise, hands tented, lowered her chin to her finger pads. 'Dickens Hart is Bobby's father.'

Daisy turned back, arms crossed. 'That's just a rumor. I told you not to believe everything Phyllis said.'

'I'm not quoting Mama. Bobby told me because he's afraid Chuck's going to arrest him for attempted murder. Apparently, Hart's will reads that Bobby is his son, and Chuck told Bobby.'

Daisy seemed to freeze once again. 'Does Ema know?'

'She'd be in the best position, don't you think?'

'Don't you be flip with me, AnnaLise Marie Griggs.' Daisy stamped her bare foot. 'Does Ema know that Chuck told Bobby what you just told me?'

'I don't know. Chuck might have told Mrs B, I guess. Bobby was going to wait until after this afternoon's tea to discuss it with his mother, alone and face-to-face.'

'Good.' Daisy had dropped her robe and was hurriedly pulling out clothes.

AnnaLise averted her eyes. 'Where are you going? I didn't think the tea started until three.'

And her mother certainly wouldn't go to Bradenham in an old sweat suit. And commando, to boot.

But Daisy was already at the door. 'I'm going early. You and I will talk later, but right now I have to see Ema.'

'Wait,' AnnaLise said, pushing up from the bed. 'I don't think Bobby would want you talking to her before he has a chance.'

'This isn't about what Bobby wants.' Daisy was heading down the stairs.

AnnaLise got to her feet, feeling awful for betraying Bobby's confidence. She hadn't told Tucker Stanton because she was afraid it would get around, and here Daisy was about to go straight to Bobby's mother, the worst possible ear to hear the information.

AnnaLise managed to reach the top of the stairs just as Daisy disappeared around the landing. 'I told you this in confidence, Daisy. You can't—'

'I can and I will.' Her mother's voice came from below. 'Sutherton's harbored too many secrets, AnnaLise. Too many that have hurt more than helped.'

AnnaLise skidded around the landing and reached the bottom of the stairs as Daisy was opening their front door. 'Wait! Please, you don't understand.'

Daisy stepped out onto the sidewalk and turned. 'No, *you* don't. I have to stop this before someone else gets hurt.'

Frightened by the look on her mother's face, AnnaLise hesitated. 'You can't honestly think Bobby Bradenham shot his own father.'

'I don't know who shot anybody, AnnaLise.' Daisy's hand on the door went white-knuckled. 'What I do know is that Dickens Hart is not his father.'

AnnaLise's feet felt as though they'd been set in concrete. 'Then who—'

'Rance Smoaks.'

TWENTY-THREE

ANNALISE STARED AT the door Daisy had just slammed behind her.

The Chrysler's engine started and AnnaLise still stood staring as the car pulled away from the curb, the sound of its motor and tires gradually receding.

Rance Smoaks as Bobby's father. Was that even possible?

Rance was fifteen years older than his wife, Kathleen. And Kathleen was Bobby's age. That meant, of course, that Rance would have been just fifteen when Bobby was born.

And likely only fourteen when the baby had been conceived.

Mrs B, now fifty-six, or six years older than Daisy, would have been…twenty-seven. A twenty-seven-year-old woman and a fourteen-year-old boy? That went beyond 'cougaring'.

All the way to statutory rape.

No wonder the lid on it was kept so tight. AnnaLise was vaguely aware that the statutory rape laws in North Carolina had been toughened in the Nineties, but even before that, the relationship would have been considered shameful, if not outright criminal.

So…what had they done? Presumably Rance Smoaks simply kept his mouth shut, though by all reports the die had been cast on his character even before he hit fifteen. An arrogant braggart and bully. Must have been hard for him to keep his 'prowess' with a hot older woman—and a 'Fawn', no less—a secret.

Then again, his dad was chief of police and, by all accounts, a violent bully himself. Maybe Rance had been frightened of his father's likely reaction—both for himself and Mrs B.

So there was never any '*Mr* Bradenham', presumably. Ema had simply gone off to have the baby and, when she returned, told people her husband, the infant's father, had died in a car accident. Even flashed a scar to prove it. And because Baby Bobby supposedly was in an infant seat, he could appear unscathed. The 'miracle'.

And Daisy had known from the get-go.

AnnaLise's mother had kept her mouth shut, honored the confidence, all these years. The two women, though, had grown apart, as Daisy put it. Probably the more often Mrs B told the fiction, the more it became reality for her. And Daisy, for all her trustworthiness, was not part of that 'reality'.

Finally turning away from the door, AnnaLise sagged into a chair at the kitchen table.

So, how did all this affect Bobby? Emotional part aside, it didn't seem to change much, at least where the crimes were concerned.

For whatever reason, Dickens Hart believed Bobby was his son, acknowledged paternity, and made him his heir. So long as Hart continued to believe that and didn't change his will, Bobby had a motive for killing him.

An even stronger motive now, since it would be to Bobby's benefit for Hart to die sooner rather than later, when the truth might nose its way out. As for Smoaks' murder, the motive remained the same. The prosecutor would say that Bobby killed Rance in order to get Kathleen and the indirect inheritance. The fact that Bobby was, in fact, having an affair with his own stepmother...

AnnaLise shuddered. Could you possibly get *more* sensational and sordid than that? The tabloids would have a field day. Hell, even AnnaLise's own, semi-staid paper back in Wisconsin would run with a story like this. Not that she intended for the publisher to get it, and certainly not from her.

James Duende, on the other hand, might jump at the opportunity. Maybe, thanks to his relationship with innkeeper Sheree Pepper, he was already on the trail and ahead of AnnaLise. Another big pay day at the expense of someone else. Bobby.

It didn't bear thinking about.

So think instead about Ichiro Katou. How did he, a late-comer, fit into the puzzle that was Sutherton? Ichiro's death couldn't have been an accident. A blow to the head and the bloodied weapon, his cane, placed in the Griggses' garage.

Compounding the situation, AnnaLise couldn't be sure who knew what. And when.

Or, for that matter, where, why, or how, either.

Bobby seemingly would have no motive, given that Rance Smoaks was his father, not Dickens Hart. Even if, in his travels, Hart had gone to Japan and fathered Ichiro, it didn't matter. Bobby and Ichiro couldn't be related and, therefore, weren't in competition for Hart's fortune.

Unless...

AnnaLise pulled Ichiro's 'genome' folder toward her. It was a little the worse for wear, given that she'd rolled the thing up and then jumped off a deck with it stuffed in her jeans.

There were two stapled reports inside. They'd apparently been sent to a Japanese address in May, two months prior to Katou's arrival in Sutherton.

The first was entitled 'PATERNAL LINEAGE TEST RESULTS FOR ICHIRO KATOU'. On its front was a map of East Asia. In the upper right hand corner was a box that read 'Paternal Haplogroup 02B'.

AnnaLise skimmed the six-page printout, the first half of which seemed pertinent. The last three pages contained general explanations of DNA testing and haplogroups (or ancestral clumpings) and teasers for why you might want to pay the provider more to dig just a little deeper.

Katou's Y-chromosome DNA, passed exclusively from father to son, showed he belonged to a subgroup of the O Haplogroup, nearly exclusive to east and southeast Asia. There was lots of other intriguing stuff, but bottom line and clear as a bell: Ichiro's biological father could not have been Dickens Hart.

The second report was Ichiro's maternal lineage record. Mitochondrial DNA (mtDNA) is inherited directly from the mother. This printout showed a map of Europe on the front page and, in the upper right corner, the box read 'Maternal Haplogroup H, the colonists.' This time, AnnaLise read the pages twice to make sure she understood them, coming to the same conclusion both times.

Ichiro Katou's other biological parent was of European descent.

Although there were no specifics about the man's maternal bloodline, the papers themselves revealed something even more interesting: the results had come as a complete shock to Ichiro.

'Haplogroup H' was vividly circled in red, not once but four times. The words 'most common mtDNA in Europe' likewise. And, on an attachment headed 'DNA Analysis of Japanese People' that looked like it was from a Japanese version of Wikipedia—but in English, thank God—Ichiro had underlined 'HV', the only H haplogroup listed in a chart of seventeen. The frequency of even that—just one tenth of one percent—was both circled and underlined.

AnnaLise set aside the reports and looked at the sheaf of envelopes Tucker had accidentally lifted from Katou's apartment. She didn't know anyone who could read Japanese, but there might be a scholar at the University of the Mountain in Sutherton who did. Or certainly somebody back in Wisconsin. Maybe Jan would know.

As AnnaLise got up to email her editor for the third time, she accidentally knocked the bound envelopes off the table. Impacting the floor, the ancient elastic broke and the letters scattered.

AnnaLise bent down to gather them. When she rose, she had the answer in her left hand. An envelope showing a return address in Sutherton, NC. And the name above that return address, as well.

Ema Sikes.

TWENTY-FOUR

EMA SIKES.

The name Daisy had called Bobby's mother when she, Daisy, had one of her flashbacks.

Sikes was the maiden name—or perhaps the only *real* name—of the woman known as Ema Bradenham.

And, apparently, the link between the two men dead and the one wounded.

Rance Smoaks had been Ema's under-aged lover and the father of her son, Bobby.

Dickens Hart believed Bobby was his own— presumably because that's what Ema Sikes had told him—and provided her child support. Or mother-and-child support.

And Ichiro Katou? He was also, somehow, Ema's child and still the piece that didn't fit.

Why would Ema have killed him and stashed the murder weapon in the garage of Daisy 'Lorraine Kuchenbacher' Griggs, the only one who seemed to know Ema's secret involving Rance Smoaks?

AnnaLise dug in a jeans pocket and pulled out the key she'd palmed when Daisy had caught her rummaging through her mother's lingerie drawer. Coast now clear, AnnaLise took the stairs two at a time. Reaching the landing, she stuck the key into the lock of the gun cabinet.

It turned like both had been oiled yesterday, and AnnaLise's heart fell. She swung open the door that had always secured three rifles and a revolver.

All four were there.

AnnaLise wasn't sure whether to laugh or cry. She lifted a deer rifle, and its butt end left a mark in the film of fine dust on the cabinet's floor.

Dust undisturbed. Meaning the firearms hadn't been moved for a long time.

Timothy Griggs's guns hadn't been involved in the shootings and, therefore, his widow hadn't been as well, no matter how loyally she'd kept Ema's secret all these years. But now Daisy was headed toward that 'friend's' isolated home to tell her that the jig was up. That the truth had to come out now, before 'anyone else was hurt'.

AnnaLise grabbed her car keys and purse before bolting out the door.

An SUV towing a trailer with a couple of standard 700-pound waverunners wheeled into the boat launch. AnnaLise nearly went off the road trying to avoid it, but her fault, as she'd been digging frantically through her handbag for the cellphone.

'Damn, damn, damn!' she yelled in frustration. Not only had AnnaLise almost killed herself and the driver of the SUV, but she'd left the cell still charging in the kitchen.

At her own apartment, AnnaLise always stuck the phone in her purse, cord running up and out of the bag into the wall, so she'd never accidentally leave the cell behind.

There, it was simply a matter of convenience.

Here, and now, it felt more like a matter of life and death. AnnaLise couldn't call for reinforcements, couldn't raise Chuck or even his office.

The only saving grace: it was just past 3:00 p.m. Mrs B, as AnnaLise continued to think of her, would have been expecting her guests to arrive at any minute for tea.

A confrontation with Daisy would need to wait until the other 'old gals' had left.

Unless the confrontation had already happened.

AnnaLise dared not think about that as she turned into the long, private drive that led to 'Bradenham' from the road. AnnaLise would have preferred to approach from the lake path, as she had on her bike the last time she'd visited. That way, Mrs B wouldn't have advance warning. Still, the cars of the other arriving guests should provide some engine noise as cover, and the ladies themselves, hopefully, would serve as AnnaLise's reinforcements in a pinch.

But, when she reached the house, there was no sign of motor vehicles except for Daisy's Chrysler, parked crookedly in front of the detached garage.

AnnaLise's bad feeling grew even worse, if that were possible.

AnnaLise snugged the Spyder close to the house, but nose-out. 'All the better to make a quick getaway,' daughter said to herself as she got out of the car.

It seemed to help, somehow. 'Herself' felt calmer.

'Don't need this,' she muttered, leaving her handbag on the passenger seat. 'But do need this.' She delved and retrieved an envelope, sticking it in her back jeans' pocket as she race-walked to the mansion's entrance.

Ignoring the urge to ring the bell or knock, AnnaLise tried the door itself. Oftentimes in Sutherton, the host or hostess would leave the entry unlocked so someone didn't have to come running each time a new guest arrived.

Of course that would require guests and a hostess and there were no signs of either. Had Daisy been lured into a trap?

In obstinate consistency, the doorknob didn't turn.

So either you ring the bell or go around the back, AnnaLise thought.

'The back it is,' she said in a whisper as she descended the porch steps. Circling the big house, AnnaLise heard voices. Female voices, but try as she might, she couldn't distinguish even syllables, much less words or phrases.

Staying close to the base of the house so she couldn't be seen from above, AnnaLise took the same outdoor staircase she had on Sunday. Climbing, the voices became clearer.

'I told you to stay away from that boy,' Daisy was saying. 'He's nothing but trouble.'

'I never should have told you,' Mrs B said. 'It's just...I was just so alone, Lorry.'

'Not alone enough,' Daisy sniffed.

AnnaLise flattened herself on the steps and slowly raised her head so she could get an ant's view onto the decking. The outdoor kitchen installation was visible, but Daisy and Mrs B weren't, unless they'd jumped into the hot tub, which AnnaLise thought unlikely.

Mrs B's voice again. 'I could say the same for you.' The conversation was coming from the outer deck, cantilevered over the lake.

'I never lied, Ema. You told the wrong man he was the daddy of your baby.' Daisy's tone was edging south.

'And just *what* was I supposed to do? Back in Florida, they would've put me in jail for having sex with someone fourteen or fifteen. I didn't know what they'd do to me in North Carolina, no matter how...mature Rance appeared. And besides, even if he was eighteen, he couldn't have supported Bobby and me.'

'Hell,' Ema continued. 'If anything, it's been the other way around for decades, what with the money Rance's been extorting from me.'

Daisy, now, voice dead-level. 'But it's only part of your allowance from Dickens for a baby he didn't father.'

A silence, as AnnaLise climbed onto the deck and, keeping low, crept toward them.

Then, Mrs B: 'You could've told him.'

AnnaLise noticed that Mrs B's cultivated timbre was slipping, replaced by the common contractions she'd managed to eradicate.

'You think Dickens will believe me?' Daisy asked. 'He already believes *you* and he's seen little Bobby.' A pause and then, in a stronger voice, 'Besides, that's not how I want things, anyway.'

AnnaLise had gained enough ground to see both women down the length of the walkway. Daisy sitting on the big chaise longue chair, Mrs B looming above her. Her mother's body language told AnnaLise what she'd suspected from the sound of her mother's voice and the fact that Daisy, but not Mrs B, was speaking in present tense.

This was not 'today's' Daisy Griggs. It was yesterday's Lorraine Kuchenbacher.

Mrs B said, 'Oh, it's so easy to be holier than thou when you have people who love you and will take care of you.'

'I am lucky, that's a fact,' Daisy said, looking up, and AnnaLise could see the light that shone from her mother. 'I have Tim who loves me no matter what. And Phyllis, too.'

'Ah, yes. Your "best" friend,' Mrs B said, and the pique in her voice almost made AnnaLise believe she, too, had reverted to a simpler time. One when you could have only a single 'best' friend.

But Mrs B just projected nasty, and grown-up nasty at that. 'You two were like...' She crossed her fingers tightly and showed their union to Daisy. 'Lorry, you didn't have time for somebody like me anymore.'

'I didn't have time for anything, what with the baby and Tim and the store. Besides, you went away. Came back "married".' Inflection, if not finger quotes, around the word 'married'.

'I *was* married,' Mrs B protested. 'I had—and have—every right to say so.'

'Married?' Daisy asked, screwing up her face. 'To who?'

Whom, AnnaLise silently corrected. But then 'Lorraine' was young and could be excused.

Ema said, 'I don't like to talk about it.'

'You can't make things go away that easy. Try as you might to forget.'

'There's nothing to remember.' Mrs B's posture was ramrod straight. 'I was married and my husband died in a car accident.'

'Just like that story you foisted on Sutherton,' Daisy said.

'Except this was a long time ago, before I ever came here.'

'So you used your true story so you'd remember?'

'No, Lorry. I used my "true" story so I wouldn't forget the one I made up.'

'But that's the same thing.' Daisy looked confused.

'Not at all. I just didn't want to get tripped up with the "facts" of the lie, so I stayed as close to the truth as I could. Right down to this.' She pushed aside that hank of hair to show her scar.

'So you were in that accident, too,' Daisy said. 'The only thing you had to sprinkle in was the "miracle" baby, because there wasn't one.'

AnnaLise, recognizing a cue when she heard it, stood up. 'Actually, there was.'

Neither Mrs B nor Daisy seemed surprised to see her there.

AnnaLise started across the bridge toward them. 'The only difference was, that little boy wasn't strapped into an infant seat like the fictional one was. Japan didn't require them.'

AnnaLise was guessing, but Mrs B made no effort to correct her.

Instead, she said, 'He died.'

'He did,' AnnaLise replied. 'But not then.' She drew the envelope from her pocket and waved it. 'You wrote this letter to your in-laws after you settled here in Sutherton.'

Ema didn't move to take it. 'They never answered and I could certainly understand.' She looked at AnnaLise. 'I was the reminder of what they'd lost and…well, they just couldn't accept it.'

'No, Mrs B,' AnnaLise said. 'It's you who can't accept that all these years your in-laws had what *you* lost. Your son. And they didn't answer because they didn't want to give him back. The more contact, the higher the possibility you'd find out your baby survived the accident. They were afraid you'd take their grandchild to the United States and they'd never see him again.'

Mrs B was shaking her head, but AnnaLise wasn't sure the woman had even heard her. 'Bobby Bradenham is my baby. My *only* son.'

A sound suspiciously like the notes from *The Twilight Zone* theme came from Daisy. When AnnaLise looked at her mother, the seated woman rotated an index finger next to her temple.

AnnaLise cleared her throat. 'Ichiro must have found your letter in the house after his grandfather died. The

DNA tests had already sparked his curiosity and the let-ter just confirmed what he already knew. His grandpar-ents had been lying to him. Just like you've been lying to Bobby.'

'Those damn tests,' Mrs B snapped. 'That's what started all this.'

'No,' AnnaLise said, gaining confidence. 'I'm pretty sure you did.'

'Why, what do you mean?' Daisy asked, eyes round.

AnnaLise leaned down and plucked something from between the planks of the decking. 'Ichiro came here Sat-urday night, when he knew Bobby would be at Sal's. Your *other* son wanted to talk to you in private.'

No reaction, even to the word 'son'.

AnnaLise plunged on. 'But you wanted nothing to do with him. An argument broke out and became violent. So violent, your pearl necklace broke, didn't it?' AnnaLise held up the object she'd snagged. 'Here, you missed one.'

She tossed the pink pearl toward Ema Bradenham, but the woman didn't seem to see it. 'That man attacked me, tried to steal my necklace. I did the only thing I could do when he lurched at me like a hulk. I pulled the cane away and hit him.'

'Ichiro wasn't stealing from you.' AnnaLise was re-membering the photo of the young Japanese woman. June Cleaver, as Tucker had put it, right down to the necklace. 'The pearls had been his grandmother's. He even had an old photograph of her wearing them. If you'd only given him the chance, he could have shown you.'

'That strand was a gift from my husband.' Her hands were at her throat, caressing pearls that weren't there. She'd loved them so much she'd destroyed them. Along with her eldest son.

'They were only jewelry.' AnnaLise wanted to cry. 'Ichiro was the gift. And you killed him in cold blood.'

'I certainly did not.' Again, with the phantom pearls. 'I merely hit him and he fell.'

'But then why didn't you call for help? Ichiro was still alive when he went into the water.'

Mrs B looked startled, and AnnaLise had a glimpse of the girl who had awakened only to be told her husband and son were dead.

Then the face changed. A wall went up, as sturdy as the deck under their feet. 'I'm afraid that was impossible.'

'Impossible?' AnnaLise echoed.

'She has too many secrets.' Daisy, suddenly lucid, was leaning forward. 'I think Ema already had killed Rance Smoaks. She couldn't admit she'd attacked another man and then have him live to talk about it.'

'I let the water close over him,' said Ema, gazing out over the lake. 'It was like he'd never been here.'

'And stashed the murder weapon in my garage,' Daisy said. 'Why?'

Mrs B pulled herself up to full height, seemingly about to deny it. Then, like a balloon pricked by a pin, the air whooshed out of her and she seemed to shrink. 'I knew the lake current would carry the body away, but I wasn't sure whether his cane would float or sink. I wiped the thing off and put it in my car's trunk, intending to dispose of it later elsewhere. When I saw the garage door open and you at Mama's, I decided it would be as good a place as any.'

'Meaning, you framed my mother,' Annalise said.

'Lorraine was already acting strangely. I thought the police would buy it.' Mrs B shrugged. 'It was worth a try.'

'Who's strange?' Daisy—or was it Lorraine?—demanded. 'I'm rubber, you're glue, Ema Sikes.'

Mrs B rolled her eyes. 'It was in the chief's office the

next day that I realized that young Lorry, crazy, was more dangerous to me than middle-aged Daisy, sane.'

'Because she knew the truth about Bobby's father.'

'And, more importantly, couldn't be depended on any longer. That's why I invited Lorry over for a private... party today.'

One that could well have resulted in another private burial, AnnaLise realized, feeling sick.

Mrs B extended a hand toward AnnaLise. 'You have to understand, Little One. It was all unraveling. First Dickens tells me my allowance has to be reduced because he's having money problems.'

'Hart's Landing is underwater,' AnnaLise said.

Mrs B dropped her hand. 'That left me with no choice but to renegotiate Rance Smoaks' stipend.'

'His blackmail, you mean. Or maybe his cut would be more accurate.'

Again, no acknowledgment. 'Rance didn't seem to understand that he needed to absorb some of the shared loss. He threatened to inform Dickens that Bobby wasn't his son.'

'Told you so,' Daisy sing-songed.

Now Ema Sikes 'Bradenham' finally lashed out. 'You shut your mouth, Lorraine Kuchenbacher. You've been sitting here preaching about how I should've told the truth.'

Mrs B nodded toward AnnaLise. 'Why don't you tell *her* the truth, Lorry?'

'I said nothing.' Daisy stood up. 'Not to Phyllis, not to anyone.'

'Until now.' This from Mrs B.

The two were toe-to-toe and nose-to-chest, given their respective heights, and far too near the low railing for AnnaLise's taste. Behind them on the lake a waverunner zipped past. 'Can you just shift—'

'I couldn't let you hurt anyone else,' Daisy said. 'The lies—'

'You're a fine one to talk about lies, Lorry. What about your own precious Tim?'

Timothy Griggs? AnnaLise thought, her head spinning. 'What does my father have to do with this?'

'Yes, Lorry. What does her father have to do with this?' Mrs B parroted.

'Tim knew the truth.' Daisy brought up both hands and shoved Mrs B. 'It didn't matter to him.'

'Yes, but do your beloved AnnaLise and her *real* father feel the—'

Daisy hurled herself into the other woman, and the two of them toppled over the rail and into the lake below.

TWENTY-FIVE

'DAMN GOOD THING neither one hit her head or we'd have another body on our hands,' said Bobby Bradenham.

'Or two, possibly,' AnnaLise amended. 'Daisy never really learned to swim and, given all the splashing and thrashing going on, I don't think either of our mothers *wanted* saving, if it meant not being able to kill the other.'

Bobby and AnnaLise were sitting on a black vinyl couch, tufts of white stuffing peeking through the seams, in the hospital waiting room. AnnaLise couldn't help but wonder if it could be the same furniture she'd sat on with Mama way back when.

AnnaLise remained slightly damp from the lake water.

Bobby and she were waiting for their mothers to be processed—Daisy to go home, Ema into police custody. Chuck had been true-blue enough to volunteer for a decent-coffee run.

AnnaLise would have preferred a shot. Of anything that assayed out at over 80-proof.

'Lucky those waverunners came by,' Bobby said.

'Lucky I didn't nail them with my car before they ever launched,' AnnaLise muttered.

'What?' Bobby looked startled.

AnnaLise did a quick mental survey. The fact that she'd nearly collided with the SUV pulling the trailer holding the Sutherton-despised waverunners that ultimately rescued their mothers should be the least of Bobby's worries right now.

'Not a big deal.' She looked over at him. 'You OK?'

'Frankly, no. You?'

'Ditto.'

Bobby sighed. 'Talk about "mother" issues. It's going to take a shit-load of therapy to get me through all of ours.'

'Not to mention the father ones.' She looked at him. 'But, while we're on the subject, who do you figure mine is?'

'From what *you* said *they* said? Dickens Hart. My once presumed, if now former, illegitimate father.'

She gave his arm a squeeze. 'Does this make us presumed bastards-in-law?'

'Once removed,' Bobby said with a weary smile.

'Randy Smoaks begat Bobby Bradenham, and Dickens Hart begat…me. Huh.' AnnaLise was probably in those journals. Or a gleam in the eye of one of them.

'Hey, things could be worse,' Bobby said. 'My father, a drunken blackmailer; my mother, a murderer.'

'There is that.' AnnaLise laid her head on his shoulder. 'I am so, so sorry.'

'Me, too.' He rested his cheek atop her head. 'I liked Ichiro and it turns out he was my half-brother. Would have been interesting to get the chance of knowing him better.'

'Given the events of the last few days, do any of us—at the risk of sounding trite—really know anyone?'

'*Sounding* trite? Trite 'R Us.'

'Trite *Is* Us.'

Bobby cuffed her on the side of the head that wasn't against his shoulder.

'That's assault.' Chuck had returned with two paper cups. 'Coffee machine was broken, so I brought you bourbon.'

AnnaLise took one. 'Ahh, the cure turns out to be better than the disease.'

'Sutherton has *bourbon* vending machines?' Bobby asked, taking the other. 'Is this a great town or what?'

AnnaLise just looked at him. 'Bobby, you're the mayor of this town.'

'I sent an officer to get it from my office,' Chuck said mildly.

'Bourbon vending machines in the police station. Even better.' AnnaLise raised her cup. 'To the High Country.'

'To the High Country,' Bobby saluted, and they bumped cardboard cups.

AnnaLise took a sip and shuddered.

'Cold?' Chuck asked. 'Here's the blanket the EMTs left.'

'Thanks, but I prefer heating myself from within right now.' AnnaLise had another hit and set her cup down on a two-year-old copy of *Good Housekeeping*. 'So, have you talked to…them?'

She really wanted to know about Daisy, but it seemed rude not to include Bobby's psycho mother.

'More like listened,' the chief said, pulling over a matching black vinyl chair to sit across from them.

'The Ema Bradenham dam has been eroded?' Bobby asked.

'More like busted and hurtling downstream,' Chuck said. 'Your mother is spewing like a volcano.'

AnnaLise said, 'Chuck, no mixing of metaphors, OK?' She tilted her head toward Bobby.

'Sorry,' Chuck said, 'I didn't mean to seem insensitive.'

Bobby shook his head. 'I think we're way past that line. Annie told me that Ma killed my half-brother—also, by the way, her own son—by hitting him with his own cane and then pushing him off our deck and into the lake.'

Chuck's eyebrows went up. 'And *I'm* insensitive?'

AnnaLise shrugged. 'I was traumatized. Thoughts just came tumbling out.'

'Speaking of trauma,' Chuck said, 'you didn't report being attacked in Daisy's garage.'

'Don't tell me,' Bobby said. 'My mother again, right?'

'Well, I don't—' AnnaLise started.

'So Mrs B herself says,' Chuck confirmed. 'She mistook you for your mother.'

AnnaLise came forward, elbows on knees. 'She was trying to kill Daisy? I mean, even before Ema pushed my mother into the lake?'

'Uh,' Bobby raised his hand. 'I think, in the interests of accuracy, that you told me *your* mother pushed *mine* into the lake.'

'Point taken,' AnnaLise said. 'But the question still stands, why did Mrs B want to hurt my Daisy?'

'She didn't, particularly, but it might have started her thinking about it. Fact is, planting the cane to divert attention had worked so well, Ema Bradenham decided maybe she should stash the rifle there, too. You surprised the woman, is all, Lise. Nearly caught her in the act.'

'The rifle?' Bobby repeated. 'The one that was used to shoot Smoaks and Hart?'

Stated that way, it sounded like a North Carolina law firm. AnnaLise, despite herself and the situation, emitted an involuntary giggle.

Side-cutting a look at her, Chuck moved both cups of bourbon to his end of the table. 'The very same. It's yours, in fact.'

'Wait just a minute.' Bobby shook his head like a horse on a cold morning. 'Ma used *my* deer rifle?'

Of all the things he'd heard, this upset Bobby the most?

'I'm sure Ema planned to put your gun back,' Anna-

Lise said, patting him on the shoulder. 'I mean, until the time she decided to plant it in our garage.'

She turned to Chuck. 'Where is it now, by the way?'

'She dropped it when you surprised her.'

AnnaLise remembered hearing something metallic hit the deck as the garage door descended on her. 'So, Ema took it with her when things didn't go as planned?'

'So she says. Then put it back in Bobby's "miscellany cabinet", as she called it.'

AnnaLise turned to Bobby. 'That's a very nice set-up there on your deck, by the way. The grill, the hot tub and...' She reached for his cup.

'Uh-uh,' Bobby said. 'You're cut off.'

'OK, OK,' AnnaLise said, settling back into the vinyl of the couch and closing her eyes to both her companions and the tufts of stuffing tickling her nose.

'Short hitter, Lise,' she heard from Chuck, as though in a dream.

'Let her sleep,' said Bobby, his voice like velvet. 'It's been a rough day all around.'

'You're telling me.' Chuck cleared his throat apologetically. 'I have to go get your mother now.'

'I know.' Silence. Then: 'Did Ma confess to everything?'

'Pretty much. Said she wanted to get it all out, then forget and move on.'

AnnaLise had that feeling of a patient listening to her doctors as the anesthesia kicks in.

Bobby laughed. 'That surely sounds like her. The past is the past, she'd say. Now I know why.' A pause. 'Funny, isn't it?'

'You're a better man than me, Bobby, if you can think of anything humorous just now.'

'I mean odd, ironic. AnnaLise is so worried about

Daisy losing her memories. And my mother? All she wants is to forget her own.'

Ironic. AnnaLise, in her fugue state, approved the choice of vocabulary.

Chuck's voice: 'Daisy's still got more on the ball than Lise might realize. Her mom heard the Spyder coming— you know, that noisy muffler?'

AnnaLise thought Bobby might have nodded. At least, he should have.

Chuck again: 'Well, Daisy kept Ema talking, pretending they were back in the day.'

Now Bobby: 'So Annie would have time to get there? That is smart, I have to say.'

'Yup.' A hesitation. 'Daisy is failing, though. It's hard to see…but impossible *not* to.'

'You think Annie'll stay?'

'I hope so.'

Another pause. AnnaLise thought she might actually be falling…asleep.

'You're going to have to ticket her for that muffler, you know.'

'I know.'

* * * * *

LARGER-PRINT BOOKS!
GET 2 FREE LARGER-PRINT NOVELS PLUS
2 FREE GIFTS!

⊞HARLEQUIN®

INTRIGUE®

BREATHTAKING ROMANTIC SUSPENSE

YES! Please send me 2 FREE LARGER-PRINT Harlequin Intrigue® novels and my 2 FREE gifts (gifts are worth about $10). After receiving them, if I don't wish to receive any more books, I can return the shipping statement marked "cancel." If I don't cancel, I will receive 6 brand-new novels every month and be billed just $5.49 per book in the U.S. or $5.99 per book in Canada. That's a saving of at least 13% off the cover price! It's quite a bargain! Shipping and handling is just 50¢ per book in the U.S. and 75¢ per book in Canada.* I understand that accepting the 2 free books and gifts places me under no obligation to buy anything. I can always return a shipment and cancel at any time. Even if I never buy another book, the two free books and gifts are mine to keep forever.

199/399 HDN F42Y

Name _____ (PLEASE PRINT) _____

Address _____ Apt. # _____

City _____ State/Prov. _____ Zip/Postal Code _____

Signature (if under 18, a parent or guardian must sign)

Mail to the **Harlequin® Reader Service:**
IN U.S.A.: P.O. Box 1867, Buffalo, NY 14240-1867
IN CANADA: P.O. Box 609, Fort Erie, Ontario L2A 5X3

Are you a subscriber to Harlequin Intrigue books
and want to receive the larger-print edition?
Call 1-800-873-8635 today or visit www.ReaderService.com.

* Terms and prices subject to change without notice. Prices do not include applicable taxes. Sales tax applicable in N.Y. Canadian residents will be charged applicable taxes. Offer not valid in Quebec. This offer is limited to one order per household. Not valid for current subscribers to Harlequin Intrigue Larger-Print books. All orders subject to credit approval. Credit or debit balances in a customer's account(s) may be offset by any other outstanding balance owed by or to the customer. Please allow 4 to 6 weeks for delivery. Offer available while quantities last.

Your Privacy—The Harlequin® Reader Service is committed to protecting your privacy. Our Privacy Policy is available online at www.ReaderService.com or upon request from the Harlequin Reader Service.

We make a portion of our mailing list available to reputable third parties that offer products we believe may interest you. If you prefer that we not exchange your name with third parties, or if you wish to clarify or modify your communication preferences, please visit us at www.ReaderService.com/consumerschoice or write to us at Harlequin Reader Service Preference Service, P.O. Box 9062, Buffalo, NY 14269. Include your complete name and address.

REQUEST YOUR FREE BOOKS!

2 FREE NOVELS
FROM THE SUSPENSE COLLECTION
PLUS 2 FREE GIFTS!

YES! Please send me 2 FREE novels from the Suspense Collection and my 2 FREE gifts (gifts are worth about $10). After receiving them, if I don't wish to receive any more books, I can return the shipping statement marked "cancel." If I don't cancel, I will receive 4 brand-new novels every month and be billed just $6.24 per book in the U.S. or $6.74 per book in Canada. That's a savings of at least 22% off the cover price. It's quite a bargain! Shipping and handling is just 50¢ per book in the U.S. and 75¢ per book in Canada.* I understand that accepting the 2 free books and gifts places me under no obligation to buy anything. I can always return a shipment and cancel at any time. Even if I never buy another book, the two free books and gifts are mine to keep forever.

191/391 MDN F4XN

Name   (PLEASE PRINT)

Address   Apt. #

City   State/Prov.   Zip/Postal Code

Signature (if under 18, a parent or guardian must sign)

Mail to the **Harlequin® Reader Service:**
IN U.S.A.: P.O. Box 1867, Buffalo, NY 14240-1867
IN CANADA: P.O. Box 609, Fort Erie, Ontario L2A 5X3

Want to try two free books from another line?
Call 1-800-873-8635 or visit www.ReaderService.com.

* Terms and prices subject to change without notice. Prices do not include applicable taxes. Sales tax applicable in N.Y. Canadian residents will be charged applicable taxes. Offer not valid in Quebec. This offer is limited to one order per household. Not valid for current subscribers to the Suspense Collection or the Romance/Suspense Collection. All orders subject to credit approval. Credit or debit balances in a customer's account(s) may be offset by any other outstanding balance owed by or to the customer. Please allow 4 to 6 weeks for delivery. Offer available while quantities last.

Your Privacy—The Harlequin® Reader Service is committed to protecting your privacy. Our Privacy Policy is available online at www.ReaderService.com or upon request from the Harlequin Reader Service.

We make a portion of our mailing list available to reputable third parties that offer products we believe may interest you. If you prefer that we not exchange your name with third parties, or if you wish to clarify or modify your communication preferences, please visit us at www.ReaderService.com/consumerschoice or write to us at Harlequin Reader Service Preference Service, P.O. Box 9062, Buffalo, NY 14269. Include your complete name and address.

ReaderService.com

Manage your account online!

- Review your order history
- Manage your payments
- Update your address

*We've designed
the Harlequin® Reader Service
website just for you.*

Enjoy all the features!

- Reader excerpts from any series
- Respond to mailings and
  special monthly offers
- Discover new series available to you
- Browse the Bonus Bucks catalog
- Share your feedback

Visit us at:
ReaderService.com